DATE DUE

MR 1 '00			
AP 2 '02			

DEMCO 38-296

The Troll Garden

A Definitive Edition
　　Edited by James Woodress
With Introduction,
　　Notes, Textual Commentary,
Emendations, and
　　Table of Revisions

Published by the
　　University of Nebraska Press
Lincoln and London
　　for the Center for Great
Plains Studies, University
　　of Nebraska–Lincoln

Publication assisted by
　　the Virginia Faulkner
Publishing Fund

Willa Cather

The Troll Garden

and durability of the Committee
on Production Guidelines for
Book Longevity of the Council
on Library Resources.

Library of Congress Cataloging
in Publication Data

Cather, Willa, 1873-1947.
The troll garden.

Contents: Flavia and her
artists – The sculptor's
funeral –
The garden lodge – [etc.]
I. Woodress, James Leslie.
II. Title.
PS3505.A87T7   1983
813'.52   82-20138
ISBN 0-8032-1417-0

First printing: 1983
Second printing: 1984

This edition

is dedicated to

the memory of

Virginia Faulkner

& Bernice Slote,

scholars, editors,

& friends

Contents

Acknowledgments

This edition of *The Troll Garden* began over a breakfast table conversation among Bernice Slote, Virginia Faulkner, and me at a Modern Language Association meeting some years ago. I proposed an edition that would record all the variants in the several stories, and both of my companions encouraged me to undertake the project. Miss Faulkner continued to support this edition as I began working on it and, before her death, arranged for support from the Center for Great Plains Studies of the University of Nebraska–Lincoln. I am grateful to Paul Olson, Rosemary Bergstrom, and the Center for this help. I also wish to thank the Research Committee of the University of California at Davis for additional support, and I owe thanks to Lee Bartlett, Pam Self, and Gary Konas for their work in collating and typing. Finally, I am indebted to Bernice Slote for giving my introduction and textual apparatus a careful reading and making suggestions; the reader for the Modern Language Association Center for Scholarly Editions, whose advice improved the textual apparatus materially; and Joan Crane and Frederick B. Adams, Jr., who answered bibliographical queries.

Introduction

Although Willa Cather mastered the art of the short story, she did not write many stories after she began publishing novels. Unlike her early master Henry James or her contemporary Edith Wharton, both of whom continued to write short fiction throughout their careers, Cather regarded her story-writing years as a literary apprenticeship. The posthumous *Willa Cather's Collected Short Fiction: 1892–1912*,[1] which spans her career from her freshman year in college to the publication of her first novel, contains forty-five stories. During the last thirty-five years of her life she wrote only sixteen more stories. Although two of them, "Neighbour Rosicky" and "Old Mrs. Harris," collected in *Obscure Destinies* (1932), are among her best work, she preferred to write novels, and one would have to say that her reputation rests largely upon her use of that genre.

Nevertheless, *The Troll Garden* represents a sort of capstone of Cather's early career. From her first story, "Peter," an amateurish early version of the suicide of a Czech neighbor that eventually became a moving episode in *My Ántonia*, to the tales collected in *The Troll Garden*, there is a steady growth in imagination and craft. During her undergraduate days at the University of Nebraska she published seven stories, all but one in college publications, but none is remarkable. Three of them, however, use Nebraska settings and characters and furnish an early glimpse of the material she was to use with consummate artistry in her maturity. She spent much of her time and energy as a junior and senior helping to work her way through college as a columnist and reviewer for the *Nebraska State Journal*. In this role she served an intensive journalistic apprenticeship as she turned out a vast amount of newspaper copy.

After graduating from the university, she stayed on in Lincoln for a year and continued her journalistic pursuits. Writing fiction was a strong interest but definitely a sideline. She did, however, place her first story in a magazine of national circulation, the *Overland Monthly*, in January 1896. This was "On the Divide," a grim story of a lonely immigrant Norwegian farmer who drinks himself into insensibility on his isolated Nebraska farm. Readers may well have thought that Cather was following in the footsteps of Hamlin Garland, whose somber tales of Midwest farm life had appeared in 1890 in *Main-Travelled Roads*. The bleakness of the prairie setting in this story anticipates the same austere note struck in "A Wagner Matinee." There is an irony here, because Cather in her later years had no use for Garland's or anyone else's naturalism; she did not even care for the commonplace realism of William Dean Howells.

Cather's big break came in 1896, when she landed a job as editor of the *Home Monthly*, a family magazine published in Pittsburgh. It was not much of a magazine, and she had to do much of the writing herself, often under pseudonyms, to fill its pages. During the year that she worked on this publication, she used seven of her own stories there. One of them, "The Count of Crow's Nest," is a two-part serial, the longest and perhaps the best thing she had done up to that time. She showed it to a member of the staff of the *Cosmopolitan*, who wanted to buy it, but she needed it to fill the pages of her own journal. This is a story laid in a Chicago boarding house that makes use of Cather's experience as a music and drama critic. Two of its characters are an impoverished European gentleman and his daughter (a third-rate singer), and the plot revolves around a struggle for possession of valuable letters. Told from a minor character's point of view, the tale marks an advance in Cather's narrative technique, and its preoccupation with art anticipates the central concerns of *The Troll Garden*. That these concerns were becoming of increasing importance to Cather may be noted also in two other stories of the *Home Monthly* period, "The Prodigies" and "Nanette, an Aside," that deal with music and singers.

In 1897 Cather moved from the *Home Monthly* back to daily journalism as a staff member of the *Pittsburgh Leader*, a position she held for nearly three years. The heavy load of reviewing and the pressure of deadlines gave her little opportunity to write fiction, and during the time she worked for the *Leader* she published only three stories. One of them, however, was "Eric Hermannson's Soul," which she placed in the *Cosmopolitan* in April 1900. This is clearly her best story yet, and its appearance in an important New York magazine must have given her confidence that someday she would be able to make her living as a creative artist.

Although Cather never reprinted this story, it is a very competent piece of fiction and marks a steady advance in her narrative skill. It is a long story and a subtle one. Eric is a blond giant, a young Siegfried, who immigrated to Nebraska at eighteen, worked in the fields, played his fiddle at all the dances, hugged the girls, and visited Lena Henson, a woman of dubious reputation. When a passionate exhorter from the fundamentalist Gospellers captures Eric's soul, Eric puts away his violin and becomes another one of the dull clods from the Old World, "sobered by toil and saddened by exile." At this juncture beautiful Margaret Elliot comes out of the East to visit on the Divide, meets Eric, is attracted to him, rides with him, and plays the organ for him, "probably the first good music he had ever heard." The hold of the Free Gospellers loosens; Eric falls in love with the accomplished Margaret. He agrees, at her urging, to play his fiddle again and to attend a dance she is giving before her departure for home. In doing so, he barters his soul, as he believes, for one evening of pleasure. The story ends with Margaret getting on the train and Eric, in possession of his soul, deaf to the reproaches of the Free Gospeller preacher.

A bare plot summary does injustice to this tale. It is the way the material is handled and the careful management of detail, as in the stories in *The Troll Garden*, that make this story interesting. One notices first of all that Cather is beginning to possess her material and to use it with a measure of aesthetic distance that makes one both see and feel the world of immigrant farmers. The prairie, the grass, the fields of wheat and rye, the western sky—all are evoked, not simply described. In one particularly effective scene Eric and Margaret climb the windmill, as Cather and her brother once had done, to view the clear night sky stretching away to the distant horizon, "which seemed to reach around the world." As they watch, the wind carries the odor of the cornfields to them, and the music of the dance sounds faintly from below. There is tension in this scene and a skillful development of the conflict between East and West. The author's sympathies lie with the West, but she understands the pull of culture and civilization.

This pull of the East was to figure more and more strongly in Cather's career for the next dozen years. Only four of the nine stories she published between 1900 and 1903 have prairie settings, and of the seven tales in *The Troll Garden* only two take place in the West. Then after her book came out, she chose western settings and characters for just three of the next nine stories. Although she went back to Nebraska several times during this period, she left Pittsburgh in 1906 for New York, which became her permanent home, except for vacations, for the rest of her life. She also was entering her Henry James phase, in which she became increasingly fascinated with the problems of artists and their relationships and with the lessons that she could learn from the master. This despite the fact that Cather had written in 1901, "The world is weary unto death of stories about artists and scholars and aesthetic freaks, and of studies of 'the artistic temperament.'"[2]

But before she left Pittsburgh for the metropolis, she quit journalism for the classroom. When she realized that the daily grind of the newspaper was making it impossible for her to do as much writing as she wanted, she became a high school teacher, first of Latin, then of English, for the next five years. As a teacher she at least had her summers free for writing. That she made good use of her free time is apparent from the fact that all of the stories appearing in *The Troll Garden* apparently were written between 1901 and 1903. Her growing mastery of the short story form also gave her the hope of putting together her first volume of fiction. The hope soon was realized when her work came to the attention of S. S. McClure, the volatile genius with whose affairs her life and her fortunes were to be inextricably linked for the next six years.

While Cather was slaving away at teaching English literature to students in Pittsburgh's Central High School, her association with McClure began dramatically. H. H. McClure, head of the McClure newspaper syndicate, passed through Lincoln scouting for talent, and Will Jones, Cather's former editor at the *State Journal*, gave him a strong talk about the fiction of his former columnist. H. H. McClure must have relayed this information to his cousin Sam, magazine editor and publisher, and the result was that Cather resubmitted her stories to *McClure's Magazine*.[3] She mailed off her work about the middle of April 1903, but without much confidence that it would be accepted. She already had submitted some of her stories to *McClure's*, and they had come back with rejection slips. A week after the parcel left Pittsburgh, however, she received a telegram from McClure summoning her to his office immediately. As soon as she could get away from school, she took the train for New York and presented herself to McClure on the morning of 1 May.

Life was never quite the same after that interview. She walked into the offices of the magazine at ten that morning, not worrying much about streetcar accidents and such; at one o'clock she left stepping carefully, she wrote Will Jones a week later. She had become a valuable property and worth saving. McClure with characteristic enthusiasm for his discoveries had offered her the world. He would publish her stories in book form. He would use them first in his magazine, and those he could not fit in, he would place in other journals for her. He wanted to publish everything she wrote from that point on. When she told him that some of the stories had already been rejected by *McClure's*, he said that he had never seen them. He then called in his manuscript readers and asked them in her presence to give an accounting of their stewardship.

That was not the end of her dealings with McClure. The ebullient Sam insisted on taking her up to his Westchester County home to meet his wife and children and Mrs. Robert Louis Stevenson, a house guest who already had read the stories. During the visit McClure wanted to know all about his new discovery, who she was, where she came from, what she had done up until then. There was no circumstance of her life that he did not go into, and he began to plan her future. She wrote Jones that if he had been a religious leader, he would have had people going to the stake for him. When she left the McClure menage, she was in a state of delirious excitement. Her future seemed assured. She was fairly launched at last after eight postgraduate years as newspaper columnist, provincial magazine editor, high school teacher, and apprentice story writer. But first she had to get back on the train and return to her Pittsburgh classroom.

One cannot be sure what stories were in that bundle that Cather mailed to McClure, but it is a good guess that five of the tales that were included in *The Troll Garden* were in the package, possibly six. One of them, "'A Death in the Desert,'" already had appeared in January in *Scribner's*. "A Wagner Matinee," which came out in *Everybody's Magazine* in February 1904, might have been one of them, but there is no doubt that "The Sculptor's Funeral" and "Paul's Case," which McClure later published in his magazine, were included. The other three stories, "Flavia and Her Artists," "The Garden Lodge," and "The

Marriage of Phædra," probably were in the parcel, but McClure was longer on promise than performance, for these three were neither published in *McClure's Magazine* nor placed in other publications. Their first and only appearance in print came in the book. McClure also did not bring out *The Troll Garden* for nearly two years after Cather's visit to New York. Cather's explanation for the delay was that they were waiting for some of the stories to appear first in the magazine. As matters turned out, the book actually was published a few weeks before "Paul's Case" finally appeared in *McClure's*, a very unusual procedure.

The first mention of *The Troll Garden* appeared in *Publisher's Weekly* on 18 March 1905, in the "Index to Spring Announcements" priced at $1.25. (A good copy bought from an antiquarian book dealer in 1980 cost $300.) A McClure advertisement in the same journal for 1 April announced publication on 5 April, which is the date that the copyright copies were deposited in the Library of Congress, and the "Weekly Record of New Publications" in *Publisher's Weekly* for 15 April lists the book. When it subsequently appeared in the book stores, buyers found a smallish volume of 256 pages bound in red cloth. It carried on its title page a quotation from Charles Kingsley: "A fairy palace, with a fairy garden; . . . . . Inside the Trolls dwell, ... Working at their magic forges, making and making always things rare and strange." Across from the title page was another epigraph from Christina Rossetti's "The Goblin Market": "We must not look at Goblin men, / We must not buy their fruits; / Who knows upon what soil they fed / Their hungry thirsty roots?" And the book carried a dedication to Cather's beloved Isabelle McClung, in whose home she had been living since 1901.

The Troll Garden is not simply a collection of stories all having something to do with art and artists. There is overall design and meaning and a careful arrangement of the tales to support the themes woven into the fabric of the text. The two epigraphs provide a clue to Cather's meaning and need to be looked at carefully. The quotation from Kingsley is taken from *The Roman and the Teuton* and is part of a parable he tells to introduce a discussion of the invasion of Rome by the barbarians. The forest people, who represent the barbarians, are attracted to the troll garden, Rome, covet it, and finally overrun it, only to discover afterwards that they have destroyed the marvels they sought.[4]

In Rossetti's poem two sisters, Laura and Lizzie, live innocently together in a fairy-tale cottage. Every morning and evening animal-like goblin men emerge from a sinister glen nearby hawking their luscious fruit. The girls know these are forbidden fruits, but Laura cannot resist the temptation and buys the fruit, paying with a golden curl. The dire consequences of this act are that Laura can no longer hear the seductive cries of the goblin men and goes into a physical decline. As she becomes prematurely old and haggard, Lizzie, who still can hear the tempting offers, sets about to save her sister. She confronts the goblin men with an offer to buy, but she will not taste. A dreadful fracas results, and the men smear the fruit over her. She rushes home, invites Laura to "eat me, drink me." Laura kisses Lizzie hungrily but finds that the juices of the fruit now are bitter, repulsive. The outcome of this encounter, however, is the restoration to health and youth of the wayward sister.

Just what Cather made of this allegory that modern feminists read as a powerful cry by a Victorian woman poet against the sexual poli-tics of the nineteenth century one can only infer.[5] The conscious or unconscious sexual-religious meaning must have been apparent to Cather, who was herself fighting her way to literary success in a male-dominated world. But the poem is complex, and it contains other lev-els of meaning, one of which fits in well with the quotation from Kingsley. The fruits of the goblin men are related in Cather's mind to the magical things rare and strange made by the trolls in their gar-den. The things desired are not only delightful and marvelous but also dangerous and capable of corrupting.

Throughout her life Cather made these juxtapositions: East against West, experience against innocence, civilization against primitivism. These opposites supplied the tension in her life, and she felt their pull throughout her career. These tensions were built into her life from her Virginia origin which contrasted sharply with Nebraska, from her study of history, literature, and the classics, which broadened the ho-rizons of her native Anglo-Saxon Protestant background, and from her life in Pittsburgh, and, later, New York, which opened a new world after a prairie childhood. She loved art like a religion and dedicated herself to it, but she also was aware that in the pursuit of any religion she might mistake false gods for the true one.

The conflict of the barbarians against the Romans, the forest chil-dren against the trolls, and primitivism against civilization long had

interested Cather. She made early use of this polarization in the previously mentioned early story "On the Divide," the tale of Canute
Canuteson, the lonely Norwegian immigrant farmer. There is more to
this story, however, than Canute's consumption of alcohol to relieve
the monotony of his isolation. The denouement of the tale consists of
Canute's decision to do something about his loneliness. He strides over
to Ole Yensen's farm and literally carries off Ole's daughter Lena, an
act that Cather describes thus:

So it was that Canute took her to his home, even as his bearded ancestors
took the fair frivolous women of the South in their hairy arms and bore them
down to their war ships. For ever and anon the soul becomes weary of the
conventions that are not of it, and with a single stroke shatters the civilized
lies with which it is unable to cope, and the strong arm reaches out and takes
by force what it cannot win by cunning.

Again the contrasts are the key element in the later story, "Eric
Hermannson's Soul," where the tensions are developed between the
easterner Margaret and the westerner Eric. Eric is one of the forest
children and Margaret the symbol of civilization—an effete civilization, as Cather's narrative makes clear to the reader—but to Eric,
Margaret's beauty and grace are overwhelming: "He felt as the Goths
before the white marbles in the Roman capitol, not knowing whether
they were men or gods." In this tale Margaret goes back to her sterile
eastern culture, leaving Eric touched by his contact with the troll garden but not corrupted by it. Primitivism in the best sense triumphs in
this story.

In Cather's arrangement of the stories in *The Troll Garden* the first
and last stories, "Flavia and Her Artists" and "Paul's Case," depict
characters seduced by art. Flavia, who operates a "hotel, habited by
freaks," as the ironical actress-commentator Miss Broadwood puts it,
is pursuing false gods in her worship of art. Cather must have observed archetypal Flavias in her years as a music and drama critic in
Pittsburgh when she attended soirées given by Pennsylvania matrons, wives of steel and coal moguls, who devoted themselves to lion-
hunting. That Flavia cannot distinguish between the true and the false
is overt enough in the talk, but her myopia is further accentuated by
Cather's abundant use of Roman allusions, always ironically. Her house
is a "temple to the gods of Victory, a sort of triumphal arch"; her relationship to her children is described as like that of Cornelia, the
mother of the Gracchi; and the story ends with Arthur Hamilton com-

pared to Gaius Marius among the ruins of Carthage.

The Jamesian flavor of this story is obvious, and the reason that Cather never reprinted this tale may well have been that she felt too much influenced by James. But her attention to James's craftsmanship was important for her developing narrative skill. The story is well told through the perspective of Imogen Willard, daughter of one of Flavia's old friends, who is invited to Flavia's menagerie because she has the distinction of being a woman who has earned a doctorate in philology. Imogen (probably suggested by Cather's old Nebraska friend Dorothy Canfield, who had a Ph.D. in Romance languages), because of her childhood friendship with Flavia's husband, can observe the relationship between the couple as Arthur's partisan. The invention of Miss Broadwood, the actress who doesn't take herself seriously, provides the running commentary on the "freaks" by one who is a real artist and not a stuffed shirt.

"Paul's Case," perhaps the best known of all Cather's stories, depicts a forest child destroyed by the delights of the troll garden. Paul, the Pittsburgh schoolboy who lives for Carnegie Hall, where he has a job ushering, cannot distinguish between the true and the false any more than Flavia can. Paul, however, does not have a patient husband to save him from his follies, and the lure of the forbidden fruit is more than he can withstand. When he commits suicide after his spree in New York financed by money stolen from his employer, the wheel comes full circle in Cather's cycle of tales. *The Troll Garden* opens "as the train neared Tarrytown" carrying Imogen Willard to Flavia's "temple" of the arts, and it ends with Paul throwing himself under the wheels of a locomotive outside Newark.

"Paul's Case" has been justly admired for its narrative skill and its psychological portraiture. It was the only story that Cather would allow to be anthologized towards the end of her life, and it is one of the three from *The Troll Garden* that she reprinted in *Youth and the Bright Medusa* and her *Novels and Stories*. It captures the very tone of Pittsburgh in 1905 and was compounded, she remembered in 1943, of two elements: the first was a boy she once had had in her Latin class, a nervous youth who was always trying to make himself interesting and to prove that he knew members of the local stock company; the other was herself, particularly the feelings she had about New York and the old Waldorf-Astoria Hotel when she was teaching in Pittsburgh and occasionally visiting the metropolis. Another ingredient that she probably had forgotten was the theft of an employer's money by two Pittsburgh boys who ran off to Chicago. They were found broke in a Chicago hotel a week later and brought back home, but not prosecuted because the families reimbursed the employer. The Pittsburgh papers were full of the story, reported the *Bookman* in a brief profile of Cather at the time *The Troll Garden* was published.[6]

"'A Death in the Desert,'" the first story in the collection to be published in a magazine, is the centerpiece of the book. The chief character, Adriance Hilgarde, who does not appear on stage at all, was suggested to Cather by Ethelbert Nevin, the composer, whom she had met during her second year in Pittsburgh. Meeting him had been one of the highlights of the year, she wrote a Nebraska friend; of all the interesting people she had encountered, Nevin, she said, was king and prince of them all—the greatest of American composers, a fellow of thirty (he actually was thirty-five) with the face of a boy and the laugh of a girl. He represented for her youth, gaiety, golden talent. His death three years later was a bitter blow, and the story captures some of her feelings about him. She must have written it soon after he died.

Cather placed this story in the middle of the book because it presents three different artists and three different kinds of careers. Katharine Gaylord, who is dying of tuberculosis in the wilds of Wyoming, is one of the forest children who has entered the garden, but only to be destroyed there. Everett Hilgarde, who is always being mistaken for his brilliant brother Adriance, is one of those who aspire to an artistic career but lack talent. Long before the story opens, he has accepted his fate and resolved "to beat no more at doors he could never enter." The least important of the three main characters, he is in the story chiefly as what James called a "ficelle," a character invented by the author as a convenience to the narrative structure. By his fortuitous meeting with Katharine in the railway depot at Cheyenne, Cather is able, through his attentive listening to Katharine's reminiscences, to develop the golden career of Adriance, the one forest child who has entered the troll garden and thrived there. But Katharine, the loser, and Adriance, the winner, are really two sides of the same coin: Nevin in his prime and Nevin who died at the age of thirty-eight. When Adriance sends the dying Katharine his latest sonata, the greatest thing he has yet written, she listens to Everett play it for her and cries out: "This is my tragedy, as I lie here spent by the race-course, listening to the feet of the runners as they pass me." Cather felt deeply the tragedy of Nevin's untimely death. Perhaps he too was a victim of the trolls.

The poignancy of Katharine's death is heightened by its being laid near Cheyenne, Wyoming, on "the grey plain that ended in the great upheaval of the Rockies." It is a bleak setting for the last days of a singer who had hoped to become a great Wagnerian soprano. Cather had visited Wyoming in 1898 with her brother Douglass, who had just gotten a job in Cheyenne, and she returned for a visit in 1901 just before writing the story. Douglass, moreover, was a railroad man, as Katharine's brother Charley Gaylord has been before coming up in the world and going into ranching. The source of the title, "A Death in the Desert" by Robert Browning, adds irony to the pathos, for Browning's poem is a dramatic monologue delivered by the apostle John as he dies in a Middle Eastern cave attended by a few faithful friends.

The second and sixth stories in *The Troll Garden* are an appropriate pair because they both deal with western characters whose lives end in defeat. "The Sculptor's Funeral" could have been set in Cather's native Red Cloud, though the stated locale is a little Kansas town. In this tale the barbarians are not noble-spirited, like Eric Hermannson, but mean and petty. The story falls into the category of revolt-from-the-village literature and invites comparison with the earlier work of E. W. Howe or Hamlin Garland and, later, the fiction of Sinclair Lewis and the poems of Edgar Lee Master's *Spoon River Anthology*. Cather no doubt placed the tale in Kansas to avoid the possible charge that she was satirizing her own townsfolk.

The story derives in part from a poem Cather wrote called "The Night Express," which was inspired by the return of the body of a Red Cloud boy who had died in another town, but she captures much more vividly in the story the opening scene of the watchers at the railway station than she had in the poem. The story also owes its origin to Cather's attendance in Pittsburgh at the funeral of a local artist, Stanley Reinhart. She wrote in her newspaper column after this event that Reinhart's family had not appreciated him, no one in Pittsburgh knew anything about him or cared, and it passed all understanding how he could have come out of that commercial city. Yet Harvey Merrick in "The Sculptor's Funeral," though he dies young and is brought home to a town that thought he was a failure, was a great artist whose fame was international. His defeat, like Nevin's, lay in his early death.

Cather's attack in this story on the narrow-mindedness of the villagers who cannot appreciate a local boy become artist is presented with no holds barred. She thought well of the story and for many years allowed it to be anthologized, but late in her life she began to feel that the criticism had been exaggerated and that the story had not been well executed. She then directed Alfred Knopf not to allow the story to be reprinted any longer, but it is one of the three tales that she reprinted in *Youth and the Bright Medusa* and *The Novels and Stories*. Despite Cather's disclaimers, it is a memorable story and one of the best productions of her early career.

"A Wagner Matinee" reverses the situation in "The Sculptor's Funeral" by bringing a Nebraska farm wife to Boston. The story fits into the overall design of *The Troll Garden* by making the narrator's Aunt Georgiana a former musician who has been denied for more than thirty years any possibility of entering the garden. She has been exiled to the barbarian country of a bleak prairie farm, where she has toiled like a slave helping her husband wrest a living from the inhospitable land. Cather paints a grim picture of Nebraska farm life in the pioneering days through her description of Georgiana with her "ill-fitting false teeth, and her skin . . . as yellow as a Mongolian's from constant exposure to a pitiless wind and to the alkaline water" and her hands that once had played the piano at the Boston Conservatory now "stretched and twisted into mere tentacles to hold and lift and knead with." The pathos in this story is overwhelming as the narrator-nephew with misguided kindness takes his aunt to a symphony concert and reawakens in her the memory of the lost garden. This is an excellent story, lean and compact, narrated with great skill from a young man's point of view, the same perspective that Cather later used in *My Ántonia*, and it is the third of the three stories that she reprinted both in *Youth and the Bright Medusa* and *The Novels and Stories*.

The last two tales to be considered from *The Troll Garden*, numbers three and five, are "The Garden Lodge" and "The Marriage of Phædra." In the first, Caroline Noble, like Aunt Georgiana, gives up art for marriage, but after that similarity the stories diverge sharply. Caroline, following her impoverished childhood and youth as the daughter of an improvident musician and sister of an unsuccessful artist, opts for marriage to a Wall Street tycoon. Denied nothing in her married life in the way of material possessions, Caroline has ample access to the music denied Aunt Georgiana and in fact retains her skill as an amateur pianist. Her life is like that of one of Cather's Pittsburgh friends, Ethel Litchfield, who had given up a career as a concert pianist to marry a prominent physician. The poignancy of this story comes in the epiphany that takes place when Caroline goes alone to the garden house where she and her recent guest, Raymond d'Esquerré, the Wagnerian tenor, have played and sung together. There Caroline realizes what strange and rare things she has lost by not entering the garden. This story dramatizes the cruel dilemma of the nineteenth-century woman artist who wanted both marriage and a career. For Cather art came first, however, and she never seriously considered subordinating her work to marriage.

"The Marriage of Phædra," like "The Garden Lodge" and "Flavia and Her Artists," was another story Cather never reprinted. It is the most Jamesian tale in the collection and probably the least effective. It fits well into the design of the book, however, as the story's conflict again focuses on the theme of the forest child versus the trolls. The barbarian this time is the wife of a great and recently deceased artist whose unfinished masterpiece she sells against his deathbed wish to an Australian art dealer. The story must have been written shortly after Cather returned from Europe in the summer of 1902, for the deceased artist is based on the Pre-Raphaelite painter Edward Burne-Jones, whose studio she visited when she was in London. The valet James, who presides over the empty studio in the story, was invented for the travel letter that Cather wrote for the *Nebraska State Journal* after her visit.[7] The invented valet, however, is appropriately named, because the narrative technique of the tale is very Henry Jamesian. The development of the character of the dead painter proceeds through the biographer-narrator's efforts to research his subject by striking up a friendship with James, the valet, and interviews with the painter's sister-in-law and wife. The tale further resonates with Jamesian meaning when one examines the great unfinished painting that gives the story its title (see Notes to the Text).

S. S. McClure's enthusiasm for his literary discovery notwithstanding, reviewers of *The Troll Garden* were not overwhelmed. The only long, signed review in a national magazine appeared in the *Bookman*, which also gave Cather a short profile accompanied by a picture. But this reviewer, Bessie du Bois, was not enchanted with the book, which she called a "collection of freak stories that are either lurid, hysterical or unwholesome, and that remind one of nothing so much as the coloured supplement to the Sunday papers." Except for Jim Laird in "The Sculptor's Funeral" and Paul in the last story, she thought the characters all "mere dummies, with fancy names, on which to hang epigrams." But this reviewer obviously was unsympathetic to the subject matter of the tales, which she thought dealt with "the ash-heap of the human mind—the thoughts and feelings that come to all of us when the pressure of the will is low, the refuse and sweepings of the mental life."[8]

Other national reviewers in the *New York Times Book Review*, the *Critic*, the *Dial*, the *Independent*, and the *Reader* treated *The Troll Garden* among their brief notices with from one hundred to two hundred words. In general these anonymous reviewers saw promise in Cather's work, but they were restrained and succinct. The *Times* thought the stories showed "deep feeling and ability," but added that "many of the stories are too ambitious, and seem to be more the work of promise than of fulfillment." Whether this reviewer even read the entire book is doubtful, for he called "Flavia and Her Artists" the best in the collection. The *Independent* reviewer would recommend the stories "strongly but not widely among his circle of acquaintances." He did, however, see "The Sculptor's Funeral" and "Paul's Case" as two of the best but had to rap Cather on the knuckles along with Hamlin Garland for seeing only the ugly side of pioneer life, its privations and rawness. The *Dial* reviewer seemed not to have read more than two of the stories and characterized the volume as "seven truly entertaining studies of somewhat abnormal human nature." The *Critic* found "real promise" and "no small degree of insight" in its two-hundred-word notice, and the *Reader Magazine* in slightly fewer words described the tales as "singularly vivid, strong, true, original."[9]

The sharpest reaction to any story in the collection already had come when "A Wagner Matinee" was published in *Everybody's Magazine* in 1904. Cather's old friend and editor Will Jones took her to task in the pages of the *Journal:* "The stranger to this state will associate Nebraska with the aunt's wretched figure, her ill-fitting false teeth, her skin yellowed by the weather. . . . If the writers of fiction who use western Nebraska as material would look up now and then and not keep their eyes and noses in the cattle yards, they might be more agreeable company."[10] Cather wrote Jones defending herself, denying that she had any intention of disparaging the state. She had placed the story back in pioneer times, she said, and she thought that everyone admitted that those were desolate days. She had thought that she was paying tribute to those uncomplaining women who weathered those times. Farm life was bad enough when she knew it, and what must it have been like before that? She had to admit, however, that she had used the farmhouse where she and her family had lived before they moved into Red Cloud and some of her recollections.[11]

She also had to admit that her family felt quite insulted. Everyone assumed that her Aunt Franc had sat for the portrait of Aunt Georgiana because Aunt Franc had graduated from Mount Holyoke Female Seminary before marrying Cather's uncle George in 1873 and moving to Nebraska. The family had told her that it was not nice to write about such things as she put into the description of Aunt Georgiana. She wrote a friend that the whole affair had been the nearest she ever had come to personal disgrace. She seemed to have done something horrid without realizing it, but someday, she supposed it would all seem humorous.[12] That she could not have intended an insult is perfectly clear from the warm, affectionate tone of all her letters to Aunt Franc.

When book-buyers did not rush out to get *The Troll Garden*, McClure, Phillips and Company did not reprint the book, and apparently the first and only printing was a small one. There were still copies left in 1906 when McClure, Phillips and Company abandoned book publishing and sold their stock to Doubleday, Page and Company. Cather took the book's lack of success philosophically and went on teaching high school. But even if McClure did not make money publishing *The Troll Garden*, he had discovered a valuable property in Cather. One year later, when an upheaval took place on his magazine, he sent for Cather to come to work for him. She then spent the next six years helping edit *McClure's Magazine*, rising to be managing editor and becoming Sam McClure's most valuable asset. If her book had been a best-seller, she probably would have begun writing novels five years sooner. In fact she already had attempted a novel that McClure's had rejected in 1905, but once she went back to magazine journalism, there was no time to revise that manuscript or to write another novel. She could only manage a few stories during the next few years.

Witter Bynner, the poet, who then was fresh out of Harvard and a lowly member of McClure's staff, had great faith in *The Troll Garden* and tried to interest Henry James in the book. He sent James a copy and then followed it up with a letter, to which James replied that he had received the book but had had no intention of reading it until getting Bynner's letter. James went on: "Being now almost in my 100th year, and with a long and weary experience of such matters [receiving complimentary works of fiction] behind me, promiscuous fiction has become abhorrent to me, and I find it the hardest thing in the world to read almost *any* new novel. Any is hard enough, but the hardest from the innocent hands of young females, young American females perhaps above all." But he added that in spite of these feelings he would do his best for Miss Cather. Bynner sent Cather a copy of the letter, to which she replied that it had given her a keen satisfaction. James's attitude was exactly the one she would have wished him to have, and she would have been very much hurt if he did not have the opinion he expressed about "promiscuous fiction." His letter she thought a kind of moral stimulant, and she promised Bynner that she would stand up with good grace to whatever punishment he might mete out in his second letter.[13] There is no evidence that James ever read the book, but if he did, he remained silent.

In 1911 Cather's friend Elizabeth Sergeant bought a secondhand copy of *The Troll Garden* and read it for the first time. She found "The Sculptor's Funeral," "A Wagner Matinee," and "Paul's Case" all exciting stories, full of passion and superbly executed, and wrote Cather of her "joy and critical estimate." Cather replied that she was pleased that her friend had found something to enjoy in *The Troll Garden*, but the stories had been written so long ago "that they now hardly seemed to belong to her. She herself had outgrown the harsh mood that had inspired the western ones. The starvation of a girl avid for a richer environment seemed to stick out, to deform, to make the picture one-sided."[14]

One of the purposes of this edition is to gather into the appendix all the changes that Cather made in successive revisions of her stories. When Dorothy Canfield Fisher, then a novelist herself, reviewed *Youth and the Bright Medusa* in 1921, she commented on Cather's ability to rework her fiction. She suggested that anyone who wanted to see how a real artist could "smooth away crudeness without rooting out the life" of a story should study the revisions made in "'A Death in the Desert'" from its initial appearance in *Scribner's* in 1903 to its final version in the volume she was reviewing.[15] Although this story underwent the most changes of any of the reprinted tales, all of the stories, except "The Wagner Matinee," underwent the same smoothing process.

The last two stories to be published serially, "The Sculptor's Funeral " and "Paul's Case," were the most polished at their first appearance, but even so, the former story underwent sixty substantive changes in its four versions. These were mostly, however, a matter of changing a word here and there, dropping a few words that seemed excessive, clarifying a detail from time to time. Some examples: the phrase "gentle bitterness" in the magazine version (MV) becomes "quiet bitterness" in *The Troll Garden* (TG) and *Youth and the Bright Medusa* (YBM), and in *The Novels and Stories* (NS) the entire sentence containing this phrase is pared away. The "red beard" of MV is merely "beard" in the later versions, and the plain "table" and "room" of MV become in later versions "side table" and "dining-room." In an effort to tone down what Cather later came to regard as excesses, she changed "orgy of grief" in MV, TG, and YBM to "behaviour" in NS and "trapseing to Paris and all that folly" in MV and TG to mere "nonsense" in YBM and NS.

"Paul's Case," which actually was published in *McClure's Magazine* after the book came out, underwent nearly ninety substantive changes from MV to NS. Between MV and TG Cather added 235 words to the story, but it is likely that she was merely restoring cuts that had been made to fit "Paul's Case" into an even number of pages in the magazine. Other changes are similar to those found in the successive versions of "The Sculptor's Funeral." For example, what is "stimulus" in MV and TG becomes "intoxication" in YBM and NS; "penetrated" becomes "permeated"; and "usually" becomes "placidly." Occasionally verb tenses and relative pronouns are touched up, and one curious change has Paul's daydreams of travel transfer their objective from Venice to California. There are minor deletions to tighten up the text and revisions for precision, such as "three" changing to "four" and a "dozen" switching to "many."

The revisions of "A Wagner Matinee" are more interesting, but the thrust of the changes is not towards artistic improvement. The criticism of her family and Will Jones made Cather soften the portrait of Aunt Georgiana between MV and TG in a few details. The following passages were deleted: "when I got her into the carriage she looked not unlike one of those charred, smoked bodies that fire-men lift from the *debris* of a burned building"; and "the most striking thing about her physiognomy, however, was an incessant twitching of the mouth and eyebrows, a form of nervous disorder resulting from isolation and monotony, and from frequent physical suffering." Two other deletions pared unnecessary detail about Wagner, as though Cather had just discovered that composer when she first wrote the story and wanted to enlighten her readers. Finally, there are several additions between MV and TG that add color to the narrative and heighten the pathos of the situation. Aunt Georgiana's skin "yellow as a Mongolian's" remained, however, along with her ill-fitting false teeth.

Between the appearance of TG in 1905 and YBM in 1920 Cather changed greatly in her attitude toward Nebraska. The affirmations in *O Pioneers!* and *My Ántonia* are reflected in a much-modified portrait of Aunt Georgiana. Missing in YBM are more than four hundred words from what is the shortest tale in TG. Gone now are seven passages, including the yellow skin and false teeth, that made the original character a grotesque figure, and in additional places the "absurdities" of Aunt Georgiana's attire give way to "her queer, country clothes"; her "misshapen figure" becomes her "battered" figure. One would have to say that the result of all this plastic surgery is to transform Aunt Georgiana from a cruelly used, worn-out farm wife from a harsh, isolated prairie farm into a quaint little old lady from the boondocks. By the time Cather revised the story once again for NS in the mid-thirties, there was not much left to change in the portrait, but still she managed three more small cuts that modify Aunt Georgiana's emotional display during the concert, and the powerful ending of the story that survived three versions is emasculated in the final one. From "she burst into tears and sobbed pleadingly. 'I don't want to go, Clark, I don't want to go!'" in MV, TG, and YBM, the final speech of Aunt Georgiana becomes in the penultimate paragraph: "She turned to me with a sad little smile. 'I don't want to go, Clark. I suppose we must.'"

The revisions in "'A Death in the Desert'" that interested Fisher are very extensive and complex. This is the first story that Cather published that she was willing to reprint, but she never was satisfied with it. As the centerpiece in her collection and a story that commemorated her short but intense friendship with Nevin, she was reluctant to abandon it, and each time she revised it, she trimmed and polished, spliced and patched. First she cut about one thousand words from MV before reprinting in TG. Many of these cuts were simply the paring of excessive detail, and one can see that even at that early date Cather was working towards the lean prose that she produced in her mature years and theorized about in her essay "The Novel Démeublé." These cuts may be clearly seen in the Table of Revisions.

When she was preparing her stories for YBM, Cather once again worked over "'A Death in the Desert'" and this time cut it from about eleven thousand words to eight thousand, making the final version only two-thirds the length of the original tale. The cuts are spread throughout the story and range from one or two sentences to entire paragraphs. The result is hardly the same story that Cather wrote in 1902. Fisher is correct in admiring the skill of the revisions, but the result is more a story of Cather's maturity than of her literary apprenticeship. Fifteen years later, when Houghton Mifflin wanted to bring out her collected works, Cather looked over the story and decided that it would have to go, and she did not reprint it again. One suspects that by the mid-thirties she was so far from the fin de siècle aestheticism out of which the story had been written that it seemed unsalvageable. The story contains more literary allusions and quotations than any of the other stories in *The Troll Garden*, embellishments that she long since had rid herself of, and in the final analysis it seems that a young artist's death in the desert no longer had the power to move her at the age of sixty-five that it had when she was twenty-nine.

Notes to the Introduction

1. Willa Cather, *Willa Cather's Collected Short Fiction, 1892–1912*, rev. ed., ed. Virginia Faulkner, introd. Mildred Bennett (Lincoln: University of Nebraska Press, 1970).

2. Willa Cather, *The World and the Parish: Willa Cather's Articles and Reviews, 1893–1902*, ed. William M. Curtin (Lincoln: University of Nebraska Press, 1970), 2:847.

3. Cather to Will Jones, 7 May 1903, University of Virginia, Charlottesville.

4. Charles Kingsley, *The Roman and the Teuton: A Series of Lectures Delivered before the University of Cambridge* (London and New York, 1891), pp. 1–5; reprinted in Willa Cather, *The Kingdom of Art: Willa Cather's First Principles and Critical Statements, 1893–1896*, ed. Bernice Slote (Lincoln: University of Nebraska Press, 1966), pp. 442–44.

Interesting readings of *The Troll Garden* by other critics may be found in E. K. Brown, *Willa Cather: A Critical Biography* (New York: Alfred A. Knopf, 1953), pp. 113–22; Edward A. and Lillian D. Bloom, *Willa Cather's Gift of Sym-*

pathy (Carbondale: Southern Illinois University Press, 1962), chap. 4 ("The Artistic 'Chain of Human Endeavor'"); Bernice Slote's introduction to *The Kingdom of Art*, pp. 92–97.

5. See Sandra Gilbert and Susan Gubar, *The Madwoman in the Attic: The Woman Writer and the Nineteenth-Century Literary Imagination* (New Haven, Conn.: Yale University Press, 1979), pp. 564–71.

6. *Bookman* 21 (July 1905): 456–57.

7. Cather, *The World and the Parish*, 2:912–16.

8. *Bookman* 21 (August 1905): 612–14.

9. *New York Times*, 6 May 1905; *Independent* 58 (29 June 1905): 1482–83; *Dial* 38 (1 June 1905): 394; *Critic* 47 (November 1905): 476; *Reader Magazine* 6 (September 1905): 477.

10. Will Jones, *Nebraska State Journal*, 27 February 1904; reprinted in Mildred Bennett, *The World of Willa Cather* (Lincoln: University of Nebraska Press, 1961), p. 254.

11. Cather to Jones, 6 March 1904, University of Virginia.

12. Cather to Viola Roseboro, n.d.; see James Woodress, *Willa Cather: Her Life and Art* (New York, 1970), pp. 117, 276.

13. Elizabeth Sergeant, *Willa Cather: A Memoir* (Philadelphia, 1953), pp. 68–69; Cather to Witter Bynner, 24 February [1906?], Harvard University, Cambridge, Mass.

14. Sergeant, *Willa Cather*, p. 67.

15. Dorothy Canfield Fisher, "Some Books of Short Stories," *Yale Review* 10 (1921): 671.

The Troll Garden

"We must not look at Goblin men,
    We must not buy their fruits;
Who knows upon what soil they fed
    Their hungry thirsty roots?"
        GOBLIN MARKET

by Willa Sibert Cather

The Troll
Garden

A fairy palace, with a fairy garden; . . . . .
Inside the trolls dwell, ... working at their
magic forges, making and making always things
rare and strange CHARLES KINGSLEY

To Isabelle McClung

Flavia and Her Artists

As the train neared Tarrytown, Imogen Willard began to wonder why she had consented to be one of Flavia's house party at all. She had not felt enthusiastic about it since leaving the city, and was experiencing a prolonged ebb of purpose, a current of chilling indecision, under which she vainly sought for the motive which had induced her to accept Flavia's invitation.

Perhaps it was a vague curiosity to see Flavia's husband, who had been the magician of her childhood and the hero of innumerable Arabian fairy tales. Perhaps it was a desire to see M. Roux, whom Flavia had announced as the especial attraction of the occasion. Perhaps it was a wish to study that remarkable woman in her own setting.

Imogen admitted a mild curiosity concerning Flavia. She was in the habit of taking people rather seriously, but somehow found it impossible to take Flavia so, because of the very vehemence and insistence with which Flavia demanded it. Submerged in her studies, Imogen had, of late years, seen very little of Flavia; but Flavia, in her hurried visits to New York, between her excursions from studio to studio—her luncheons with this lady who had to play at a matinée, and her dinners with that singer who had an evening concert—had seen enough of her friend's handsome daughter to conceive for her an inclination of such violence and assurance as only Flavia could afford. The fact that Imogen had shown rather marked capacity in certain esoteric lines of scholarship, and had decided to specialize in a well-sounding branch of philology at the Ecole des Chartes, had fairly placed her in that category of "interesting people" whom Flavia considered her natural affinities, and lawful prey.

When Imogen stepped upon the station platform she was immediately appropriated by her hostess, whose commanding figure and assurance of attire she had recognized from a distance. She was hurried into a high tilbury and Flavia, taking the driver's cushion beside her, gathered up the reins with an experienced hand.

"My dear girl," she remarked, as she turned the horses up the street, "I was afraid the train might be late. M. Roux insisted upon coming up by boat and did not arrive until after seven."

"To think of M. Roux's being in this part of the world at all, and subject to the vicissitudes of river boats! Why in the world did he come over?" queried Imogen with lively interest. "He is the sort of man who must dissolve and become a shadow outside of Paris."

"Oh, we have a houseful of the most interesting people," said Flavia, professionally. "We have actually managed to get Ivan Schemetzkin. He was ill in California at the close of his concert tour, you know, and he is recuperating with us, after his wearing journey from the coast. Then there is Jules Martel, the painter; Signor Donati, the tenor; Professor Schotte, who has dug up Assyria, you know; Restzhoff, the Russian chemist; Alcée Buisson, the philologist; Frank Wellington, the novelist; and Will Maidenwood, the editor of *Woman*. Then there is my second cousin, Jemima Broadwood, who made such a hit in Pinero's comedy last winter, and Frau Lichtenfeld. *Have* you read her?"

Imogen confessed her utter ignorance of Frau Lichtenfeld, and Flavia went on.

"Well, she is a most remarkable person; one of those advanced German women, a militant iconoclast, and this drive will not be long enough to permit of my telling you her history. Such a story! Her novels were the talk of all Germany when I was there last, and several of them have been suppressed—an honour in Germany, I understand. 'At Whose Door' has been translated. I am so unfortunate as not to read German."

"I'm all excitement at the prospect of meeting Miss Broadwood," said Imogen. "I've seen her in nearly everything she does. Her stage personality is delightful. She always reminds me of a nice, clean, pink-and-white boy who has just had his cold bath, and come down all aglow for a run before breakfast."

"Yes, but isn't it unfortunate that she will limit herself to those minor comedy parts that are so little appreciated in this country? One ought to be satisfied with nothing less than the best, ought one?" The peculiar, breathy tone in which Flavia always uttered that word "best," the most worn in her vocabulary, always jarred on Imogen and always made her obdurate.

"I don't at all agree with you," she said reservedly. "I thought every one admitted that the most remarkable thing about Miss Broadwood is her admirable sense of fitness, which is rare enough in her profession."

Flavia could not endure being contradicted; she always seemed to regard it in the light of a defeat, and usually coloured unbecomingly. Now she changed the subject.

"Look, my dear," she cried, "there is Frau Lichtenfeld now, coming to meet us. Doesn't she look as if she had just escaped out of Walhalla? She is actually over six feet."

Imogen saw a woman of immense stature, in a very short skirt and a broad, flapping sun hat, striding down the hillside at a long, swinging gait. The refugee from Walhalla approached, panting. Her heavy, Teutonic features were scarlet from the rigour of her exercise, and her hair, under her flapping sun hat, was tightly befrizzled about her brow. She fixed her sharp little eyes upon Imogen and extended both her hands.

"So this is the little friend?" she cried, in a rolling baritone.

Imogen was quite as tall as her hostess; but everything, she reflected, is comparative. After the introduction Flavia apologized.

"I wish I could ask you to drive up with us, Frau Lichtenfeld."

"Ah, no!" cried the giantess, drooping her head in humorous caricature of a time-honoured pose of the heroines of sentimental romances. "It has never been my fate to be fitted into corners. I have never known the sweet privileges of the tiny."

Laughing, Flavia started the ponies, and the colossal woman, standing in the middle of the dusty road, took off her wide hat and waved them a farewell which, in scope of gesture, recalled the salute of a plumed cavalier.

When they arrived at the house, Imogen looked about her with keen curiosity, for this was veritably the work of Flavia's hands, the materialization of hopes long deferred. They passed directly into a large, square hall with a gallery on three sides, studio fashion. This opened at one end into a Dutch breakfast-room, beyond which was the large dining-room. At the other end of the hall was the music-room. There was a smoking-room, which one entered through the li-

brary behind the staircase. On the second floor there was the same
general arrangement; a square hall, and, opening from it, the guest
chambers, or, as Miss Broadwood termed them, the "cages."

When Imogen went to her room, the guests had begun to return
from their various afternoon excursions. Boys were gliding through
the halls with ice-water, covered trays, and flowers, colliding with
maids and valets who carried shoes and other articles of wearing ap-
parel. Yet, all this was done in response to inaudible bells, on felt
soles, and in hushed voices, so that there was very little confusion
about it.

Flavia had at last builded her house and hewn out her seven pil-
lars; there could be no doubt, now, that the asylum for talent, the
sanatorium of the arts, so long projected, was an accomplished fact.
Her ambition had long ago outgrown the dimensions of her house on
Prairie Avenue; besides, she had bitterly complained that in Chicago
traditions were against her. Her project had been delayed by Arthur's doggedly standing out for the Michigan woods, but Flavia knew
well enough that certain of the *aves rares*—"the best"—could not be
lured so far away from the seaport, so she declared herself for the
historic Hudson and knew no retreat. The establishing of a New York
office had at length overthrown Arthur's last valid objection to quit-
ting the lake country for three months of the year; and Arthur could
be wearied into anything, as those who knew him knew.

Flavia's house was the mirror of her exultation; it was a temple to
the gods of Victory, a sort of triumphal arch. In her earlier days she
had swallowed experiences that would have unmanned one of less tor-
rential enthusiasm or blind pertinacity. But, of late years, her deter-
mination had told; she saw less and less of those mysterious persons
with mysterious obstacles in their path and mysterious grievances
against the world, who had once frequented her house on Prairie Avenue. In the stead of this multitude of the unarrived, she had now the
few, the select, "the best." Of all that band of indigent retainers who
had once fed at her board like the suitors in the halls of Penelope, only
Alcée Buisson still retained his right of entrée. He alone had remembered that ambition hath a knapsack at his back, wherein he puts
alms to oblivion, and he alone had been considerate enough to do what
Flavia had expected of him, and give his name a current value in the
world. Then, as Miss Broadwood put it, "he was her first real one,"—
and Flavia, like Mahomet, could remember her first believer.

The "House of Song," as Miss Broadwood had called it, was the outcome of Flavia's more exalted strategies. A woman who made less a point of sympathizing with their delicate organisms, might have sought to plunge these phosphorescent pieces into the tepid bath of domestic life; but Flavia's discernment was deeper. This must be a refuge where the shrinking soul, the sensitive brain, should be unconstrained; where the caprice of fancy should outweigh the civil code, if necessary. She considered that this much Arthur owed her; for she, in her turn, had made concessions. Flavia, had, indeed, quite an equipment of epigrams to the effect that our century creates the iron genii which evolve its fairy tales: but the fact that her husband's name was annually painted upon some ten thousand threshing machines, in reality contributed very little to her happiness.

Arthur Hamilton was born, and had spent his boyhood in the West Indies, and physically he had never lost the brand of the tropics. His father, after inventing the machine which bore his name, had returned to the States to patent and manufacture it. After leaving college, Arthur had spent five years ranching in the West and travelling abroad. Upon his father's death he had returned to Chicago and, to the astonishment of all his friends, had taken up the business,—without any demonstration of enthusiasm, but with quiet perseverance, marked ability, and amazing industry. Why or how a self-sufficient, rather ascetic man of thirty, indifferent in manner, wholly negative in all other personal relations, should have doggedly wooed and finally married Flavia Malcolm, was a problem that had vexed older heads than Imogen's.

While Imogen was dressing she heard a knock at her door, and a young woman entered whom she at once recognized as Jemima Broadwood—"Jimmy" Broadwood, she was called by people in her own profession. While there was something unmistakably professional in her frank *savoir-faire*, "Jimmy's" was one of those faces to which the rouge never seems to stick. Her eyes were keen and grey as a windy April sky, and so far from having been seared by calcium lights, you might have fancied they had never looked on anything less bucolic than growing fields and country fairs. She wore her thick, brown hair short and parted at the side; and, rather than hinting at freakishness, this seemed admirably in keeping with her fresh boyish countenance. She extended to Imogen a large, well-shaped hand which it was a pleasure to clasp.

"Ah! you are Miss Willard, and I see I need not introduce myself. Flavia said you were kind enough to express a wish to meet me, and I preferred to meet you alone. Do you mind if I smoke?"

"Why, certainly not," said Imogen, somewhat disconcerted and looking hurriedly about for matches.

"There, be calm, I'm always prepared," said Miss Broadwood, checking Imogen's flurry with a soothing gesture, and producing an oddly-fashioned silver match-case from some mysterious recess in her dinner-gown. She sat down in a deep chair, crossed her patent-leather Oxfords, and lit her cigarette. "This match-box," she went on meditatively, "once belonged to a Prussian officer. He shot himself in his bath-tub, and I bought it at the sale of his effects."

Imogen had not yet found any suitable reply to make to this rather irrelevant confidence, when Miss Broadwood turned to her cordially: "I'm awfully glad you've come, Miss Willard, though I've not quite decided why you did it. I wanted very much to meet you. Flavia gave me your thesis to read."

"Why, how funny!" ejaculated Imogen.

"On the contrary," remarked Miss Broadwood. "I thought it decidedly lacked humour."

"I meant," stammered Imogen, beginning to feel very much like Alice in Wonderland, "I meant that I thought it rather strange Mrs. Hamilton should fancy you would be interested."

Miss Broadwood laughed heartily. "Now, don't let my rudeness frighten you. Really, I found it very interesting, and no end impressive. You see, most people in my profession are good for absolutely nothing else, and, therefore, they have a deep and abiding conviction that in some other line they might have shone. Strange to say, scholarship is the object of our envious and particular admiration. Anything in type impresses us greatly; that's why so many of us marry authors or newspaper men and lead miserable lives." Miss Broadwood saw that she had rather disconcerted Imogen, and blithely tacked in another direction. "You see," she went on, tossing aside her half-consumed cigarette, "some years ago Flavia would not have deemed me worthy to open the pages of your thesis—nor to be one of her house party of the chosen, for that matter. I've Pinero to thank for both pleasures. It all depends on the class of business I'm playing whether I'm in favour or not. Flavia is my second cousin, you know, so I can say whatever disagreeable things I choose with perfect good grace. I'm quite desperate for some one to laugh with, so I'm going to fasten myself upon you—for, of course, one can't expect any of these gypsy-dago people to see anything funny. I don't intend you shall lose the humour of the situation. What do you think of Flavia's infirmary for the arts, anyway?"

"Well, it's rather too soon for me to have any opinion at all," said Imogen, as she again turned to her dressing. "So far, you are the only one of the artists I've met."

"One of them?" echoed Miss Broadwood. "One of the *artists?* My offence may be rank, my dear, but I really don't deserve that. Come, now, whatever badges of my tribe I may bear upon me, just let me divest you of any notion that I take myself seriously."

Imogen turned from the mirror in blank astonishment, and sat down on the arm of a chair, facing her visitor. "I can't fathom you at all, Miss Broadwood," she said frankly. "Why shouldn't you take yourself seriously? What's the use of beating about the bush? Surely you know that you are one of the few players on this side of the water who have at all the spirit of natural or ingenuous comedy?"

"Thank you, my dear. Now we are quite even about the thesis, aren't we? Oh! did you mean it? Well, you *are* a clever girl. But you see it doesn't do to permit oneself to look at it in that light. If we do, we always go to pieces, and waste our substance a-starring as the unhappy daughter of the Capulets. But there, I hear Flavia coming to take you down; and just remember I'm not one of them; the artists, I mean."

Flavia conducted Imogen and Miss Broadwood downstairs. As they reached the lower hall they heard voices from the music-room, and dim figures were lurking in the shadows under the gallery, but their hostess led straight to the smoking-room. The June evening was chilly, and a fire had been lighted in the fireplace. Through the deepening dusk the firelight flickered upon the pipes and curious weapons on the wall, and threw an orange glow over the Turkish hangings. One side of the smoking-room was entirely of glass, separating it from the conservatory, which was flooded with white light from the electric bulbs. There was about the darkened room some suggestion of certain chambers in the Arabian Nights, opening on a court of palms. Perhaps it was partially this memory-evoking suggestion that caused Imogen to start so violently when she saw dimly, in a blur of shadow, the figure of a man, who sat smoking in a low, deep chair before the fire. He was long, and thin, and brown. His long, nerveless hands drooped from the arms of his chair. A brown moustache shaded his mouth, and his eyes were sleepy and apathetic. When Imogen entered, he rose indolently and gave her his hand, his manner barely courteous.

"I am glad you arrived promptly, Miss Willard," he said with an indifferent drawl. "Flavia was afraid you might be late. You had a pleasant ride up, I hope?"

"O, very, thank you, Mr. Hamilton," she replied, feeling that he did not particularly care whether she replied at all.

Flavia explained that she had not yet had time to dress for dinner, as she had been attending to Mr. Will Maidenwood, who had become faint after hurting his finger in an obdurate window, and immediately excused herself. As she left, Hamilton turned to Miss Broadwood with a rather spiritless smile.

"Well, Jimmy," he remarked, "I brought up a piano box full of fireworks for the boys. How do you suppose we'll manage to keep them until the Fourth?"

"We can't, unless we steel ourselves to deny there are any on the premises," said Miss Broadwood, seating herself on a low stool by Hamilton's chair, and leaning back against the mantel. "Have you seen Helen, and has she told you the tragedy of the tooth?"

"She met me at the station, with her tooth wrapped up in tissue paper. I had tea with her an hour ago. Better sit down, Miss Willard"; he rose and pushed a chair toward Imogen, who was standing peering into the conservatory. "We are scheduled to dine at seven, but they seldom get around before eight."

By this time Imogen had made out that here the plural pronoun, third person, always referred to the artists. As Hamilton's manner did not spur one to cordial intercourse, and as his attention seemed directed to Miss Broadwood, in so far as it could be said to be directed to any one, she sat down facing the conservatory and watched him, unable to decide in how far he was identical with the man who had first met Flavia Malcolm in her mother's house, twelve years ago. Did he at all remember having known her as a little girl, and why did his indifference hurt her so, after all these years? Had some remnant of her childish affection for him gone on living, somewhere down in the sealed caves of her consciousness, and had she really expected to find it possible to be fond of him again? Suddenly she saw a light in the

man's sleepy eyes, an unmistakable expression of interest and pleasure that fairly startled her. She turned quickly in the direction of his
glance, and saw Flavia, just entering, dressed for dinner and lit by
the effulgence of her most radiant manner. Most people considered
Flavia handsome, and there was no gainsaying that she carried her
five-and-thirty years splendidly. Her figure had never grown ma-
tronly, and her face was of the sort that does not show wear. Its blond
tints were as fresh and enduring as enamel,—and quite as hard. Its
usual expression was one of tense, often strained, animation, which
compressed her lips nervously. A perfect scream of animation, Miss
Broadwood had called it—created and maintained by sheer, indomi-
table force of will. Flavia's appearance on any scene whatever made a
ripple, caused a certain agitation and recognition, and, among im-
pressionable people, a certain uneasiness. For all her sparkling assurance of manner, Flavia was certainly always ill at ease, and even more
certainly anxious. She seemed not convinced of the established order
of material things, seemed always trying to conceal her feeling that
walls might crumble, chasms open, or the fabric of her life fly to the
winds in irretrievable entanglement. At least this was the impression
Imogen got from that note in Flavia which was so manifestly false.

Hamilton's keen, quick, satisfied glance at his wife had recalled to
Imogen all her inventory of speculations about them. She looked at
him with compassionate surprise. As a child she had never permitted
herself to believe that Hamilton cared at all for the woman who had
taken him away from her; and since she had begun to think about
them again, it had never occurred to her that any one could become
attached to Flavia in that deeply personal and exclusive sense. It
seemed quite as irrational as trying to possess oneself of Broadway
at noon.

When they went out to dinner, Imogen realized the completeness
of Flavia's triumph. They were people of one name, mostly, like kings;
people whose names stirred the imagination like a romance or a melody. With the notable exception of M. Roux, Imogen had seen most of
them before, either in concert halls or lecture rooms; but they looked
noticeably older and dimmer than she remembered them.

Opposite her sat Schemetzkin, the Russian pianist, a short, corpulent man, with an apoplectic face and purplish skin, his thick, iron-
grey hair tossed back from his forehead. Next the German giantess
sat the Italian tenor—the tiniest of men—pale, with soft, light hair,

much in disorder, very red lips and fingers yellowed by cigarettes. Frau Lichtenfeld shone in a gown of emerald green, fitting so closely as to enhance her natural floridness. However, to do the good lady justice, let her attire be never so modest, it gave an effect of barbaric splendour. At her left sat Herr Schotte, the Assyriologist, whose features were effectually concealed by the convergence of his hair and beard, and whose glasses were continually falling into his plate. This gentleman had removed more tons of earth in the course of his explorations than had any of his confrères, and his vigorous attack upon his food seemed to suggest the strenuous nature of his accustomed toil. His eyes were small and deeply set, and his forehead bulged fiercely above his eyes in a bony ridge. His heavy brows completed the leonine suggestion of his face. Even to Imogen, who knew something of his work and greatly respected it, he was entirely too reminiscent of the stone age to be altogether an agreeable dinner companion. He seemed, indeed, to have absorbed something of the savagery of those early types of life which he continually studied.

Frank Wellington, the young Kansas man who had been two years out of Harvard and had published three historical novels, sat next Mr. Will Maidenwood, who was still pale from his recent sufferings, and carried his hand bandaged. They took little part in the general conversation, but, like the lion and the unicorn, were always at it; discussing, every time they met, whether there were or were not passages in Mr. Wellington's works which should be eliminated, out of consideration for the Young Person. Wellington had fallen into the hands of a great American syndicate which most effectually befriended struggling authors whose struggles were in the right direction, and which had guaranteed to make him famous before he was thirty. Feeling the security of his position, he stoutly defended those passages which jarred upon the sensitive nerves of the young editor of *Woman*. Maidenwood, in the smoothest of voices, urged the necessity of the author's recognizing certain restrictions at the outset, and Miss Broadwood, who joined the argument quite without invitation or encouragement, seconded him with pointed and malicious remarks which caused the young editor manifest discomfort. Restzhoff, the chemist, demanded the attention of the entire company for his exposition of his devices for manufacturing ice-cream from vegetable oils, and for administering drugs in bonbons.

Flavia, always noticeably restless at dinner, was somewhat apathetic toward the advocate of peptonized chocolate, and was plainly concerned about the sudden departure of M. Roux, who had announced that it would be necessary for him to leave to-morrow. M. Emile Roux, who sat at Flavia's right, was a man in middle life and quite bald, clearly without personal vanity, though his publishers preferred to circulate only those of his portraits taken in his ambrosial youth. Imogen was considerably shocked at his unlikeness to the slender, black-stocked Rolla he had looked at twenty. He had declined into the florid, settled heaviness of indifference and approaching age. There was, however, a certain look of durability and solidity about him; the look of a man who has earned the right to be fat and bald, and even silent at dinner if he chooses.

Throughout the discussion between Wellington and Will Maidenwood, though they invited his participation, he remained silent, betraying no sign either of interest or contempt. Since his arrival he had directed most of his conversation to Hamilton, who had never read one of his twelve great novels. This perplexed and troubled Flavia. On the night of his arrival, Jules Martel had enthusiastically declared, "There are schools and schools, manners and manners; but Roux is Roux, and Paris sets its watches by his clock." Flavia had already repeated this remark to Imogen. It haunted her, and each time she quoted it she was impressed anew.

Flavia shifted the conversation uneasily, evidently exasperated and excited by her repeated failures to draw the novelist out. "Monsieur Roux," she began abruptly, with her most animated smile, "I remember so well a statement I read some years ago in your 'Mes Etudes des Femmes,' to the effect that you had never met a really intellectual woman. May I ask, without being impertinent, whether that assertion still represents your experience?"

"I meant, madame," said the novelist conservatively, "intellectual in a sense very special, as we say of men in whom the purely intellectual functions seem almost independent."

"And you still think a woman so constituted a mythical personage?" persisted Flavia, nodding her head encouragingly.

"*Une Méduse*, madame, who, if she were discovered, would transmute us all into stone," said the novelist, bowing gravely. "If she existed at all," he added deliberately, "it was my business to find her, and she has cost me many a vain pilgrimage. Like Rudel of Tripoli, I have crossed seas and penetrated deserts to seek her out. I have, indeed, encountered women of learning whose industry I have been compelled to respect; many who have possessed beauty and charm and perplexing cleverness; a few with remarkable information, and a sort of fatal facility."

"And Mrs. Browning, George Eliot, and your own Mme. Dudevant?" queried Flavia with that fervid enthusiasm with which she could, on occasion, utter things simply incomprehensible for their banality—at her feats of this sort Miss Broadwood was wont to sit breathless with admiration.

"Madame, while the intellect was undeniably present in the performances of those women, it was only the stick of the rocket. Although this woman has eluded me, I have studied her conditions and perturbations as astronomers conjecture the orbits of planets they have never seen. If she exists, she is probably neither an artist nor a woman with a mission, but an obscure personage, with imperative intellectual needs, who absorbs rather than produces."

Flavia, still nodding nervously, fixed a strained glance of interrogation upon M. Roux. "Then you think she would be a woman whose first necessity would be to know, whose instincts would be satisfied only with the best, who could draw from others; appreciative, merely?"

The novelist lifted his dull eyes to his interlocutress with an untranslatable smile, and a slight inclination of his shoulders. "Exactly so; you are really remarkable, madame," he added, in a tone of cold astonishment.

After dinner the guests took their coffee in the music-room, where Schemetzkin sat down at the piano to drum rag-time, and give his celebrated imitation of the boarding-school girl's execution of Chopin. He flatly refused to play anything more serious, and would practise only in the morning, when he had the music-room to himself. Hamilton and M. Roux repaired to the smoking-room to discuss the necessity of extending the tax on manufactured articles in France,—one of those conversations which particularly exasperated Flavia.

After Schemetzkin had grimaced and tortured the keyboard with malicious vulgarities for half an hour, Signor Donati, to put an end to his torture, consented to sing, and Flavia and Imogen went to fetch Arthur to play his accompaniments. Hamilton rose with an annoyed look, and placed his cigarette on the mantel. "Why yes, Flavia, I'll accompany him, provided he sings something with a melody, Italian arias or ballads, and provided the recital is not interminable."

"You will join us, M. Roux?"

"Thank you, but I have some letters to write," replied the novelist bowing.

As Flavia had remarked to Imogen, "Arthur really played accompaniments remarkably well." To hear him recalled vividly the days of her childhood, when he always used to spend his business vacations at her mother's home in Maine. He had possessed for her that almost hypnotic influence which young men sometimes exert upon little girls. It was a sort of phantom love affair, subjective and fanciful, a precocity of instinct, like that tender and maternal concern which some little girls feel for their dolls. Yet this childish infatuation is capable of all the depressions and exaltations of love itself; it has its bitter jealousies, cruel disappointments, its exacting caprices.

Summer after summer she had awaited his coming and wept at his departure, indifferent to the gayer young men who had called her their sweetheart, and laughed at everything she said. Although Hamilton never said so, she had been always quite sure that he was fond of her. When he pulled her up the river to hunt for fairy knolls shut about by low, hanging willows, he was often silent for an hour at a time, yet she never felt that he was bored or was neglecting her. He would lie in the sand smoking, his eyes half closed, watching her play and she was always conscious that she was entertaining him. Sometimes he would take a copy of "Alice in Wonderland" in his pocket, and no one could read it as he could, laughing at her with his dark eyes, when anything amused him. No one else could laugh so, with just their eyes, and without moving a muscle of their face. Though he usually smiled at passages that seemed not at all funny to the child, she always laughed gleefully, because he was so seldom moved to mirth that any such demonstration delighted her and she took the credit of it entirely to herself. Her own inclination had been for serious stories with sad endings, like the Little Mermaid, which he had once told her in an unguarded moment when she had a cold, and was put to bed early on her birthday night and cried because she could not have her party. But he highly disapproved of this preference, and had called it a morbid taste, and always shook his finger at her when she asked for the story. When she had been particularly good, or particularly neglected by other people, then he would sometimes melt and tell her the story, and never laugh at her if she enjoyed the "sad ending" even to tears. When Flavia had taken him away and he came no more, she wept inconsolably for the space of two weeks, and refused to learn her lessons. Then she found the story of the Little Mermaid herself, and forgot him.

Imogen had discovered at dinner that he could still smile at one secretly, out of his eyes, and that he had the old manner of outwardly seeming bored, but letting you know that he was not. She was intensely curious about his exact state of feeling toward his wife, and more curious still to catch a sense of his final adjustment to the conditions of life in general. This, she could not help feeling, she might get again—if she could have him alone for an hour, in some place where there was a little river and a sandy cove bordered by drooping willows, and a blue sky seen through white sycamore boughs.

That evening, before retiring, Flavia entered her husband's room, where he sat in his smoking-jacket, in one of his favourite low chairs.

"I suppose it's a grave responsibility to bring an ardent, serious young thing like Imogen here among all these fascinating personages," she remarked reflectively. "But, after all, one can never tell. These grave, silent girls have their own charm, even for facile people."

"O, so that is your plan?" queried her husband dryly. "I was wondering why you got her up here. She doesn't seem to mix well with the faciles. At least, so it struck me."

Flavia paid no heed to this jeering remark, but repeated, "No, after all, it may not be a bad thing."

"Then do consign her to that shaken reed, the tenor," said her husband yawning. "I remember she used to have a taste for the pathetic."

"And then," remarked Flavia coquettishly, "after all, I owe her mother a return in kind. She was not afraid to trifle with destiny."

But Hamilton was asleep in his chair.

Next morning Imogen found only Miss Broadwood in the breakfast-room.

"Good-morning, my dear girl, whatever are you doing up so early? They never breakfast before eleven. Most of them take their coffee in their room. Take this place by me."

Miss Broadwood looked particularly fresh and encouraging in her blue serge walking-skirt, her open jacket displaying an expanse of stiff, white, shirt bosom, dotted with some almost imperceptible figure, and a dark blue-and-white necktie, neatly knotted under her wide, rolling collar. She wore a white rosebud in the lapel of her coat, and decidedly she seemed more than ever like a nice, clean boy on his holiday. Imogen was just hoping that they would breakfast alone when Miss Broadwood exclaimed, "Ah, there comes Arthur with the children. That's the reward of early rising in this house; you never get to see the youngsters at any other time."

Hamilton entered, followed by two dark, handsome little boys. The girl, who was very tiny, blonde like her mother, and exceedingly frail, he carried in his arms. The boys came up and said good-morning with an ease and cheerfulness uncommon, even in well-bred children, but the little girl hid her face on her father's shoulder.

"She's a shy little lady," he explained, as he put her gently down in her chair. "I'm afraid she's like her father; she can't seem to get used to meeting people. And you, Miss Willard, did you dream of the white rabbit or the little mermaid?"

"O, I dreamed of them all! All the personages of that buried civilization," cried Imogen, delighted that his estranged manner of the night before had entirely vanished, and feeling that, somehow, the old confidential relations had been restored during the night.

"Come, William," said Miss Broadwood, turning to the younger of the two boys, "and what did you dream about?"

"We dreamed," said William gravely—he was the more assertive of the two and always spoke for both—"we dreamed that there were fireworks hidden in the basement of the carriage-house; lots and lots of fireworks."

His elder brother looked up at him with apprehensive astonishment, while Miss Broadwood hastily put her napkin to her lips, and Hamilton dropped his eyes. "If little boys dream things, they are so apt not to come true," he reflected sadly. This shook even the redoubtable William, and he glanced nervously at his brother. "But do things vanish just because they have been dreamed?" he objected.

"Generally that is the very best reason for their vanishing," said Arthur gravely.

"But, father, people can't help what they dream," remonstrated Edward gently.

"Oh, come! You're making these children talk like a Maeterlinck dialogue," laughed Miss Broadwood.

Flavia presently entered, a book in her hand, and bade them all good-morning. "Come, little people, which story shall it be this morning?" she asked winningly. Greatly excited, the children followed her into the garden. "She does then, sometimes," murmured Imogen as they left the breakfast-room.

"Oh, yes, to be sure," said Miss Broadwood cheerfully. "She reads a story to them every morning in the most picturesque part of the garden. The mother of the Gracchi, you know. She does so long, she says, for the time when they will be intellectual companions for her. What do you say to a walk over the hills?"

As they left the house they met Frau Lichtenfeld and the bushy Herr Schotte—the professor cut an astonishing figure in golf stockings—returning from a walk and engaged in an animated conversation on the tendencies of German fiction.

"Aren't they the most attractive little children," exclaimed Imogen as they wound down the road toward the river.

"Yes, and you must not fail to tell Flavia that you think so. She will look at you in a sort of startled way and say, 'Yes, aren't they?' and maybe she will go off and hunt them up and have tea with them, to fully appreciate them. She is awfully afraid of missing anything good, is Flavia. The way those youngsters manage to conceal their guilty presence in the House of Song is a wonder."

"But don't any of the artist-folk fancy children?" asked Imogen.

"Yes, they just fancy them and no more. The chemist remarked the other day that children are like certain salts which need not be actualized because the formulæ are quite sufficient for practical purposes. I don't see how even Flavia can endure to have that man about."

"I have always been rather curious to know what Arthur thinks of it all," remarked Imogen cautiously.

"Thinks of it!" ejaculated Miss Broadwood. "Why, my dear, what would any man think of having his house turned into an hotel, habited by freaks who discharge his servants, borrow his money, and insult his neighbours? This place is shunned like a lazaretto!"

"Well, then, why does he—why does he—" persisted Imogen.

"Bah!" interrupted Miss Broadwood impatiently, "why did he in the first place? That's the question."

"Marry her, you mean?" said Imogen colouring.

"Exactly so," said Miss Broadwood sharply, as she snapped the lid of her match-box.

"I suppose that is a question rather beyond us, and certainly one which we cannot discuss," said Imogen. "But his toleration on this one point puzzles me, quite apart from other complications."

"Toleration? Why this point, as you call it, simply *is* Flavia. Who could conceive of her without it? I don't know where it's all going to end, I'm sure, and I'm equally sure that, if it were not for Arthur, I shouldn't care," declared Miss Broadwood, drawing her shoulders together.

"But will it end at all, now?"

"Such an absurd state of things can't go on indefinitely. A man isn't going to see his wife make a guy of herself forever, is he? Chaos has already begun in the servants' quarters. There are six different languages spoken there now. You see, it's all on an entirely false basis. Flavia hasn't the slightest notion of what these people are really like, their good and their bad alike escape her. They, on the other hand, can't imagine what she is driving at. Now, Arthur is worse off than either faction; he is not in the fairy story in that he sees these people exactly as they are, *but* he is utterly unable to see Flavia as they see her. There you have the situation. Why can't he see her as we do? My dear, that has kept me awake o' nights. This man who has thought so much and lived so much, who is naturally a critic, really takes Flavia at very nearly her own estimate. But now I am entering upon a wilderness. From a brief acquaintance with her, you can know nothing of the icy fastnesses of Flavia's self-esteem. It's like St. Peter's; you can't realize its magnitude at once. You have to grow into a sense of it by living under its shadow. It has perplexed even Emile Roux, that merciless dissector of egoism. She has puzzled him the more because he saw at a glance what some of them do not perceive at once, and what will be mercifully concealed from Arthur until the trump sounds; namely, that all Flavia's artists have done or ever will do means exactly as much to her as a symphony means to an oyster; that there is no bridge by which the significance of any work of art could be conveyed to her."

"Then, in the name of goodness, why does she bother?" gasped Imogen. "She is pretty, wealthy, well-established; why should she bother?"

"That's what M. Roux has kept asking himself. I can't pretend to analyse it. She reads papers on the Literary Landmarks of Paris, and the Loves of the Poets, and that sort of thing, to clubs out in Chicago. To Flavia it is more necessary to be called clever than to breathe. I would give a good deal to know that glum Frenchman's diagnosis. He has been watching her out of those fishy eyes of his as a biologist watches a hemisphereless frog."

For several days after M. Roux's departure, Flavia gave an embarrassing share of her attention to Imogen. Embarrassing, because Imogen had the feeling of being energetically and futilely explored, she knew not for what. She felt herself under the globe of an air pump, expected to yield up something. When she confined the conversation to matters of general interest, Flavia conveyed to her with some pique that her one endeavour in life had been to fit herself to converse with her friends upon those things which vitally interested them. "One has no right to accept their best from people unless one gives, isn't it so? I want to be able to give—!" she declared vaguely. Yet whenever Imogen strove to pay her tithes and plunged bravely into her plans for study next winter, Flavia grew absent-minded and interrupted her by amazing generalizations or by such embarrassing questions as, "And these grim studies really have charm for you; you are quite buried in them; they make other things seem light and ephemeral?"

"I rather feel as though I had got in here under false pretences," Imogen confided to Miss Broadwood. "I'm sure I don't know what it is that she wants of me."

"Ah," chuckled Jemima, "you are not equal to these heart to heart talks with Flavia. You utterly fail to communicate to her the atmosphere of that untroubled joy in which you dwell. You must remember that she gets no feeling out of things herself, and she demands that you impart yours to her by some process of psychic transmission. I once met a blind girl, blind from birth, who could discuss the peculiarities of the Barbizon school with just Flavia's glibness and enthusiasm. Ordinarily Flavia knows how to get what she wants from people, and her memory is wonderful. One evening I heard her giving Frau Lichtenfeld some random impressions about Hedda Gabler which she extracted from me five years ago; giving them with an impassioned conviction of which I was never guilty. But I have known other people who could appropriate your stories and opinions; Flavia is infinitely more subtle than that; she can soak up the very thrash and drift of your day dreams, and take the very thrills off your back, as it were."

After some days of unsuccessful effort, Flavia withdrew herself, and Imogen found Hamilton ready to catch her when she was tossed a-field. He seemed only to have been awaiting this crisis, and at once their old intimacy re-established itself as a thing inevitable and beautifully prepared for. She convinced herself that she had not been mistaken in him, despite all the doubts that had come up in later years, and this renewal of faith set more than one question thumping in her brain. "How did he, how can he?" she kept repeating with a tinge of her childish resentment, "what right had he to waste anything so fine?"

When Imogen and Arthur were returning from a walk before luncheon one morning about a week after M. Roux's departure, they noticed an absorbed group before one of the hall windows. Herr Schotte and Restzhoff sat on the window seat with a newspaper between them, while Wellington, Schemetzkin and Will Maidenwood looked over their shoulders. They seemed intensely interested, Herr Schotte occasionally pounding his knees with his fists in ebullitions of barbaric glee. When Imogen entered the hall, however, the men were all sauntering toward the breakfast-room and the paper was lying innocently on the divan. During luncheon the personnel of that window group were unwontedly animated and agreeable,—all save Schemetzkin, whose stare was blanker than ever, as though Roux's mantle of insulting indifference had fallen upon him, in addition to his own oblivious self absorption. Will Maidenwood seemed embarrassed and annoyed; the chemist employed himself with making polite speeches to Hamilton.—Flavia did not come down to lunch—and there was a malicious gleam under Herr Schotte's eyebrows. Frank Wellington announced nervously that an imperative letter from his protecting syndicate summoned him to the city.

After luncheon the men went to the golf links, and Imogen, at the first opportunity, possessed herself of the newspaper which had been left on the divan. One of the first things that caught her eye was an article headed "Roux on Tuft Hunters; The Advanced American Woman As He Sees Her; Aggressive, Superficial and Insincere." The entire interview was nothing more nor less than a satiric characterization of Flavia, a-quiver with irritation and vitriolic malice. No one could mistake it; it was done with all his deftness of portraiture. Imogen had not finished the article when she heard a footstep, and clutching the paper she started precipitately toward the stairway as Arthur entered. He put out his hand, looking critically at her distressed face.

"Wait a moment, Miss Willard," he said peremptorily, "I want to see whether we can find what it was that so interested our friends this morning. Give me the paper, please."

Imogen grew quite white as he opened the journal. She reached forward and crumpled it with her hands. "Please don't, please don't," she pleaded, "it's something I don't want you to see. Oh! why will you? It's just something low and despicable that you can't notice."

Arthur had gently loosed her hands and he pointed her to a chair. He lit a cigar and read the article through without comment. When he had finished it, he walked to the fireplace, struck a match, and tossed the flaming journal between the brass andirons.

"You are right," he remarked as he came back, dusting his hands with his handkerchief. "It's quite impossible to comment. There are extremes of blackguardism for which we have no name. The only thing necessary is to see that Flavia gets no wind of this. This seems to be my cue to act; poor girl."

Imogen looked at him tearfully; she could only murmur, "Oh, why did you read it!"

Hamilton laughed spiritlessly. "Come, don't you worry about it. You always took other people's troubles too seriously. When you were little and all the world was gay and everybody happy, you must needs get the Little Mermaid's troubles to grieve over. Come with me into the music-room. You remember the musical setting I once made for you for the Lay of the Jabberwock? I was trying it over the other night, long after you were in bed, and I decided it was quite as fine as the Erl-King music. How I wish I could give you some of the cake that Alice ate and make you a little girl again. Then, when you had got through the glass door into the little garden, you could call to me, perhaps, and tell me all the fine things that were going on there. What a pity it is that you ever grew up!" he added, laughing, and Imogen, too, was thinking just that.

At dinner that evening, Flavia, with fatal persistence, insisted upon turning the conversation to M. Roux. She had been reading one of his novels and had remembered anew that Paris set its watches by his clock. Imogen surmised that she was tortured by a feeling that she had not sufficiently appreciated him while she had had him. When she first mentioned his name, she was answered only by the pall of silence that fell over the company. Then every one began to talk at once, as though to correct a false position. They spoke of him with fervid, defiant admiration, with the sort of hot praise that covers a double purpose. Imogen fancied she could see that they felt a kind of relief at what the man had done, even those who despised him for doing it; that they felt a spiteful hate against Flavia, as though she had tricked them, and a certain contempt for themselves that they had been beguiled. She was reminded of the fury of the crowd in the fairy tale, when once the child had called out that the king was in his nightclothes. Surely these people knew no more about Flavia than they had known before, but the mere fact that the thing had been said, altered the situation. Flavia, meanwhile, sat chattering amiably, pathetically unconscious of her nakedness.

Hamilton lounged, fingering the stem of his wine glass, gazing down the table at one face after another and studying the various degrees of self-consciousness they exhibited. Imogen's eyes followed his, fearfully. When a lull came in the spasmodic flow of conversation, Arthur, leaning back in his chair, remarked deliberately, "As for M. Roux, his very profession places him in that class of men whom society has never been able to accept unconditionally because it has never been able to assume that they have any ordered notion of taste. He and his ilk remain, with the mountebanks and snake charmers, people indispensable to our civilization, but wholly unreclaimed by it; people whom we receive, but whose invitations we do not accept."

Fortunately for Flavia, this mine was not exploded until just before the coffee was brought. Her laughter was pitiful to hear; it echoed through the silent room as in a vault, while she made some tremulously light remark about her husband's drollery, grim as a jest from the dying. No one responded and she sat nodding her head like a mechanical toy and smiling her white, set smile through her teeth, until Alcée Buisson and Frau Lichtenfeld came to her support.

After dinner the guests retired immediately to their rooms, and Imogen went upstairs on tip-toe, feeling the echo of breakage and the dust of crumbling in the air. She wondered whether Flavia's habitual note of uneasiness were not, in a manner, prophetic, and a sort of unconscious premonition, after all. She sat down to write a letter, but she found herself so nervous, her head so hot and her hands so cold, that she soon abandoned the effort. Just as she was about to seek Miss Broadwood, Flavia entered and embraced her hysterically.

"My dearest girl," she began, "was there ever such an unfortunate and incomprehensible speech made before? Of course it is scarcely

necessary to explain to you poor Arthur's lack of tact, and that he
meant nothing. But they! Can they be expected to understand? He
will feel wretchedly about it when he realizes what he has done, but
in the meantime? And M. Roux, of all men! When we were so fortunate as to get him, and he made himself so unreservedly agreeable,
and I fancied that, in his way, Arthur quite admired him. My dear,
you have no idea what that speech has done. Schemetzkin and Herr
Schotte have already sent me word that they must leave us to-morrow.
Such a thing from a host!" Flavia paused, choked by tears of vexation
and despair.

Imogen was thoroughly disconcerted; this was the first time she
had ever seen Flavia betray any personal emotion which was indub-
itably genuine. She replied with what consolation she could. "Need
they take it personally at all? It was a mere observation upon a class
of people—"

"Which he knows nothing whatever about, and with whom he has
no sympathy," interrupted Flavia. "Ah, my dear, you could not be
expected to understand. You can't realize, knowing Arthur as you do,
his entire lack of any æsthetic sense whatever. He is absolutely *nil*,
stone deaf and stark blind, on that side. He doesn't mean to be brutal,
it is just the brutality of utter ignorance. They always feel it—they
are so sensitive to unsympathetic influences, you know; they know it
the moment they come into the house. I have spent my life apologiz-
ing for him and struggling to conceal it; but in spite of me, he wounds
them; his very attitude, even in silence, offends them. Heavens! do I
not know, is it not perpetually and forever wounding me? But there
has never been anything so dreadful as this, never! If I could conceive
of any possible motive, even!"

"But, surely, Mrs. Hamilton, it was, after all, a mere expression
of opinion, such as we are any of us likely to venture upon any subject
whatever. It was neither more personal nor more extravagant than
many of M. Roux's remarks."

"But, Imogen, certainly M. Roux has the right. It is a part of his
art, and that is altogether another matter. Oh, this is not the only
instance!" continued Flavia passionately, "I've always had that narrow, bigoted prejudice to contend with. It has always held me back.
But this—!"

"I think you mistake his attitude," replied Imogen, feeling a flush
that made her ears tingle, "that is, I fancy he is more appreciative

than he seems. A man can't be very demonstrative about those things—not if he is a real man. I should not think you would care much about saving the feelings of people who are too narrow to admit of any other point of view than their own." She stopped, finding herself in the impossible position of attempting to explain Hamilton to his wife; a task which, if once begun, would necessitate an entire course of enlightenment which she doubted Flavia's ability to receive, and which she could offer only with very poor grace.

"That's just where it stings most," here Flavia began pacing the floor, "it is just because they have all shown such tolerance, and have treated Arthur with such unfailing consideration, that I can find no reasonable pretext for his rancour. How can he fail to see the value of such friendships on the children's account, if for nothing else! What an advantage for them to grow up among such associations! Even though he cares nothing about these things himself he might realize that. Is there nothing I could say by way of explanation? To them, I mean? If some one were to explain to them how unfortunately limited he is in these things—"

"I'm afraid I cannot advise you," said Imogen decidedly, "but that, at least, seems to me impossible."

Flavia took her hand and glanced at her affectionately, nodding nervously. "Of course, dear girl, I can't ask you to be quite frank with me. Poor child, you are trembling and your hands are icy. Poor Arthur! But you must not judge him by this altogether; think how much he misses in life. What a cruel shock you've had. I'll send you some sherry. Good-night, my dear."

When Flavia shut the door, Imogen burst into a fit of nervous weeping.

Next morning she awoke after a troubled and restless night. At eight o'clock, Miss Broadwood entered in a red and white striped bath-robe.

"Up, up, and see the great doom's image!" she cried, her eyes sparkling with excitement. "The hall is full of trunks, they are packing. What bolt has fallen? It's you, *ma chérie*, you've brought Ulysses home again and the slaughter has begun!" She blew a cloud of smoke triumphantly from her lips and threw herself into a chair beside the bed.

Imogen, rising on her elbow, plunged excitedly into the story of the Roux interview, which Miss Broadwood heard with the keenest interest, frequently interrupting her by exclamations of delight. When

Imogen reached the dramatic scene which terminated in the destruction of the newspaper, Miss Broadwood rose and took a turn about the room, violently switching the tasselled cords of her bath-robe.

"Stop a moment," she cried, "you mean to tell me that he had such a heaven-sent means to bring her to her senses and didn't use it, that he held such a weapon and threw it away?"

"Use it?" cried Imogen unsteadily, "of course he didn't. He bared his back to the tormentor, signed himself over to punishment in that speech he made at dinner, which every one understands but Flavia. She was here for an hour last night and disregarded every limit of taste in her maledictions."

"My dear!" cried Miss Broadwood, catching her hand in inordinate delight at the situation, "do you see what he has done? There'll be no end to it. Why he has sacrificed himself to spare the very vanity that devours him, put rancours in the vessels of his peace, and his eternal jewel given to the common enemy of man, to make them kings, the seed of Banquo kings! He is magnificent!"

"Isn't he always that?" cried Imogen hotly. "He's like a pillar of sanity and law in this house of shams and swollen vanities, where people stalk about with a sort of mad-house dignity, each one fancying himself a king or a pope. If you could have heard that woman talk of him! Why she thinks him stupid, bigoted, blinded by middle-class prejudices. She talked about his having no æsthetic sense, and insisted that her artists had always shown him tolerance. I don't know why it should get on my nerves so, I'm sure, but her stupidity and assurance are enough to drive one to the brink of collapse."

"Yes, as opposed to his singular fineness, they are calculated to do just that," said Miss Broadwood gravely, wisely ignoring Imogen's tears. "But what has been is nothing to what will be. Just wait until Flavia's black swans have flown! You ought not to try to stick it out; that would only make it harder for every one. Suppose you let me telephone your mother to wire you to come home by the evening train?"

"Anything, rather than have her come at me like that again. It puts me in a perfectly impossible position, and he *is* so fine!"

"Of course it does," said Miss Broadwood sympathetically, "and there is no good to be got from facing it. I will stay, because such things interest me, and Frau Lichtenfeld will stay because she has no money to get away, and Buisson will stay because he feels somewhat responsible. These complications are interesting enough to cold-blooded folk like myself who have an eye for the dramatic element, but they are distracting and demoralizing to young people with any serious purpose in life."

Miss Broadwood's counsel was all the more generous seeing that, for her, the most interesting element of this dénouement would be eliminated by Imogen's departure. "If she goes now, she'll get over it," soliloquized Miss Broadwood, "if she stays she'll be wrung for him, and the hurt may go deep enough to last. I haven't the heart to see her spoiling things for herself." She telephoned Mrs. Willard, and helped Imogen to pack. She even took it upon herself to break the news of Imogen's going to Arthur, who remarked, as he rolled a cigarette in his nerveless fingers:

"Right enough, too. What should she do here with old cynics like you and me, Jimmy? Seeing that she is brim full of dates and formulæ and other positivisms, and is so girt about with illusions that she still casts a shadow in the sun. You've been very tender of her, haven't you? I've watched you. And to think it may all be gone when we see her next. 'The common fate of all things rare,' you know. What a good fellow you are, anyway, Jimmy," he added, putting his hands affectionately on her shoulders.

Arthur went with them to the station. Flavia was so prostrated by the concerted action of her guests that she was able to see Imogen only for a moment in her darkened sleeping chamber, where she kissed her hysterically, without lifting her head, bandaged in aromatic vinegar. On the way to the station both Arthur and Imogen threw the burden of keeping up appearances entirely upon Miss Broadwood, who blithely rose to the occasion. When Hamilton carried Imogen's bag into the car, Miss Broadwood detained her for a moment, whispering as she gave her a large, warm handclasp, "I'll come to see you when I get back to town; and, in the meantime, if you meet any of our artists, tell them you have left Gaius Marius among the ruins of Carthage."

The Sculptor's Funeral

A group of the townspeople stood on the station siding of a little Kansas town, awaiting the coming of the night train, which was already twenty minutes overdue. The snow had fallen thick over everything; in the pale starlight the line of bluffs across the wide, white meadows south of the town made soft, smoke-coloured curves against the clear sky. The men on the siding stood first on one foot and then on the other, their hands thrust deep into their trousers pockets, their overcoats open, their shoulders screwed up with the cold; and they glanced from time to time toward the southeast, where the railroad track wound along the river shore. They conversed in low tones and moved about restlessly, seeming uncertain as to what was expected of them. There was but one of the company who looked as though he knew exactly why he was there; and he kept conspicuously apart; walking to the far end of the platform, returning to the station door, then pacing up the track again, his chin sunk in the high collar of his overcoat, his burly shoulders drooping forward, his gait heavy and dogged. Presently he was approached by a tall, spare, grizzled man clad in a faded Grand Army suit, who shuffled out from the group and advanced with a certain deference, craning his neck forward until his back made the angle of a jack-knife three-quarters open.

"I reckon she's a-goin' to be pretty late agin to-night, Jim," he remarked in a squeaky falsetto. "S'pose it's the snow?"

"I don't know," responded the other man with a shade of annoyance, speaking from out an astonishing cataract of red beard that grew fiercely and thickly in all directions.

The spare man shifted the quill toothpick he was chewing to the other side of his mouth. "It ain't likely that anybody from the

East will come with the corpse, I s'pose," he went on reflectively.

"I don't know," responded the other, more curtly than before.

"It's too bad he didn't belong to some lodge or other. I like an order funeral myself. They seem more appropriate for people of some re-pytation," the spare man continued, with an ingratiating concession in his shrill voice, as he carefully placed his toothpick in his vest pocket. He always carried the flag at the G. A. R. funerals in the town.

The heavy man turned on his heel, without replying, and walked up the siding. The spare man shuffled back to the uneasy group. "Jim's ez full ez a tick, ez ushel," he commented commiseratingly.

Just then a distant whistle sounded, and there was a shuffling of feet on the platform. A number of lanky boys of all ages appeared as suddenly and slimily as eels wakened by the crack of thunder; some came from the waiting-room, where they had been warming them-selves by the red stove, or half asleep on the slat benches; others uncoiled themselves from baggage trucks or slid out of express wag-ons. Two clambered down from the driver's seat of a hearse that stood backed up against the siding. They straightened their stooping shoul-ders and lifted their heads, and a flash of momentary animation kin-dled their dull eyes at that cold, vibrant scream, the world-wide call for men. It stirred them like the note of a trumpet; just as it had often stirred the man who was coming home to-night, in his boyhood.

The night express shot, red as a rocket, from out the eastward marsh lands and wound along the river shore under the long lines of shivering poplars that sentinelled the meadows, the escaping steam hanging in grey masses against the pale sky and blotting out the Milky Way. In a moment the red glare from the headlight streamed up the snow-covered track before the siding and glittered on the wet, black rails. The burly man with the dishevelled red beard walked swiftly up the platform toward the approaching train, uncovering his head as he went. The group of men behind him hesitated, glanced questioningly at one another, and awkwardly followed his example. The train stopped, and the crowd shuffled up to the express car just as the door was thrown open, the spare man in the G. A. R. suit thrusting his head forward with curiosity. The express messenger appeared in the door-way, accompanied by a young man in a long ulster and travelling cap.

"Are Mr. Merrick's friends here?" inquired the young man.

The group on the platform swayed and shuffled uneasily. Philip

Phelps, the banker, responded with dignity: "We have come to take charge of the body. Mr. Merrick's father is very feeble and can't be about."

"Send the agent out here," growled the express messenger, "and tell the operator to lend a hand."

The coffin was got out of its rough box and down on the snowy platform. The townspeople drew back enough to make room for it and then formed a close semicircle about it, looking curiously at the palm leaf which lay across the black cover. No one said anything. The baggage man stood by his truck, waiting to get at the trunks. The engine panted heavily, and the fireman dodged in and out among the wheels with his yellow torch and long oil-can, snapping the spindle boxes. The young Bostonian, one of the dead sculptor's pupils who had come with the body, looked about him helplessly. He turned to the banker, the only one of that black, uneasy, stoop-shouldered group who seemed enough of an individual to be addressed.

"None of Mr. Merrick's brothers are here?" he asked uncertainly.

The man with the red beard for the first time stepped up and joined the group. "No, they have not come yet; the family is scattered. The body will be taken directly to the house." He stooped and took hold of one of the handles of the coffin.

"Take the long hill road up, Thompson, it will be easier on the horses," called the liveryman as the undertaker snapped the door of the hearse and prepared to mount to the driver's seat.

Laird, the red-bearded lawyer, turned again to the stranger: "We didn't know whether there would be any one with him or not," he explained. "It's a long walk, so you'd better go up in the hack." He pointed to a single battered conveyance, but the young man replied stiffly: "Thank you, but I think I will go up with the hearse. If you don't object," turning to the undertaker, "I'll ride with you."

They clambered up over the wheels and drove off in the starlight up the long, white hill toward the town. The lamps in the still village were shining from under the low, snow-burdened roofs; and beyond, on every side, the plains reached out into emptiness, peaceful and wide as the soft sky itself, and wrapped in a tangible, white silence.

When the hearse backed up to a wooden sidewalk before a naked, weather-beaten frame house, the same composite, ill-defined group that had stood upon the station siding was huddled about the gate. The front yard was an icy swamp, and a couple of warped planks, extending from the sidewalk to the door, made a sort of rickety foot-bridge. The gate hung on one hinge, and was opened wide with diffi-culty. Steavens, the young stranger, noticed that something black was tied to the knob of the front door.

The grating sound made by the casket, as it was drawn from the hearse, was answered by a scream from the house; the front door was wrenched open, and a tall, corpulent woman rushed out bareheaded into the snow and flung herself upon the coffin, shrieking: "My boy, my boy! And this is how you've come home to me!"

As Steavens turned away and closed his eyes with a shudder of unutterable repulsion, another woman, also tall, but flat and angular, dressed entirely in black, darted out of the house and caught Mrs. Merrick by the shoulders, crying sharply: "Come, come, mother; you musn't go on like this!" Her tone changed to one of obsequious sol-emnity as she turned to the banker: "The parlour is ready, Mr. Phelps."

The bearers carried the coffin along the narrow boards, while the undertaker ran ahead with the coffin-rests. They bore it into a large, unheated room that smelled of dampness and disuse and furniture polish, and set it down under a hanging lamp ornamented with jin-gling glass prisms and before a "Rogers group" of John Alden and Priscilla, wreathed with smilax. Henry Steavens stared about him with the sickening conviction that there had been some horrible mis-take, and that he had somehow arrived at the wrong destination. He looked painfully about over the clover-green Brussels, the fat plush upholstery; among the hand-painted china placques and panels and vases, for some mark of identification, for something that might once conceivably have belonged to Harvey Merrick. It was not until he recognized his friend in the crayon portrait of a little boy in kilts and curls, hanging above the piano, that he felt willing to let any of these people approach the coffin.

"Take the lid off, Mr. Thompson; let me see my boy's face," wailed the elder woman between her sobs. This time Steavens looked fear-fully, almost beseechingly into her face, red and swollen under its masses of strong, black, shiny hair. He flushed, dropped his eyes, and then, almost incredulously, looked again. There was a kind of power about her face—a kind of brutal handsomeness, even; but it was scarred and furrowed by violence, and so coloured and coarsened by fiercer passions that grief seemed never to have laid a gentle finger there. The long nose was distended and knobbed at the end, and there were deep lines on either side of it; her heavy, black brows almost met across her forehead, her teeth were large and square, and set far apart— teeth that could tear. She filled the room; the men were obliterated, seemed tossed about like twigs in an angry water, and even Steavens felt himself being drawn into the whirlpool.

The daughter—the tall, raw-boned woman in crêpe, with a mourning comb in her hair which curiously lengthened her long face— sat stiffly upon the sofa, her hands, conspicuous for their large knuc- kles, folded in her lap, her mouth and eyes drawn down, solemnly awaiting the opening of the coffin. Near the door stood a mulatto woman, evidently a servant in the house, with a timid bearing and an emaciated face pitifully sad and gentle. She was weeping silently, the corner of her calico apron lifted to her eyes, occasionally suppressing a long, quivering sob. Steavens walked over and stood beside her.

Feeble steps were heard on the stairs, and an old man, tall and frail, odorous of pipe smoke, with shaggy, unkept grey hair and a dingy beard, tobacco stained about the mouth, entered uncertainly. He went slowly up to the coffin and stood rolling a blue cotton hand- kerchief between his hands, seeming so pained and embarrassed by his wife's orgy of grief that he had no consciousness of anything else.

"There, there, Annie, dear, don't take on so," he quavered timidly, putting out a shaking hand and awkwardly patting her elbow. She turned with a cry, and sank upon his shoulder with such violence that he tottered a little. He did not even glance toward the coffin, but con- tinued to look at her with a dull, frightened, appealing expression, as a spaniel looks at the whip. His sunken cheeks slowly reddened and burned with miserable shame. When his wife rushed from the room, her daughter strode after her with set lips. The servant stole up to the coffin, bent over it for a moment, and then slipped away to the kitchen, leaving Steavens, the lawyer, and the father to themselves. The old man stood trembling and looking down at his dead son's face. The sculptor's splendid head seemed even more noble in its rigid still- ness than in life. The dark hair had crept down upon the wide fore- head; the face seemed strangely long, but in it there was not that beautiful and chaste repose which we expect to find in the faces of the dead. The brows were so drawn that there were two deep lines above the beaked nose, and the chin was thrust forward defiantly. It was as though the strain of life had been so sharp and bitter that death could not at once wholly relax the tension and smooth the countenance into perfect peace—as though he were still guarding something precious and holy, which might even yet be wrested from him.

The old man's lips were working under his stained beard. He turned to the lawyer with timid deference: "Phelps and the rest are comin' back to set up with Harve, ain't they?" he asked. "Thank 'ee, Jim, thank 'ee." He brushed the hair back gently from his son's forehead. "He was a good boy, Jim; always a good boy. He was ez gentle ez a child and the kindest of 'em all—only we didn't none of us ever onderstand him." The tears trickled slowly down his beard and dropped upon the sculptor's coat.

"Martin, Martin. Oh, Martin! come here," his wife wailed from the top of the stairs. The old man started timorously: "Yes, Annie, I'm coming." He turned away, hesitated, stood for a moment in miserable indecision; then reached back and patted the dead man's hair softly, and stumbled from the room.

"Poor old man, I didn't think he had any tears left. Seems as if his eyes would have gone dry long ago. At his age nothing cuts very deep," remarked the lawyer.

Something in his tone made Steavens glance up. While the mother had been in the room, the young man had scarcely seen any one else; but now, from the moment he first glanced into Jim Laird's florid face and blood-shot eyes, he knew that he had found what he had been heartsick at not finding before—the feeling, the understanding, that must exist in some one, even here.

The man was red as his beard, with features swollen and blurred by dissipation, and a hot, blazing blue eye. His face was strained—that of a man who is controlling himself with difficulty—and he kept plucking at his beard with a sort of fierce resentment. Steavens, sitting by the window, watched him turn down the glaring lamp, still its jangling pendants with an angry gesture, and then stand with his hands locked behind him, staring down into the master's face. He could not help wondering what link there could have been between the porcelain vessel and so sooty a lump of potter's clay.

From the kitchen an uproar was sounding; when the dining-room door opened, the import of it was clear. The mother was abusing the maid for having forgotten to make the dressing for the chicken salad which had been prepared for the watchers. Steavens had never heard anything in the least like it; it was injured, emotional, dramatic abuse, unique and masterly in its excruciating cruelty, as violent and unrestrained as had been her grief of twenty minutes before. With a shudder of disgust the lawyer went into the dining-room and closed the door into the kitchen.

"Poor Roxy's getting it now," he remarked when he came back. "The Merricks took her out of the poor-house years ago; and if her loyalty would let her, I guess the poor old thing could tell tales that would curdle your blood. She's the mulatto woman who was standing in here a while ago, with her apron to her eyes. The old woman is a fury; there never was anybody like her for demonstrative piety and ingenious cruelty. She made Harvey's life a hell for him when he lived at home; he was so sick ashamed of it. I never could see how he kept himself so sweet."

"He was wonderful," said Steavens slowly, "wonderful; but until to-night I have never known how wonderful."

"That is the true and eternal wonder of it, anyway; that it can come even from such a dung heap as this," the lawyer cried, with a sweeping gesture which seemed to indicate much more than the four walls within which they stood.

"I think I'll see whether I can get a little air. The room is so close I am beginning to feel rather faint," murmured Steavens, struggling with one of the windows. The sash was stuck, however, and would not yield, so he sat down dejectedly and began pulling at his collar. The lawyer came over, loosened the sash with one blow of his red fist and sent the window up a few inches. Steavens thanked him, but the nausea which had been gradually climbing into his throat for the last half hour left him with but one desire—a desperate feeling that he must get away from this place with what was left of Harvey Merrick. Oh, he comprehended well enough now the quiet bitterness of the smile that he had seen so often on his master's lips!

He remembered that once, when Merrick returned from a visit home, he brought with him a singularly feeling and suggestive bas-relief of a thin, faded old woman, sitting and sewing something pinned to her knee; while a full-lipped, full-blooded little urchin, his trousers held up by a single gallows, stood beside her, impatiently twitching her gown to call her attention to a butterfly he had caught. Steavens, impressed by the tender and delicate modelling of the thin, tired face, had asked him if it were his mother. He remembered the dull flush that had burned up in the sculptor's face.

The lawyer was sitting in a rocking-chair beside the coffin, his head thrown back and his eyes closed. Steavens looked at him earnestly, puzzled at the line of the chin, and wondering why a man should conceal a feature of such distinction under that disfiguring shock of beard. Suddenly, as though he felt the young sculptor's keen glance, he opened his eyes.

"Was he always a good deal of an oyster?" he asked abruptly. "He was terribly shy as a boy."

"Yes, he was an oyster, since you put it so," rejoined Steavens. "Although he could be very fond of people, he always gave one the impression of being detached. He disliked violent emotion; he was reflective, and rather distrustful of himself—except, of course, as regarded his work. He was sure-footed enough there. He distrusted men pretty thoroughly and women even more, yet somehow without believing ill of them. He was determined, indeed, to believe the best, but he seemed afraid to investigate."

"A burnt dog dreads the fire," said the lawyer grimly, and closed his eyes.

Steavens went on and on, reconstructing that whole miserable boyhood. All this raw, biting ugliness had been the portion of the man whose tastes were refined beyond the limits of the reasonable—whose mind was an exhaustless gallery of beautiful impressions, and so sensitive that the mere shadow of a poplar leaf flickering against a sunny wall would be etched and held there forever. Surely, if ever a man had the magic word in his finger tips, it was Merrick. Whatever he touched, he revealed its holiest secret; liberated it from enchantment and restored it to its pristine loveliness, like the Arabian prince who fought the enchantress spell for spell. Upon whatever he had come in contact with, he had left a beautiful record of the experience—a sort of ethereal signature; a scent, a sound, a colour that was his own.

Steavens understood now the real tragedy of his master's life; neither love nor wine, as many had conjectured; but a blow which had fallen earlier and cut deeper than these could have done—a shame not his, and yet so unescapably his, to hide in his heart from his very boyhood. And without—the frontier warfare; the yearning of a boy, cast ashore upon a desert of newness and ugliness and sordidness, for all that is chastened and old, and noble with traditions.

At eleven o'clock the tall, flat woman in black crêpe entered and announced that the watchers were arriving, and asked them "to step into the dining-room." As Steavens rose, the lawyer said dryly: "You go on—it'll be a good experience for you, doubtless; as for me, I'm not equal to that crowd to-night; I've had twenty years of them."

As Steavens closed the door after him he glanced back at the lawyer, sitting by the coffin in the dim light, with his chin resting on his hand.

The same misty group that had stood before the door of the express car shuffled into the dining-room. In the light of the kerosene lamp they separated and became individuals. The minister, a pale, feeble-looking man with white hair and blond chin-whiskers, took his seat beside a small side table and placed his Bible upon it. The Grand Army man sat down behind the stove and tilted his chair back comfortably against the wall, fishing his quill toothpick from his waistcoat pocket. The two bankers, Phelps and Elder, sat off in a corner behind the dinner-table, where they could finish their discussion of the new usury law and its effect on chattel security loans. The real estate agent, an old man with a smiling, hypocritical face, soon joined them. The coal and lumber dealer and the cattle shipper sat on opposite sides of the hard coal-burner, their feet on the nickel-work. Steavens took a book from his pocket and began to read. The talk around him ranged through various topics of local interest while the house was quieting down. When it was clear that the members of the family were in bed, the Grand Army man hitched his shoulders and, untangling his long legs, caught his heels on the rounds of his chair.

"S'pose there'll be a will, Phelps?" he queried in his weak falsetto.

The banker laughed disagreeably, and began trimming his nails with a pearl-handled pocket-knife.

"There'll scarcely be any need for one, will there?" he queried in his turn.

The restless Grand Army man shifted his position again, getting his knees still nearer his chin. "Why, the ole man says Harve's done right well lately," he chirped.

The other banker spoke up. "I reckon he means by that Harve ain't asked him to mortgage any more farms lately, so as he could go on with his education."

"Seems like my mind don't reach back to a time when Harve wasn't bein' edycated," tittered the Grand Army man.

There was a general chuckle. The minister took out his handkerchief and blew his nose sonorously. Banker Phelps closed his knife with a snap. "It's too bad the old man's sons didn't turn out better," he remarked with reflective authority. "They never hung together. He spent money enough on Harve to stock a dozen cattle-farms, and he might as well have poured it into Sand Creek. If Harve had stayed at home and helped nurse what little they had, and gone into stock on the old man's bottom farm, they might all have been well fixed. But the old man had to trust everything to tenants and was cheated right and left."

"Harve never could have handled stock none," interposed the cattleman. "He hadn't it in him to be sharp. Do you remember when he bought Sander's mules for eight-year olds, when everybody in town knew that Sander's father-in-law give 'em to his wife for a wedding present eighteen years before, an' they was full-grown mules then?"

Every one chuckled, and the Grand Army man rubbed his knees with a spasm of childish delight.

"Harve never was much account for anything practical, and he shore was never fond of work," began the coal and lumber dealer. "I mind the last time he was home; the day he left, when the old man was out to the barn helpin' his hand hitch up to take Harve to the train, and Cal Moots was patchin' up the fence, Harve, he come out on the step and sings out, in his ladylike voice: 'Cal Moots, Cal Moots! please come cord my trunk.'"

"That's Harve for you," approved the Grand Army man gleefully. "I kin hear him howlin' yet, when he was a big feller in long pants and his mother used to whale him with a rawhide in the barn for lettin' the cows git foundered in the cornfield when he was drivin' 'em home from pasture. He killed a cow of mine that-a-way onct—a pure Jersey and the best milker I had, an' the ole man had to put up for her. Harve, he was watchin' the sun set acrost the marshes when the anamile got away; he argued that sunset was oncommon fine."

"Where the old man made his mistake was in sending the boy East to school," said Phelps, stroking his goatee and speaking in a deliberate, judicial tone. "There was where he got his head full of trapseing to Paris and all such folly. What Harve needed, of all people, was a course in some first-class Kansas City business college."

The letters were swimming before Steavens's eyes. Was it possible that these men did not understand, that the palm on the coffin meant nothing to them? The very name of their town would have remained forever buried in the postal guide had it not been now and again mentioned in the world in connection with Harvey Merrick's.

He remembered what his master had said to him on the day of his death, after the congestion of both lungs had shut off any probability of recovery, and the sculptor had asked his pupil to send his body home. "It's not a pleasant place to be lying while the world is moving and doing and bettering," he had said with a feeble smile, "but it rather seems as though we ought to go back to the place we came from in the end. The townspeople will come in for a look at me; and after they have had their say, I shan't have much to fear from the judgment of God. The wings of the Victory, in there"—with a weak gesture toward his studio—"will not shelter me."

The cattleman took up the comment. "Forty's young for a Merrick to cash in; they usually hang on pretty well. Probably he helped it along with whisky."

"His mother's people were not long lived, and Harvey never had a robust constitution," said the minister mildly. He would have liked to say more. He had been the boy's Sunday-school teacher, and had been fond of him; but he felt that he was not in a position to speak. His own sons had turned out badly, and it was not a year since one of them had made his last trip home in the express car, shot in a gambling-house in the Black Hills.

"Nevertheless, there is no disputin' that Harve frequently looked upon the wine when it was red, also variegated, and it shore made an oncommon fool of him," moralized the cattleman.

Just then the door leading into the parlour rattled loudly and every one started involuntarily, looking relieved when only Jim Laird came out. His red face was convulsed with anger, and the Grand Army man ducked his head when he saw the spark in his blue, blood-shot eye. They were all afraid of Jim; he was a drunkard, but he could twist the law to suit his client's needs as no other man in all western Kansas could do; and there were many who tried. The lawyer closed the door gently behind him, leaned back against it and folded his arms, cocking his head a little to one side. When he assumed this attitude in the court-room, ears were always pricked up, as it usually foretold a flood of withering sarcasm.

"I've been with you gentlemen before," he began in a dry, even tone, "when you've sat by the coffins of boys born and raised in this town; and, if I remember rightly, you were never any too well satisfied when you checked them up. What's the matter, anyhow? Why is it that reputable young men are as scarce as millionaires in Sand City?

It might almost seem to a stranger that there was some way something the matter with your progressive town. Why did Ruben Sayer, the brightest young lawyer you ever turned out, after he had come home from the university as straight as a die, take to drinking and forge a check and shoot himself? Why did Bill Merrit's son die of the shakes in a saloon in Omaha? Why was Mr. Thomas's son, here, shot in a gambling-house? Why did young Adams burn his mill to beat the insurance companies and go to the pen?"

The lawyer paused and unfolded his arms, laying one clenched fist quietly on the table. "I'll tell you why. Because you drummed nothing but money and knavery into their ears from the time they wore knickerbockers; because you carped away at them as you've been carping here to-night, holding our friends Phelps and Elder up to them for their models, as our grandfathers held up George Washington and John Adams. But the boys, worse luck, were young, and raw at the business you put them to; and how could they match coppers with such artists as Phelps and Elder? You wanted them to be successful rascals; they were only unsuccessful ones—that's all the difference. There was only one boy ever raised in this borderland between ruffianism and civilization who didn't come to grief, and you hated Harvey Merrick more for winning out than you hated all the other boys who got under the wheels. Lord, Lord, how you did hate him! Phelps, here, is fond of saying that he could buy and sell us all out any time he's a mind to; but he knew Harve wouldn't have given a tinker's damn for his bank and all his cattle-farms put together; and a lack of appreciation, that way, goes hard with Phelps.

"Old Nimrod, here, thinks Harve drank too much; and this from such as Nimrod and me!

"Brother Elder says Harve was too free with the old man's money—fell short in filial consideration, maybe. Well, we can all remember the very tone in which brother Elder swore his own father was a liar, in the county court; and we all know that the old man came out of that partnership with his son as bare as a sheared lamb. But maybe I'm getting personal, and I'd better be driving ahead at what I want to say."

The lawyer paused a moment, squared his heavy shoulders, and went on: "Harvey Merrick and I went to school together, back East. We were dead in earnest, and we wanted you all to be proud of us some day. We meant to be great men. Even I, and I haven't lost my sense of humour, gentlemen, I meant to be a great man. I came back here to practise, and I found you didn't in the least want me to be a great man. You wanted me to be a shrewd lawyer—oh, yes! Our veteran here wanted me to get him an increase of pension, because he had dyspepsia; Phelps wanted a new county survey that would put the widow Wilson's little bottom farm inside his south line; Elder wanted to lend money at 5 per cent a month, and get it collected; old Stark here wanted to wheedle old women up in Vermont into investing their annuities in real-estate mortgages that are not worth the paper they are written on. Oh, you needed me hard enough, and you'll go on needing me; and that's why I'm not afraid to plug the truth home to you this once.

"Well, I came back here and became the damned shyster you wanted me to be. You pretend to have some sort of respect for me; and yet you'll stand up and throw mud at Harvey Merrick, whose soul you couldn't dirty and whose hands you couldn't tie. Oh, you're a discriminating lot of Christians! There have been times when the sight of Harvey's name in some Eastern paper has made me hang my head like a whipped dog; and, again, times when I liked to think of him off there in the world, away from all this hog-wallow, doing his great work and climbing the big, clean up-grade he'd set for himself.

"And we? Now that we've fought and lied and sweated and stolen, and hated as only the disappointed strugglers in a bitter, dead little Western town know how to do, what have we got to show for it? Harvey Merrick wouldn't have given one sunset over your marshes for all you've got put together, and you know it. It's not for me to say why, in the inscrutable wisdom of God, a genius should ever have been called from this place of hatred and bitter waters; but I want this Boston man to know that the drivel he's been hearing here to-night is the only tribute any truly great man could ever have from such a lot of sick, side-tracked, burnt-dog, land-poor sharks as the here-present financiers of Sand City—upon which town may God have mercy!"

The lawyer thrust out his hand to Steavens as he passed him, caught up his overcoat in the hall, and had left the house before the Grand Army man had had time to lift his ducked head and crane his long neck about at his fellows.

Next day Jim Laird was drunk and unable to attend the funeral services. Steavens called twice at his office, but was compelled to start East without seeing him. He had a presentiment that he would hear from him again, and left his address on the lawyer's table; but if Laird found it, he never acknowledged it. The thing in him that Harvey Merrick had loved must have gone under ground with Harvey Merrick's coffin; for it never spoke again, and Jim got the cold he died of driving across the Colorado mountains to defend one of Phelps's sons who had got into trouble out there by cutting government timber.

The Garden Lodge

When Caroline Noble's friends learned that Raymond d'Esquerré was to spend a month at her place on the Sound before he sailed to fill his engagement for the London opera season, they considered it another striking instance of the perversity of things. That the month was May, and the most mild and florescent of all the blue-and-white Mays the middle coast had known in years, but added to their sense of wrong. D'Esquerré, they learned, was ensconced in the lodge in the apple orchard, just beyond Caroline's glorious garden, and report went that at almost any hour the sound of the tenor's voice and of Caroline's crashing accompaniment could be heard floating through the open windows, out among the snowy apple boughs. The Sound, steel-blue and dotted with white sails, was splendidly seen from the windows of the lodge. The garden to the left and the orchard to the right had never been so riotous with spring, and had burst into impassioned bloom, as if to accommodate Caroline, though she was certainly the last woman to whom the witchery of Freya could be attributed; the last woman, as her friends affirmed, to at all adequately appreciate and make the most of such a setting for the great tenor.

Of course, they admitted, Caroline was musical—well, she ought to be!—but in that as in everything she was paramountly cool-headed, slow of impulse, and disgustingly practical; in that, as in everything else, she had herself so provokingly well in hand. Of course it would be she, always mistress of herself in any situation, she who would never be lifted one inch from the ground by it, and who would go on superintending her gardeners and workmen as usual, it would be she who got him. Perhaps some of them suspected that this was exactly why she did get him, and it but nettled them the more.

Caroline's coolness, her capableness, her general success, especially exasperated people because they felt that, for the most part, she had made herself what she was; that she had cold-bloodedly set about complying with the demands of life and making her position comfortable and masterful. That was why, every one said, she had married Howard Noble. Women who did not get through life so well as Caroline, who could not make such good terms either with fortune or their husbands, who did not find their health so unfailingly good, or hold their looks so well, or manage their children so easily, or give such distinction to all they did, were fond of stamping Caroline as a materialist and called her hard.

The impression of cold calculation, of having a definite policy, which Caroline gave, was far from a false one; but there was this to be said for her, that there were extenuating circumstances which her friends could not know.

If Caroline held determinedly to the middle course, if she was apt to regard with distrust everything which inclined toward extravagance, it was not because she was unacquainted with other standards than her own, or had never seen another side of life. She had grown up in Brooklyn, in a shabby little house under the vacillating administration of her father, a music teacher who usually neglected his duties to write orchestral compositions for which the world seemed to have no especial need. His spirit was warped by bitter vindictiveness and puerile self-commiseration, and he spent his days in scorn of the labour that brought him bread and in pitiful devotion to the labour that brought him only disappointment, writing interminable scores which demanded of the orchestra everything under heaven except melody.

It was not a cheerful home for a girl to grow up in. The mother, who idolized her husband as the music lord of the future, was left to a life-long battle with broom and dust-pan, to never ending conciliatory overtures to the butcher and grocer, to the making of her own gowns and of Caroline's, and to the delicate task of mollifying Auguste's neglected pupils.

The son, Heinrich, a painter, Caroline's only brother, had inherited all his father's vindictive sensitiveness without his capacity for slavish application. His little studio on the third floor had been much frequented by young men as unsuccessful as himself, who met there to give themselves over to contemptuous derision of this or that artist whose industry and stupidity had won him recognition. Heinrich, when he worked at all, did newspaper sketches at twenty-five dollars a week. He was too indolent and vacillating to set himself seriously to his art, too irascible and poignantly self-conscious to make a living, too much addicted to lying late in bed, to the incontinent reading of poetry and to the use of chloral, to be anything very positive except painful. At twenty-six he shot himself in a frenzy, and the whole wretched affair had effectually shattered his mother's health and brought on the decline of which she died. Caroline had been fond of him, but she felt a certain relief when he no longer wandered about the little house, commenting ironically upon its shabbiness, a Turkish cap on his head and a cigarette hanging from between his long, tremulous fingers.

After her mother's death, Caroline assumed the management of that bankrupt establishment. The funeral expenses were unpaid, and Auguste's pupils had been frightened away by the shock of successive disasters and the general atmosphere of wretchedness that pervaded the house. Auguste himself was writing a symphonic poem, Icarus, dedicated to the memory of his son. Caroline was barely twenty when she was called upon to face this tangle of difficulties, but she reviewed the situation candidly. The house had served its time as the shrine of idealism; vague, distressing, unsatisfied yearnings had brought it low enough. Her mother, thirty years before, had eloped and left Germany with her music teacher, to give herself over to life-long, drudging bondage at the kitchen range. Ever since Caroline could remember, the law in the house had been a sort of mystic worship of things distant, intangible and unattainable. The family had lived in successive ebullitions of generous enthusiasm, in talk of masters and masterpieces, only to come down to the cold facts in the case; to boiled mutton and to the necessity of turning the dining-room carpet. All these emotional pyrotechnics had ended in petty jealousies, in neglected duties and in cowardly fear of the little grocer on the corner.

From her childhood she had hated it, that humiliating and uncertain existence, with its glib tongue and empty pockets, its poetic ideals and sordid realities, its indolence and poverty tricked out in paper roses. Even as a little girl, when vague dreams beset her, when she wanted to lie late in bed and commune with visions, or to leap and sing because the sooty little trees along the street were putting out their first pale leaves in the sunshine, she would clench her hands and go to help her mother sponge the spots from her father's waistcoat or press Heinrich's trousers. Her mother never permitted the slightest question concerning anything Auguste or Heinrich saw fit to do, but from the time Caroline could reason at all she could not help thinking that many things went wrong at home. She knew, for example, that her father's pupils ought not to be kept waiting half an hour while he discussed Schopenhauer with some bearded socialist over a dish of herrings and a spotted table cloth. She knew that Heinrich ought not to give a dinner on Heine's birthday, when the laundress had not been paid for a month and when he frequently had to ask his mother for car fare. Certainly Caroline had served her apprenticeship to idealism and to all the embarrassing inconsistencies which it sometimes entails, and she decided to deny herself this diffuse, ineffectual answer to the sharp questions of life.

When she came into the control of herself and the house, she refused to proceed any further with her musical education. Her father, who had intended to make a concert pianist of her, set this down as another item in his long list of disappointments and his grievances against the world. She was young and pretty, and she had worn turned gowns and soiled gloves and improvised hats all her life. She wanted the luxury of being like other people, of being honest from her hat to her boots, of having nothing to hide, not even in the matter of stockings, and she was willing to work for it. She rented a little studio away from that house of misfortune, and began to give lessons. She managed well and was the sort of girl people liked to help. The bills were paid and Auguste went on composing, growing indignant only when she refused to insist that her pupils should study his compositions for the piano. She began to get engagements in New York to play accompaniments at song recitals. She dressed well, made herself agreeable, and gave herself a chance. She never permitted herself to look further than a step ahead, and set herself with all the strength of her will to see things as they are and meet them squarely in the broad day. There were two things she feared even more than poverty; the part of one that sets up an idol and the part of one that bows down and worships it.

When Caroline was twenty-four she married Howard Noble, then a widower of forty, who had been for ten years a power in Wall Street. Then, for the first time, she had paused to take breath. It took a substantialness as unquestionable as his; his money, his position, his energy, the big vigour of his robust person, to satisfy her that she was entirely safe. Then she relaxed a little, feeling that there was a barrier to be counted upon between her and that world of visions and quagmires and failure.

Caroline had been married for six years when Raymond d'Esquerré came to stay with them. He came chiefly because Caroline was what she was; because he, too, felt occasionally the need of getting out of Klingsor's garden, of dropping down somewhere for a time near a quiet nature, a cool head, a strong hand. The hours he had spent in the garden lodge were hours of such concentrated study as, in his fevered life, he seldom got in anywhere. She had, as he told Noble, a fine appreciation of the seriousness of work.

One evening two weeks after d'Esquerré had sailed, Caroline was in the library giving her husband an account of the work she had laid out for the gardeners. She superintended the care of the grounds herself. Her garden, indeed, had become quite a part of her; a sort of beautiful adjunct, like gowns or jewels. It was a famous spot, and Noble was very proud of it.

"What do you think, Caroline, of having the garden lodge torn down and putting a new summer house there at the end of the arbour; a big rustic affair where you could have tea served in mid-summer?" he asked.

"The lodge?" repeated Caroline looking at him quickly. "Why, that seems almost a shame, doesn't it, after d'Esquerré has used it?"

Noble put down his book with a smile of amusement.

"Are you going to be sentimental about it? Why, I'd sacrifice the whole place to see that come to pass. But I don't believe you could do it for an hour together."

"I don't believe so, either," said his wife, smiling.

Noble took up his book again and Caroline went into the music-room to practise. She was not ready to have the lodge torn down. She had gone there for a quiet hour every day during the two weeks since d'Esquerré had left them. It was the sheerest sentiment she had ever permitted herself. She was ashamed of it, but she was childishly unwilling to let it go.

Caroline went to bed soon after her husband, but she was not able to sleep. The night was close and warm, presaging storm. The wind had fallen and the water slept, fixed and motionless as the sand. She rose and thrust her feet into slippers and putting a dressing-gown over her shoulders opened the door of her husband's room; he was sleeping soundly. She went into the hall and down the stairs; then, leaving the house through a side door, stepped into the vine covered arbour that led to the garden lodge. The scent of the June roses was heavy in the still air, and the stones that paved the path felt pleasantly cool through the thin soles of her slippers. Heat-lightning flashed continuously from the bank of clouds that had gathered over the sea, but the shore was flooded with moonlight and, beyond, the rim of the Sound lay smooth and shining. Caroline had the key of the lodge, and the door creaked as she opened it. She stepped into the long, low room radiant with the moonlight which streamed through the bow window and lay in a silvery pool along the waxed floor. Even that part of the room which lay in the shadow was vaguely illuminated; the piano, the tall candlesticks, the picture frames and white casts standing out as clearly in the half-light as did the sycamores and black poplars of the garden against the still, expectant night sky. Caroline sat down to think it all over. She had come here to do just that every day of the two weeks since d'Esquerré's departure, but, far from ever having reached a conclusion, she had succeeded only in losing her way in a maze of memories—sometimes bewilderingly confused, sometimes too acutely distinct—where there was neither path, nor clue, nor any hope of finality. She had, she realized, defeated a life-long regimen; completely confounded herself by falling unaware and incontinently into that luxury of revery which, even as a little girl, she had so determinedly denied herself; she had been developing with alarming celerity that part of one which sets up an idol and that part of one which bows down and worships it.

It was a mistake, she felt, ever to have asked d'Esquerré to come at all. She had an angry feeling that she had done it rather in self-defiance, to rid herself finally of that instinctive fear of him which had always troubled and perplexed her. She knew that she had reckoned with herself before he came; but she had been equal to so much that she had never really doubted she would be equal to this. She had come to believe, indeed, almost arrogantly in her own malleability and endurance; she had done so much with herself that she had come to think that there was nothing which she could not do; like swimmers, overbold, who reckon upon their strength and their power to hoard it, forgetting the ever changing moods of their adversary, the sea.

And d'Esquerré was a man to reckon with. Caroline did not deceive herself now upon that score. She admitted it humbly enough, and since she had said good-bye to him she had not been free for a moment from the sense of his formidable power. It formed the undercurrent of her consciousness; whatever she might be doing or thinking, it went on, involuntarily, like her breathing; sometimes welling up until suddenly she found herself suffocating. There was a moment of this to-night, and Caroline rose and stood shuddering, looking about her in the blue duskiness of the silent room. She had not been here at night before, and the spirit of the place seemed more troubled and insistent than ever it had been in the quiet of the afternoons. Caroline brushed her hair back from her damp forehead and went over to the bow window. After raising it she sat down upon the low seat. Leaning her head against the sill, and loosening her night-gown at the throat, she half closed her eyes and looked off into the troubled night, watching the play of the sheet-lightning upon the massing clouds between the pointed tops of the poplars.

Yes, she knew, she knew well enough, of what absurdities this spell was woven; she mocked, even while she winced. His power she knew, lay not so much in anything that he actually had—though he had so much—or in anything that he actually was; but in what he suggested, in what he seemed picturesque enough to have or be—and that was just anything that one chose to believe or to desire. His appeal was all the more persuasive and alluring that it was to the imagination alone, that it was as indefinite and impersonal as those cults of idealism which so have their way with women. What he had was that, in his mere personality, he quickened and in a measure gratified that something without which—to women—life is no better than sawdust, and to the desire for which most of their mistakes and tragedies and astonishingly poor bargains are due.

D'Esquerré had become the centre of a movement, and the Metropolitan had become the temple of a cult. When he could be induced to cross the Atlantic, the opera season in New York was successful; when he could not, the management lost money; so much every one knew. It was understood, too, that his superb art had disproportionately little to do with his peculiar position. Women swayed the balance this way or that; the opera, the orchestra, even his own glorious art, achieved at such a cost, were but the accessories of himself; like the scenery and costumes and even the soprano, they all went to produce atmosphere, were the mere mechanics of the beautiful illusion.

Caroline understood all this; to-night was not the first time that she had put it to herself so. She had seen the same feeling in other people; watched for it in her friends, studied it in the house night after night when he sang, candidly putting herself among a thousand others.

D'Esquerré's arrival in the early winter was the signal for a feminine hegira toward New York. On the nights when he sang, women flocked to the Metropolitan from mansions and hotels, from typewriter desks, school-rooms, shops and fitting-rooms. They were of all conditions and complexions. Women of the world who accepted him knowingly, as they sometimes took champagne for its agreeable effect; sisters of charity and overworked shop-girls, who received him devoutly; withered women who had taken doctorate degrees and who worshipped furtively through prism spectacles; business women and women of affairs, the Amazons who dwelt afar from men in the stony fastnesses of apartment houses. They all entered into the same romance; dreamed, in terms as various as the hues of phantasy, the same dream; drew the same quick breath when he stepped upon the stage, and, at his exit, felt the same dull pain of shouldering the pack again.

There were the maimed, even; those who came on crutches, who were pitted by smallpox or grotesquely painted by cruel birth stains. These, too, entered with him into enchantment. Stout matrons became slender girls again; worn spinsters felt their cheeks flush with the tenderness of their lost youth. Young and old, however hideous, however fair, they yielded up their heat—whether quick or latent— sat hungering for the mystic bread wherewith he fed them at this eucharist of sentiment.

Sometimes when the house was crowded from the orchestra to the last row of the gallery, when the air was charged with this ecstasy of fancy, he himself was the victim of the burning reflection of his power. They acted upon him in turn; he felt their fervent and despairing appeal to him; it stirred him as the spring drives the sap up into an old tree; he, too, burst into bloom. For the moment, he, too, believed again, desired again, he knew not what, but something.

But it was not in these exalted moments that Caroline had learned to fear him most. It was in the quiet, tired reserve, the dullness, even, that kept him company between these outbursts that she found that exhausting drain upon her sympathies which was the very pith and substance of their alliance. It was the tacit admission of disappointment under all this glamour of success—the helplessness of the enchanter to at all enchant himself—that awoke in her an illogical, womanish desire to in some way compensate, to make it up to him.

She had observed drastically to herself that it was her eighteenth year he awoke in her—those hard years she had spent in turning gowns and placating tradesmen, and which she had never had time to live. After all, she reflected, it was better to allow one's self a little youth; to dance a little at the carnival and to live these things when they are natural and lovely, not to have them coming back on one and demanding arrears when they are humiliating and impossible. She went over to-night all the catalogue of her self-deprivations; recalled how, in the light of her father's example, she had even refused to humour her innocent taste for improvising at the piano; how, when she began to teach, after her mother's death, she had struck out one little indulgence after another, reducing her life to a relentless routine, unvarying as clockwork. It seemed to her that ever since d'Esquerré first came into the house she had been haunted by an imploring little girlish ghost that followed her about, wringing its hands and entreating for an hour of life.

The storm had held off unconscionably long; the air within the lodge was stifling, and without the garden waited, breathless. Everything seemed pervaded by a poignant distress; the hush of feverish, intolerable expectation. The still earth, the heavy flowers, even the growing darkness, breathed the exhaustion of protracted waiting. Caroline felt that she ought to go; that it was wrong to stay; that the hour and the place were as treacherous as her own reflections. She rose and began to pace the floor, stepping softly, as though in fear of awakening some one, her figure, in its thin drapery, diaphanously vague and white. Still unable to shake off the obsession of the intense stillness, she sat down at the piano and began to run over the first act of the *Walküre*, the last of his rôles they had practised together; playing listlessly and absently at first, but with gradually increasing seriousness. Perhaps it was the still heat of the summer night, perhaps it was the heavy odours from the garden that came in through the open windows; but as she played there grew and grew the feeling that he was there, beside her, standing in his accustomed place. In the duet at the end of the first act she heard him clearly: *"Thou art the Spring for which I sighed in Winter's cold embraces."* Once as he sang it, he had put his arm about her, his one hand under her heart, while with the other he took her right from the keyboard, holding her as he always held *Sieglinde* when he drew her toward the window. She had been wonderfully the mistress of herself at the time; neither repellent nor acquiescent. She remembered that she had rather exulted, then, in her self-control—which he had seemed to take for granted, though there was perhaps the whisper of a question from the hand under her heart. *"Thou art the Spring for which I sighed in Winter's cold embraces."* Caroline lifted her hands quickly from the keyboard, and she bowed her head in them, sobbing.

The storm broke and the rain beat in, spattering her night-dress until she rose and lowered the windows. She dropped upon the couch and began fighting over again the battles of other days, while the ghosts of the slain rose as from a sowing of dragon's teeth. The shadows of things always so scorned and flouted, bore down upon her merciless and triumphant. It was not enough; this happy, useful, well-ordered life was not enough. It did not satisfy, it was not even real. No, the other things, the shadows—they were the realities. Her father, poor Heinrich, even her mother, who had been able to sustain her poor romance and keep her little illusions amid the tasks of a scullion, were nearer happiness than she. Her sure foundation was but made ground, after all, and the people in Klingsor's garden were more fortunate, however barren the sands from which they conjured their paradise.

The lodge was still and silent; her fit of weeping over, Caroline made no sound, and within the room, as without in the garden, was the blackness of storm. Only now and then a flash of lightning showed a woman's slender figure rigid on the couch, her face buried in her hands.

Toward morning, when the occasional rumbling of thunder was heard no more and the beat of the rain drops upon the orchard leaves was steadier, she fell asleep and did not waken until the first red streaks of dawn shone through the twisted boughs of the apple trees. There was a moment between world and world, when, neither asleep nor awake, she felt her dream grow thin, melting away from her, felt the warmth under her heart growing cold. Something seemed to slip from the clinging hold of her arms, and she groaned protestingly through her parted lips, following it a little way with fluttering hands. Then her eyes opened wide and she sprang up and sat holding dizzily to the cushions of the couch, staring at her bare, cold feet, at her labouring breast, rising and falling under her open night-dress.

The dream was gone, but the feverish reality of it still pervaded her and she held it as the vibrating string holds a tone. In the last hour the shadows had had their way with Caroline. They had shown her the nothingness of time and space, of system and discipline, of closed doors and broad waters. Shuddering, she thought of the Arabian fairy tale in which the Genii brought the princess of China to the sleeping prince of Damascus, and carried her through the air back to her palace at dawn. Caroline closed her eyes and dropped her elbows weakly upon her knees, her shoulders sinking together. The horror was that it had not come from without, but from within. The dream was no blind chance; it was the expression of something she had kept so close a prisoner that she had never seen it herself; it was the wail from the donjon deeps when the watch slept. Only as the outcome of such a night of sorcery could the thing have been loosed to straighten its limbs and measure itself with her; so heavy were the chains upon it, so many a fathom deep it was crushed down into darkness. The fact that d'Esquerré happened to be on the other side of the world meant nothing; had he been here, beside her, it could scarcely have hurt her self-respect so much. She could scarcely have despised herself more had she come to him here in the night three weeks ago and thrown herself down upon the stone slab at the door there.

Caroline rose unsteadily and crept guiltily from the lodge and along the path under the arbour, terrified lest the servants should be stirring, trembling with the chill air, while the wet shrubbery, brushing against her, drenched her night-dress until it clung about her limbs.

At breakfast her husband looked across the table at her with concern. "It seems to me that you are looking rather fagged, Caroline. It was a beastly night to sleep. Why don't you go up to the mountains until this hot weather is over? By the way, were you in earnest about letting the lodge stand?"

Caroline laughed quietly. "No, I find I was not very serious. I haven't sentiment enough to forego a summer-house. Will you tell Baker to come to-morrow to talk it over with me? If we are to have a house party, I should like to put him to work on it at once."

Noble gave her a glance, half humorous, half vexed. "Do you know I am rather disappointed?" he said. "I had almost hoped that, just for once, you know, you would be a little bit foolish."

"Not now that I've slept over it," replied Caroline, and they both rose from the table, laughing.

"A Death in the Desert"

Everett Hilgarde was conscious that the man in the seat across the aisle was looking at him intently. He was a large, florid man, wore a conspicuous diamond solitaire upon his third finger, and Everett judged him to be a travelling salesman of some sort. He had the air of an adaptable fellow who had been about the world and who could keep cool and clean under almost any circumstances.

The "High Line Flyer," as this train was derisively called among railroad men, was jerking along through the hot afternoon over the monotonous country between Holdrege and Cheyenne. Besides the blond man and himself the only occupants of the car were two dusty, bedraggled-looking girls who had been to the Exposition at Chicago, and who were earnestly discussing the cost of their first trip out of Colorado. The four uncomfortable passengers were covered with a sediment of fine, yellow dust which clung to their hair and eyebrows like gold powder. It blew up in clouds from the bleak, lifeless country through which they passed, until they were one colour with the sage-brush and sand-hills. The grey and yellow desert was varied only by occasional ruins of deserted towns, and by the little red boxes of station-houses, where the spindling trees and sickly vines in the blue-grass yards made little green reserves fenced off in that confusing wilderness of sand.

As the slanting rays of the sun beat in stronger and stronger through the car-windows, the blond gentleman asked the ladies' permission to remove his coat, and sat in his lavender striped shirt-sleeves, with a black silk handkerchief tucked carefully about his collar. He had seemed interested in Everett since they had boarded the train at Holdrege, and kept glancing at him curiously and then looking reflectively out of the window, as though he were trying to recall something. But wherever Everett went some one was almost sure to look at him with that curious interest, and it had ceased to embarrass or annoy him. Presently the stranger, seeming satisfied with his observation, leaned back in his seat, half closed his eyes, and began softly to whistle the Spring Song from *Proserpine*, the cantata that a dozen years before had made its young composer famous in a night. Everett had heard that air on guitars in Old Mexico, on mandolins at college glees, on cottage organs in New England hamlets, and only two weeks ago he had heard it played on sleighbells at a variety theatre in Denver. There was literally no way of escaping his brother's precocity. Adriance could live on the other side of the Atlantic, where his youthful indiscretions were forgotten in his mature achievements, but his brother had never been able to outrun *Proserpine*, and here he found it again in the Colorado sand-hills. Not that Everett was exactly ashamed of *Proserpine;* only a man of genius could have written it, but it was the sort of thing that a man of genius outgrows as soon as he can.

Everett unbent a trifle, and smiled at his neighbour across the aisle. Immediately the large man rose and coming over dropped into the seat facing Hilgarde, extending his card.

"Dusty ride, isn't it? I don't mind it myself; I'm used to it. Born and bred in de briar patch, like Br'er Rabbit. I've been trying to place you for a long time; I think I must have met you before."

"Thank you," said Everett, taking the card; "my name is Hilgarde. You've probably met my brother, Adriance; people often mistake me for him."

The travelling-man brought his hand down upon his knee with such vehemence that the solitaire blazed.

"So I was right after all, and if you're not Adriance Hilgarde you're his double. I thought I couldn't be mistaken. Seen him? Well, I guess! I never missed one of his recitals at the Auditorium, and he played the piano score of *Proserpine* through to us once at the Chicago Press Club. I used to be on the *Commercial* there before I began to travel for the publishing department of the concern. So you're Hilgarde's brother, and here I've run into you at the jumping-off place. Sounds like a newspaper yarn, doesn't it?"

The travelling-man laughed and offered Everett a cigar and plied him with questions on the only subject that people ever seemed to care to talk to Everett about. At length the salesman and the two girls alighted at a Colorado way station, and Everett went on to Cheyenne alone.

The train pulled into Cheyenne at nine o'clock, late by a matter of four hours or so; but no one seemed particularly concerned at its tardiness except the station agent, who grumbled at being kept in the office over time on a summer night. When Everett alighted from the train he walked down the platform and stopped at the track crossing, uncertain as to what direction he should take to reach a hotel. A phaeton stood near the crossing and a woman held the reins. She was dressed in white, and her figure was clearly silhouetted against the cushions, though it was too dark to see her face. Everett had scarcely noticed her, when the switch-engine came puffing up from the opposite direction, and the head-light threw a strong glare of light on his face. Suddenly the woman in the phaeton uttered a low cry and dropped the reins. Everett started forward and caught the horse's head, but the animal only lifted its ears and whisked its tail in impatient surprise. The woman sat perfectly still, her head sunk between her shoulders and her handkerchief pressed to her face. Another woman came out of the depot and hurried toward the phaeton, crying, "Katharine, dear, what is the matter?"

Everett hesitated a moment in painful embarrassment, then lifted his hat and passed on. He was accustomed to sudden recognitions in the most impossible places, especially by women, but this cry out of the night had shaken him.

While Everett was breakfasting the next morning, the head waiter leaned over his chair to murmur that there was a gentleman waiting to see him in the parlour. Everett finished his coffee, and went in the direction indicated, where he found his visitor restlessly pacing the floor. His whole manner betrayed a high degree of agitation, though his physique was not that of a man whose nerves lie near the surface. He was something below medium height, square-shouldered and solidly built. His thick, closely cut hair was beginning to show grey about the ears, and his bronzed face was heavily lined. His square brown hands were locked behind him, and he held his shoulders like a man conscious of responsibilities, yet, as he turned to greet Everett, there was an incongruous diffidence in his address.

"Good-morning, Mr. Hilgarde," he said, extending his hand; "I found your name on the hotel register. My name is Gaylord. I'm afraid my sister startled you at the station last night, Mr. Hilgarde, and I've come around to apologize."

"Ah! the young lady in the phaeton? I'm sure I didn't know whether I had anything to do with her alarm or not. If I did, it is I who owe the apology."

The man coloured a little under the dark brown of his face.

"Oh, it's nothing you could help, sir, I fully understand that. You see, my sister used to be a pupil of your brother's, and it seems you favour him; and when the switch-engine threw a light on your face it startled her."

Everett wheeled about in his chair. "Oh! *Katharine* Gaylord! Is it possible! Now it's you who have given me a turn. Why I used to know her when I was a boy. What on earth—"

"Is she doing here?" said Gaylord, grimly filling out the pause. "You've got at the heart of the matter. You knew my sister had been in bad health for a long time?"

"No, I had never heard a word of that. The last I knew of her she was singing in London. My brother and I correspond infrequently, and seldom get beyond family matters. I am deeply sorry to hear this. There are many more reasons why I am concerned than I can tell you."

The lines in Charley Gaylord's brow relaxed a little.

"What I'm trying to say, Mr. Hilgarde, is that she wants to see you. I hate to ask you, but she's so set on it. We live several miles out of town, but my rig's below, and I can take you out any time you can go."

"I can go now, and it will give me real pleasure to do so," said Everett, quickly. "I'll get my hat and be with you in a moment."

When he came downstairs Everett found a cart at the door, and Charley Gaylord drew a long sigh of relief as he gathered up the reins and settled back into his own element.

"You see, I think I'd better tell you something about my sister before you see her, and I don't know just where to begin. She travelled in Europe with your brother and his wife, and sang at a lot of his concerts; but I don't know just how much you know about her."

"Very little, except that my brother always thought her the most gifted of his pupils, and that when I knew her she was very young and very beautiful and turned my head sadly for a while."

Everett saw that Gaylord's mind was quite engrossed by his grief. He was wrought up to the point where his reserve and sense of proportion had quite left him, and his trouble was the one vital thing in the world. "That's the whole thing," he went on, flicking his horses with the whip.

"She was a great woman, as you say, and she didn't come of a great family. She had to fight her own way from the first. She got to Chicago, and then to New York, and then to Europe, where she went up like lightning, and got a taste for it all; and now she's dying here like a rat in a hole, out of her own world, and she can't fall back into ours. We've grown apart, some way—miles and miles apart—and I'm afraid she's fearfully unhappy."

"It's a very tragic story that you are telling me, Gaylord," said Everett. They were well out into the country now, spinning along over the dusty plains of red grass, with the ragged blue outline of the mountains before them.

"Tragic!" cried Gaylord, starting up in his seat, "my God, man, nobody will ever know how tragic. It's a tragedy I live with and eat with and sleep with, until I've lost my grip on everything. You see she had made a good bit of money, but she spent it all going to health resorts. It's her lungs, you know. I've got money enough to send her anywhere, but the doctors all say it's no use. She hasn't the ghost of a chance. It's just getting through the days now. I had no notion she was half so bad before she came to me. She just wrote that she was all run down. Now that she's here, I think she'd be happier anywhere under the sun, but she won't leave. She says it's easier to let go of life here, and that to go East would be dying twice. There was a time when I was a brakeman with a run out of Bird City, Iowa, and she was a little thing I could carry on my shoulder, when I could get her everything on earth she wanted, and she hadn't a wish my $80 a month didn't cover; and now, when I've got a little property together, I can't buy her a night's sleep!"

Everett saw that, whatever Charley Gaylord's present status in the world might be, he had brought the brakeman's heart up the ladder with him, and the brakeman's frank avowal of sentiment. Presently Gaylord went on:

"You can understand how she has outgrown her family. We're all a pretty common sort, railroaders from away back. My father was a conductor. He died when we were kids. Maggie, my other sister, who lives with me, was a telegraph operator here while I was getting my grip on things. We had no education to speak of. I have to hire a stenographer because I can't spell straight—the Almighty couldn't teach me to spell. The things that make up life to Kate are all Greek to me, and there's scarcely a point where we touch any more, except in our recollections of the old times when we were all young and happy together, and Kate sang in a church choir in Bird City. But I believe, Mr. Hilgarde, that if she can see just one person like you, who knows about the things and people she's interested in, it will give her about the only comfort she can have now."

The reins slackened in Charley Gaylord's hand as they drew up before a showily painted house with many gables and a round tower. "Here we are," he said, turning to Everett, "and I guess we understand each other."

They were met at the door by a thin, colourless woman, whom Gaylord introduced as "My sister, Maggie." She asked her brother to show Mr. Hilgarde into the music-room, where Katharine wished to see him alone.

When Everett entered the music-room he gave a little start of surprise, feeling that he had stepped from the glaring Wyoming sunlight into some New York studio that he had always known. He wondered which it was of those countless studios, high up under the roofs, over banks and shops and wholesale houses, that this room resembled, and he looked incredulously out of the window at the grey plain which ended in the great upheaval of the Rockies.

The haunting air of familiarity about the room perplexed him. Was it a copy of some particular studio he knew, or was it merely the studio atmosphere that seemed so individual and poignantly reminiscent here in Wyoming? He sat down in a reading-chair and looked keenly about him. Suddenly his eye fell upon a large photograph of his brother above the piano. Then it all became clear to him: this was veritably his brother's room. If it were not an exact copy of one of the many studios that Adriance had fitted up in various parts of the world, wearying of them and leaving almost before the renovator's varnish had dried, it was at least in the same tone. In every detail Adriance's taste was so manifest that the room seemed to exhale his personality.

Among the photographs on the wall there was one of Katharine Gaylord, taken in the days when Everett had known her, and when the flash of her eye or the flutter of her skirt was enough to set his boyish heart in a tumult. Even now, he stood before the portrait with a certain degree of embarrassment. It was the face of a woman already old in her first youth, thoroughly sophisticated and a trifle hard, and it told of what her brother had called her fight. The *camaraderie* of her frank, confident eyes was qualified by the deep lines about her mouth and the curve of the lips, which was both sad and cynical. Certainly she had more good-will than confidence toward the world, and the bravado of her smile could not conceal the shadow of an unrest that was almost discontent. The chief charm of the woman, as Everett had known her, lay in her superb figure and in her eyes, which possessed a warm, life-giving quality like the sunlight; eyes which glowed with a sort of perpetual *salutat* to the world. Her head, Everett remembered as peculiarly well shaped and proudly poised. There had been always a little of the imperatrix about her, and her pose in the photograph revived all his old impressions of her unattachedness, of how absolutely and valiantly she stood alone.

Everett was still standing before the picture, his hands behind him and his head inclined, when he heard the door open. A very tall woman advanced toward him, holding out her hand. As she started to speak she coughed slightly, then, laughing, said, in a low, rich voice, a trifle husky: "You see I make the traditional Camille entrance—with the cough. How good of you to come, Mr. Hilgarde."

Everett was acutely conscious that while addressing him she was not looking at him at all, and, as he assured her of his pleasure in coming, he was glad to have an opportunity to collect himself. He had not reckoned upon the ravages of a long illness. The long, loose folds of her white gown had been especially designed to conceal the sharp outlines of her emaciated body, but the stamp of her disease was there; simple and ugly and obtrusive, a pitiless fact that could not be disguised or evaded. The splendid shoulders were stooped, there was a swaying unevenness in her gait, her arms seemed disproportionately long, and her hands were transparently white, and cold to the touch. The changes in her face were less obvious; the proud carriage of the head, the warm, clear eyes, even the delicate flush of colour in her cheeks, all defiantly remained, though they were all in a lower key— older, sadder, softer.

She sat down upon the divan and began nervously to arrange the pillows. "I know I'm not an inspiring object to look upon, but you must be quite frank and sensible about that and get used to it at once, for we've no time to lose. And if I'm a trifle irritable you won't mind?— for I'm more than usually nervous."

"Don't bother with me this morning, if you are tired," urged Everett. "I can come quite as well to-morrow."

"Gracious, no!" she protested, with a flash of that quick, keen humour that he remembered as a part of her. "It's solitude that I'm tired to death of—solitude and the wrong kind of people. You see, the minister, not content with reading the prayers for the sick, called on me this morning. He happened to be riding by on his bicycle and felt it his duty to stop. Of course, he disapproves of my profession, and I think he takes it for granted that I have a dark past. The funniest feature of his conversation is that he is always excusing my own vocation to me—condoning it, you know—and trying to patch up my peace with my conscience by suggesting possible noble uses for what he kindly calls my talent."

Everett laughed. "Oh! I'm afraid I'm not the person to call after such a serious gentleman—I can't sustain the situation. At my best I don't reach higher than low comedy. Have you decided to which one of the noble uses you will devote yourself?"

Katharine lifted her hands in a gesture of renunciation and exclaimed: "I'm not equal to any of them, not even the least noble. I didn't study that method."

She laughed and went on nervously: "The parson's not so bad. He has read Gibbon's 'Decline and Fall,' all five volumes, and that's something. Then, he has been to New York, and that's a great deal. But how we are losing time! Do tell me about New York; Charley says you're just on from there. How does it look and taste and smell just now? I think a whiff of the Jersey ferry would be as flagons of cod-liver oil to me. Who conspicuously walks the Rialto now, and what does he or she wear? Are the trees still green in Madison Square, or have they grown brown and dusty? Does the chaste Diana on the Garden Theatre still keep her vestal vows through all the exasperating changes of weather? Who has your brother's old studio now, and what misguided aspirants practise their scales in the rookeries about Carnegie Hall? What do people go to see at the theatres, and what do they eat and drink there in the world nowadays? You see, I'm homesick for it all, from the Battery to Riverside. Oh, let me die in Harlem!" she was interrupted by a violent attack of coughing, and Everett, embarrassed by her discomfort, plunged into gossip about the professional people he had met in town during the summer, and the musical outlook for the winter. He was diagramming with his pencil, on the back of an old envelope he found in his pocket, some new mechanical device to be used at the Metropolitan in the production of the *Rheingold*, when he became conscious that she was looking at him intently, and that he was talking to the four walls.

Katharine was lying back among the pillows, watching him through half-closed eyes, as a painter looks at a picture. He finished his explanation vaguely enough and put the envelope back in his pocket. As he did so, she said, quietly: "How wonderfully like Adriance you are!" and he felt as though a crisis of some sort had been met and tided over.

He laughed, looking up at her with a touch of pride in his eyes that made them seem quite boyish. "Yes, isn't it absurd? It's almost as awkward as looking like Napoleon—But, after all, there are some advantages. It has made some of his friends like me, and I hope it will make you."

Katharine smiled and gave him a quick, meaning glance from under her lashes. "Oh, it did that long ago. What a haughty, reserved youth you were then, and how you used to stare at people, and then blush and look cross if they paid you back in your own coin. Do you remember that night when you took me home from a rehearsal, and scarcely spoke a word to me?"

"It was the silence of admiration," protested Everett, "very crude and boyish, but very sincere and not a little painful. Perhaps you suspected something of the sort? I remember you saw fit to be very grown up and worldly."

"I believe I suspected a pose; the one that college boys usually affect with singers—'an earthen vessel in love with a star,' you know. But it rather surprised me in you, for you must have seen a good deal of your brother's pupils. Or had you an omnivorous capacity, and elasticity that always met the occasion?"

"Don't ask a man to confess the follies of his youth," said Everett, smiling a little sadly; "I am sensitive about some of them even now. But I was not so sophisticated as you imagined. I saw my brother's pupils come and go, but that was about all. Sometimes I was called on to play accompaniments, or to fill out a vacancy at a rehearsal, or to order a carriage for an infuriated soprano who had thrown up her part. But they never spent any time on me, unless it was to notice the resemblance you speak of."

"Yes," observed Katharine, thoughtfully. "I noticed it then, too;

but it has grown as you have grown older. That is rather strange, when you have lived such different lives. It's not merely an ordinary family likeness of feature, you know, but a sort of interchangeable individuality; the suggestion of the other man's personality in your face—like an air transposed to another key. But I'm not attempting to define it; it's beyond me; something altogether unusual and a trifle—well, uncanny," she finished, laughing.

"I remember," Everett said, seriously, twirling the pencil between his fingers and looking, as he sat with his head thrown back, out under the red window-blind which was raised just a little, and as it swung back and forth in the wind revealed the glaring panorama of the desert—a blinding stretch of yellow, flat as the sea in dead calm, splotched here and there with deep purple shadows; and, beyond, the ragged blue outline of the mountains and the peaks of snow, white as the white clouds—"I remember, when I was a little fellow I used to be very sensitive about it. I don't think it exactly displeased me, or that I would have had it otherwise if I could, but it seemed to me like a birthmark, or something not to be lightly spoken of. People were naturally always fonder of Ad than of me, and I used to feel the chill of reflected light pretty often. It came into even my relations with my mother. Ad went abroad to study when he was absurdly young, you know, and mother was all broken up over it. She did her whole duty by each of us, but it was sort of generally understood among us that she'd have made burnt offerings of us all for Ad any day. I was a little fellow then, and when she sat alone on the porch in the summer dusk, she used sometimes to call me to her and turn my face up in the light that streamed out through the shutters and kiss me, and then I always knew she was thinking of Adriance."

"Poor little chap," said Katharine, and her tone was a trifle huskier than usual. "How fond people have always been of Adriance! Now tell me the latest news of him. I haven't heard, except through the press, for a year or more. He was in Algiers then, in the valley of the Chelif, riding horseback night and day in an Arabian costume, and in his usual enthusiastic fashion he had quite made up his mind to adopt the Mahometan faith and become as nearly an Arab as possible. How many countries and faiths has he adopted, I wonder? Probably he was playing Arab to himself all the time. I remember he was a sixteenth-century duke in Florence once for weeks together."

"Oh, that's Adriance," chuckled Everett. "He is himself barely long enough to write checks and be measured for his clothes. I didn't hear from him while he was an Arab; I missed that."

"He was writing an Algerian *suite* for the piano then; it must be in the publisher's hands by this time. I have been too ill to answer his letter, and have lost touch with him."

Everett drew a letter from his pocket. "This came about a month ago. It's chiefly about his new opera which is to be brought out in London next winter. Read it at your leisure."

"I think I shall keep it as a hostage, so that I may be sure you will come again. Now I want you to play for me. Whatever you like; but if there is anything new in the world, in mercy let me hear it. For nine months I have heard nothing but 'The Baggage Coach Ahead' and 'She is My Baby's Mother.'"

He sat down at the piano, and Katharine sat near him, absorbed in his remarkable physical likeness to his brother, and trying to discover in just what it consisted. She told herself that it was very much as though a sculptor's finished work had been rudely copied in wood. He was of a larger build than Adriance, and his shoulders were broad and heavy, while those of his brother were slender and rather girlish. His face was of the same oval mould, but it was grey, and darkened about the mouth by continual shaving. His eyes were of the same inconstant April colour, but they were reflective and rather dull; while Adriance's were always points of high light, and always meaning another thing than the thing they meant yesterday. But it was hard to see why this earnest man should so continually suggest that lyric, youthful face that was as gay as his was grave. For Adriance, though he was ten years the elder, and though his hair was streaked with silver, had the face of a boy of twenty, so mobile that it told his thoughts before he could put them into words. A contralto, famous for the extravagance of her vocal methods and of her affections had once said of him that the shepherd-boys who sang in the Vale of Tempe must certainly have looked like young Hilgarde; and the comparison had been apppropriated by a hundred shyer women who preferred to quote.

As Everett sat smoking on the veranda of the Inter-Ocean House that night, he was a victim to random recollections. His infatuation for Katharine Gaylord, visionary as it was, had been the most serious of his boyish love-affairs, and had long disturbed his bachelor dreams. He was painfully timid in everything relating to the emotions, and his hurt had withdrawn him from the society of women. The fact that it was all so done and dead and far behind him, and that the woman had lived her life out since then, gave him an oppressive sense of age and loss. He bethought himself of something he had read about "sitting by the hearth and remembering the faces of women without desire," and felt himself an octogenarian.

He remembered how bitter and morose he had grown during his stay at his brother's studio when Katharine Gaylord was working there, and how he had wounded Adriance on the night of his last concert in New York. He had sat there in the box while his brother and Katharine were called back again and again after the last number, watching the roses go up over the footlights until they were stacked half as high as the piano, brooding, in his sullen boy's heart, upon the pride those two felt in each other's work—spurring each other to their best and beautifully contending in song. The footlights had seemed a hard, glittering line drawn sharply between their life and his; a circle of flame set about those splendid children of genius. He walked back to his hotel alone, and sat in his window staring out on Madison Square until long after midnight, resolving to beat no more at doors that he could never enter, and realizing more keenly than ever before how far this glorious world of beautiful creations lay from the paths of men like himself. He told himself that he had in common with this woman only the baser uses of life.

Everett's week in Cheyenne stretched to three, and he saw no prospect of release except through the thing he dreaded. The bright, windy days of the Wyoming autumn passed swiftly. Letters and telegrams came urging him to hasten his trip to the coast, but he resolutely postponed his business engagements. The mornings he spent on one of Charley Gaylord's ponies, or fishing in the mountains, and in the evenings he sat in his room writing letters or reading. In the afternoon he was usually at his post of duty. Destiny, he reflected, seems to have very positive notions about the sort of parts we are fitted to play. The scene changes and the compensation varies, but in the end we usually find that we have played the same class of business from first to last. Everett had been a stop-gap all his life. He remembered going through a looking-glass labyrinth when he was a boy, and trying gallery after gallery, only at every turn to bump his nose against his own face—which, indeed, was not his own, but his brother's. No matter what his mission, east or west, by land or sea, he was sure to find himself employed in his brother's business, one of the tributary lives which helped to swell the shining current of Adriance Hilgarde's. It was not the first time that his duty had been to comfort, as best he could, one of the broken things his brother's imperious speed had cast aside and forgotten. He made no attempt to analyse the situation or to state it in exact terms; but he felt Katharine Gaylord's need for him, and he accepted it as a commission from his brother to help this woman to die. Day by day he felt her demands on him grow more imperious, her need for him grow more acute and positive; and day by day he felt that in his peculiar relation to her, his own individuality played a smaller and smaller part. His power to minister to her comfort, he saw, lay solely in his link with his brother's life. He understood all that his physical resemblance meant to her. He knew that she sat by him always watching for some common trick of gesture, some familiar play of expression, some illusion of light and shadow, in which he should seem wholly Adriance. He knew that she lived upon this and that her disease fed upon it; that it sent shudders of remembrance through her and that in the exhaustion which followed this turmoil of her dying senses, she slept deep and sweet, and dreamed of youth and art and days in a certain old Florentine garden, and not of bitterness and death.

The question which most perplexed him was, "How much shall I know? How much does she wish me to know?" A few days after his first meeting with Katharine Gaylord, he had cabled his brother to write her. He had merely said that she was mortally ill; he could depend on Adriance to say the right thing—that was a part of his gift. Adriance always said not only the right thing, but the opportune, graceful, exquisite thing. His phrases took the colour of the moment and the then present condition, so that they never savoured of perfunctory compliment or frequent usage. He always caught the lyric essence of the moment, the poetic suggestion of every situation. Moreover, he usually did the right thing, the opportune, graceful, exquisite thing—except, when he did very cruel things—bent upon making people happy when their existence touched his, just as he insisted that his material environment should be beautiful; lavishing upon those near him all the warmth and radiance of his rich nature, all the homage of the poet and troubadour, and, when they were no longer near, forgetting—for that also was a part of Adriance's gift.

Three weeks after Everett had sent his cable, when he made his daily call at the gayly painted ranch-house, he found Katharine laughing like a school-girl. "Have you ever thought," she said, as he entered the music-room, "how much these séances of ours are like Heine's 'Florentine Nights,' except that I don't give you an opportunity to monopolize the conversation as Heine did?" She held his hand longer than usual as she greeted him, and looked searchingly up into his face. "You are the kindest man living, the kindest," she added, softly.

Everett's grey face coloured faintly as he drew his hand away, for he felt that this time she was looking at him, and not at a whimsical caricature of his brother. "Why, what have I done now?" he asked, lamely. "I can't remember having sent you any stale candy or champagne since yesterday."

She drew a letter with a foreign postmark from between the leaves of a book and held it out, smiling. "You got him to write it. Don't say you didn't, for it came direct, you see, and the last address I gave him was a place in Florida. This deed shall be remembered of you when I am with the just in Paradise. But one thing you did not ask him to do, for you didn't know about it. He has sent me his latest work, the new sonata, the most ambitious thing he has ever done, and you are to play it for me directly, though it looks horribly intricate. But first for the letter; I think you would better read it aloud to me."

Everett sat down in a low chair facing the window-seat in which she reclined with a barricade of pillows behind her. He opened the letter, his lashes half-veiling his kind eyes, and saw to his satisfaction that it was a long one; wonderfully tactful and tender, even for Adriance, who was tender with his valet and his stable-boy, with his old gondolier and the beggar-women who prayed to the saints for him.

The letter was from Granada, written in the Alhambra, as he sat by the fountain of the Patio di Lindaraxa. The air was heavy with the warm fragrance of the South and full of the sound of splashing, running water, as it had been in a certain old garden in Florence, long ago. The sky was one great turquoise, heated until it glowed. The wonderful Moorish arches threw graceful blue shadows all about him. He had sketched an outline of them on the margin of his note-paper. The subtleties of Arabic decoration had cast an unholy spell over him, and the brutal exaggerations of Gothic art were a bad dream, easily forgotten. The Alhambra itself had, from the first, seemed perfectly familiar to him, and he knew that he must have trod that court, sleek and brown and obsequious, centuries before Ferdinand rode into Andalusia. The letter was full of confidences about his work, and delicate allusions to their old happy days of study and comradeship, and of her own work, still so warmly remembered and appreciatively discussed everywhere he went.

As Everett folded the letter he felt that Adriance had divined the thing needed and had risen to it in his own wonderful way. The letter was consistently egotistical, and seemed to him even a trifle patronizing, yet it was just what she had wanted. A strong realization of his brother's charm and intensity and power came over him; he felt the breath of that whirlwind of flame in which Adriance passed, consuming all in his path, and himself even more resolutely than he consumed others. Then he looked down at this white, burnt-out brand that lay before him. "Like him, isn't it?" she said, quietly.

"I think I can scarcely answer his letter, but when you see him next you can do that for me. I want you to tell him many things for me, yet they can all be summed up in this: I want him to grow wholly into his best and greatest self, even at the cost of the dear boyishness that is half his charm to you and me. Do you understand me?"

"I know perfectly well what you mean," answered Everett, thoughtfully. "I have often felt so about him myself. And yet it's difficult to prescribe for those fellows; so little makes, so little mars."

Katharine raised herself upon her elbow, and her face flushed with feverish earnestness. "Ah, but it is the waste of himself that I mean; his lashing himself out on stupid and uncomprehending people until they take him at their own estimate. He can kindle marble, strike fire from putty, but is it worth what it costs him?"

"Come, come," expostulated Everett, alarmed at her excitement. "Where is the new sonata? Let him speak for himself."

He sat down at the piano and began playing the first movement which was indeed the voice of Adriance, his proper speech. The sonata was the most ambitious work he had done up to that time, and marked the transition from his purely lyric vein to a deeper and nobler style. Everett played intelligently and with that sympathetic comprehension which seems peculiar to a certain lovable class of men who never accomplish anything in particular. When he had finished he turned to Katharine.

"How he has grown!" she cried. "What the three last years have done for him! He used to write only the tragedies of passion; but this is the tragedy of the soul, the shadow coexistent with the soul. This is the tragedy of effort and failure, the thing Keats called hell. This is my tragedy, as I lie here spent by the race-course, listening to the feet of the runners as they pass me—ah, God! the swift feet of the runners!"

She turned her face away and covered it with her straining hands. Everett crossed over to her quickly and knelt beside her. In all the days he had known her she had never before, beyond an occasional ironical jest, given voice to the bitterness of her own defeat. Her courage had become a point of pride with him, and to see it going sickened him.

"Don't do it," he gasped. "I can't stand it, I really can't, I feel it too much. We mustn't speak of that; it's too tragic and too vast."

When she turned her face back to him there was a ghost of the old, brave, cynical smile on it, more bitter than the tears she could not shed. "No, I won't be so ungenerous; I will save that for the watches of the night when I have no better company. Now you may mix me another drink of some sort. Formerly, when it was not *if* I should ever sing Brunhilda, but quite simply when I *should* sing Brunhilda, I was always starving myself, and thinking what I might drink and what I might not. But broken music-boxes may drink whatsoever they list, and no one cares whether they lose their figure. Run over that theme at the beginning again. That, at least, is not new. It was running in his head when we were in Venice years ago, and he used to drum it on his glass at the dinner-table. He had just begun to work it out when the late autumn came on, and the paleness of the Adriatic oppressed him, and he decided to go to Florence for the winter, and lost touch with the theme during his illness. Do you remember those frightful days? All the people who have loved him are not strong enough to save him from himself! When I got word from Florence that he had been ill, I was in Nice filling a concert engagement. His wife was hurrying to him from Paris, but I reached him first. I arrived at dusk, in a terrific storm. They had taken an old palace there for the winter, and I found him in the library—a long, dark room full of old Latin books and heavy furniture and bronzes. He was sitting by a wood fire at one end of the room, looking, oh, so worn and pale!—as he always does when he is ill, you know. Ah, it is so good that you *do* know! Even his red smoking-jacket lent no colour to his face. His first words were not to tell me how ill he had been, but that that morning he had been well enough to put the last strokes to the score of his 'Souvenirs d'Au-

tomne,' and he was, as I most like to remember him; so calm and happy and tired; not gay, as he usually is, but just contented and tired with that heavenly tiredness that comes after a good work done at last. Outside, the rain poured down in torrents, and the wind moaned for the pain of all the world and sobbed in the branches of the shivering olives and about the walls of that desolated old palace. How that night comes back to me! There were no lights in the room, only the wood fire which glowed upon the hard features of the bronze Dante like the reflection of purgatorial flames, and threw long black shadows about us; beyond us it scarcely penetrated the gloom at all. Adriance sat staring at the fire with the weariness of all his life in his eyes, and of all the other lives that must aspire and suffer to make up one such life as his. Somehow the wind with all its world-pain had got into the room, and the cold rain was in our eyes, and the wave came up in both of us at once—that awful vague, universal pain, that cold fear of life and death and God and hope—and we were like two clinging together on a spar in mid-ocean after the shipwreck of everything. Then we heard the front door open with a great gust of wind that shook even the walls, and the servants came running with lights, announcing that Madame had returned, *'and in the book we read no more that night.'*"

She gave the old line with a certain bitter humour, and with the hard, bright smile in which of old she had wrapped her weakness as in a glittering garment. That ironical smile, worn like a mask through so many years, had gradually changed even the lines of her face completely, and when she looked in the mirror she saw not herself, but the scathing critic, the amused observer and satirist of herself. Everett dropped his head upon his hand and sat looking at the rug. "How much you have cared!" he said.

"Ah, yes, I cared," she replied, closing her eyes with a long-drawn sigh of relief; and lying perfectly still, she went on: "You can't imagine what a comfort it is to have you know how I cared, what a relief it is to be able to tell it to some one. I used to want to shriek it out to the world in the long nights when I could not sleep. It seemed to me that I could not die with it. It demanded some sort of expression. And now that you know, you would scarcely believe how much less sharp the anguish of it is."

Everett continued to look helplessly at the floor. "I was not sure how much you wanted me to know," he said.

"Oh, I intended you should know from the first time I looked into your face, when you came that day with Charley. I flatter myself that I have been able to conceal it when I chose, though I suppose women always think that. The more observing ones may have seen, but discerning people are usually discreet and often kind, for we usually bleed a little before we begin to discern. But I wanted you to know; you are so like him that it is almost like telling him himself. At least, I feel now that he will know some day, and then I shall be quite sacred from his compassion, for we none of us dare pity the dead. Since it was what my life has chiefly meant, I should like him to know. On the whole, I am not ashamed of it. I have fought a good fight."

"And has he never known at all?" asked Everett, in a thick voice.

"Oh! never at all in the way you mean. Of course, he is accustomed to looking into the eyes of women and finding love there; when he doesn't find it there he thinks he must have been guilty of some discourtesy and is miserable about it. He has a genuine fondness for every one who is not stupid or gloomy, or old or preternaturally ugly. Granted youth and cheerfulness, and a moderate amount of wit and some tact, and Adriance will always be glad to see you coming round the corner. I shared with the rest; shared the smiles and the gallantries and the droll little sermons. It was quite like a Sunday-school picnic; we wore our best clothes and a smile and took our turns. It was his kindness that was hardest. I have pretty well used my life up at standing punishment."

"Don't; you'll make me hate him," groaned Everett.

Katharine laughed and began to play nervously with her fan. "It wasn't in the slightest degree his fault; that is the most grotesque part of it. Why, it had really begun before I ever met him. I fought my way to him, and I drank my doom greedily enough."

Everett rose and stood hesitating. "I think I must go. You ought to be quiet, and I don't think I can hear any more just now."

She put out her hand and took his playfully. "You've put in three weeks at this sort of thing, haven't you? Well, it may never be to your glory in this world, perhaps, but it's been the mercy of heaven to me, and it ought to square accounts for a much worse life than yours will ever be."

Everett knelt beside her, saying, brokenly: "I stayed because I wanted to be with you, that's all. I have never cared about other women since I met you in New York when I was a lad. You are a part of my destiny, and I could not leave you if I would."

She put her hands on his shoulders and shook her head. "No, no; don't tell me that. I have seen enough of tragedy, God knows: don't show me any more just as the curtain is going down. No, no, it was only a boy's fancy, and your divine pity and my utter pitiableness have recalled it for a moment. One does not love the dying, dear friend. If some fancy of that sort had been left over from boyhood, this would rid you of it, and that were well. Now go, and you will come again to-morrow, as long as there are to-morrows, will you not?" She took his hand with a smile that lifted the mask from her soul, that was both courage and despair, and full of infinite loyalty and tenderness, as she said softly:

> "For ever and for ever, farewell, Cassius;
> If we do meet again, why, we shall smile;
> If not, why then, this parting was well made."

The courage in her eyes was like the clear light of a star to him as he went out.

On the night of Adriance Hilgarde's opening concert in Paris, Everett sat by the bed in the ranch-house in Wyoming, watching over the last battle that we have with the flesh before we are done with it and free of it forever. At times it seemed that the serene soul of her must have left already and found some refuge from the storm, and only the tenacious animal life were left to do battle with death. She laboured under a delusion at once pitiful and merciful, thinking that she was in the Pullman on her way to New York, going back to her life and her work. When she aroused from her stupor, it was only to ask the porter to waken her half an hour out of Jersey City, or to remonstrate with him about the delays and the roughness of the road. At midnight Everett and the nurse were left alone with her. Poor Charley Gaylord had lain down on a couch outside the door. Everett sat looking at the sputtering night-lamp until it made his eyes ache. His head dropped forward on the foot of the bed, and he sank into a heavy, distressful slumber. He was dreaming of Adriance's concert in Paris, and of Adriance, the troubadour, smiling and debonair, with his boyish face and the touch of silver grey in his hair. He heard the applause and he saw the roses going up over the footlights until they were stacked half as high as the piano, and the petals fell and scattered, making crimson splotches on the floor. Down this crimson pathway came Adriance with his youthful step, leading his prima donna by the hand; a dark woman this time, with Spanish eyes.

The nurse touched him on the shoulder, he started and awoke. She screened the lamp with her hand. Everett saw that Katharine was awake and conscious, and struggling a little. He lifted her gently upon his arm and began to fan her. She laid her hands lightly on his hair and looked into his face with eyes that seemed never to have wept or doubted. "Ah, dear Adriance, dear, dear," she whispered.

Everett went to call her brother, but when they came back the madness of art was over for Katharine.

Two days later Everett was pacing the station siding, waiting for the west-bound train. Charley Gaylord walked beside him, but the two men had nothing to say to each other. Everett's bags were piled on the truck, and his step was hurried and his eyes were full of impatience, as he gazed again and again up the track, watching for the train. Gaylord's impatience was not less than his own; these two, who had grown so close, had now become painful and impossible to each other, and longed for the wrench of farewell.

As the train pulled in, Everett wrung Gaylord's hand among the crowd of alighting passengers. The people of a German opera company, *en route* for the coast, rushed by them in frantic haste to snatch their breakfast during the stop. Everett heard an exclamation in a broad German dialect, and a massive woman whose figure persistently escaped from her stays in the most improbable places rushed up to him, her blond hair disordered by the wind, and glowing with joyful surprise she caught his coat-sleeve with her tightly gloved hands.

"*Herr Gott*, Adriance, *lieber Freund*," she cried, emotionally.

Everett quickly withdrew his arm, and lifted his hat, blushing. "Pardon me, madame, but I see that you have mistaken me for Adriance Hilgarde. I am his brother," he said, quietly, and turning from the crestfallen singer he hurried into the car.

The Marriage of Phædra

The sequence of events was such that MacMaster did not make his pilgrimage to Hugh Treffinger's studio until three years after that painter's death. MacMaster was himself a painter, an American of the Gallicized type, who spent his winters in New York, his summers in Paris, and no inconsiderable amount of time on the broad waters between. He had often contemplated stopping in London on one of his return trips in the late autumn, but he had always deferred leaving Paris until the prick of necessity drove him home by the quickest and shortest route.

Treffinger was a comparatively young man at the time of his death, and there had seemed no occasion for haste until haste was of no avail. Then, possibly, though there had been some correspondence between them, MacMaster felt certain qualms about meeting in the flesh a man who in the flesh was so diversely reported. His intercourse with Treffinger's work had been so deep and satisfying, so apart from other appreciations, that he rather dreaded a critical juncture of any sort. He had always felt himself singularly inadept in personal relations, and in this case he had avoided the issue until it was no longer to be feared or hoped for. There still remained, however, Treffinger's great unfinished picture, the *Marriage of Phædra*, which had never left his studio, and of which MacMaster's friends had now and again brought report that it was the painter's most characteristic production.

The young man arrived in London in the evening, and the next morning went out to Kensington to find Treffinger's studio. It lay in one of the perplexing by-streets off Holland Road, and the number he found on a door set in a high garden wall, the top of which was covered with broken green glass and over which a budding lilac-bush nodded. Treffinger's plate was still there, and a card requesting visitors to ring for the attendant. In response to MacMaster's ring, the door was opened by a cleanly built little man, clad in a shooting jacket and trousers that had been made for an ampler figure. He had a fresh complexion, eyes of that common uncertain shade of grey, and was closely shaven except for the incipient mutton-chops on his ruddy cheeks. He bore himself in a manner strikingly capable, and there was a sort of trimness and alertness about him, despite the too-generous shoulders of his coat. In one hand he held a bulldog pipe, and in the other a copy of *Sporting Life*. While MacMaster was explaining the purpose of his call, he noticed that the man surveyed him critically, though not impertinently. He was admitted into a little tank of a lodge made of white-washed stone, the back door and windows opening upon a garden. A visitor's book and a pile of catalogues lay on a deal table, together with a bottle of ink and some rusty pens. The wall was ornamented with photographs and coloured prints of racing favourites.

"The studio is h'only open to the public on Saturdays and Sundays," explained the man—he referred to himself as "Jymes"—"but of course we make exceptions in the case of pynters. Lydy Elling Treffinger 'erself is on the Continent, but Sir 'Ugh's orders was that pynters was to 'ave the run of the place." He selected a key from his pocket and threw open the door into the studio which, like the lodge, was built against the wall of the garden.

MacMaster entered a long, narrow room, built of smoothed planks, painted a light green; cold and damp even on that fine May morning. The room was utterly bare of furniture—unless a step-ladder, a model throne, and a rack laden with large leather portfolios could be accounted such—and was windowless, without other openings than the door and the skylight, under which hung the unfinished picture itself. MacMaster had never seen so many of Treffinger's paintings together. He knew the painter had married a woman with money and had been able to keep such of his pictures as he wished. These, with all of his replicas and studies, he had left as a sort of common legacy to the younger men of the school he had originated.

As soon as he was left alone, MacMaster sat down on the edge of the model throne before the unfinished picture. Here indeed was what he had come for; it rather paralysed his receptivity for the moment, but gradually the thing found its way to him.

At one o'clock he was standing before the collection of studies done for *Boccaccio's Garden* when he heard a voice at his elbow.

"Pardon, sir, but I was just about to lock up and go to lunch. Are you lookin' for the figure study of Boccaccio 'imself?" James queried respectfully, "Lydy Elling Treffinger give it to Mr. Rossiter to take down to Oxford for some lectures he's been a-giving there."

"Did he never paint out his studies, then?" asked MacMaster with perplexity. "Here are two completed ones for this picture. Why did he keep them?"

"I don't know as I could say as to that, sir," replied James, smiling indulgently, "but that was 'is way. That is to say, 'e pynted out very frequent, but 'e always made two studies to stand; one in water colours and one in oils, before 'e went at the final picture,—to say nothink of all the pose studies 'e made in pencil before he begun on the composition proper at all. He was that particular. You see 'e wasn't so keen for the final effect as for the proper pyntin' of 'is pictures. 'E used to say they ought to be well made, the same as any other h'article of trade. I can lay my 'and on the pose studies for you, sir." He rummaged in one of the portfolios and produced half a dozen drawings. "These three," he continued, "was discarded; these two was the pose he finally accepted; this one without alteration, as it were."

"That's in Paris, as I remember," James continued reflectively. "It went with the *Saint Cecilia* into the Baron H——'s collection. Could you tell me, sir, 'as 'e it still? I don't like to lose account of them, but some 'as changed 'ands since Sir 'Ugh's death."

"H——'s collection is still intact, I believe," replied MacMaster. "You were with Treffinger long?"

"From my boyhood, sir," replied James with gravity. "I was a stable boy when 'e took me."

"You were his man, then?"

"That's it, sir. Nobody else ever done anything around the studio. I always mixed 'is colours and 'e taught me to do a share of the varnishin'; 'e said as 'ow there wasn't a 'ouse in England as could do it proper. You aynt looked at the *Marriage* yet, sir?" he asked abruptly, glancing doubtfully at MacMaster, and indicating with his thumb the picture under the north light.

"Not very closely. I prefer to begin with something simpler; that's rather appalling, at first glance," replied MacMaster.

"Well may you say that, sir," said James warmly. "That one regular killed Sir 'Ugh; it regular broke 'im up, and nothink will ever convince me as 'ow it didn't bring on 'is second stroke."

When MacMaster walked back to High Street to take his bus, his mind was divided between two exultant convictions. He felt that he had not only found Treffinger's greatest picture, but that, in James, he had discovered a kind of cryptic index to the painter's personality—a clue which, if tactfully followed, might lead to much.

Several days after his first visit to the studio, MacMaster wrote to Lady Mary Percy, telling her that he would be in London for some time and asking her if he might call. Lady Mary was an only sister of Lady Ellen Treffinger, the painter's widow, and MacMaster had known her during one winter he spent at Nice. He had known her, indeed, very well, and Lady Mary, who was astonishingly frank and communicative upon all subjects, had been no less so upon the matter of her sister's unfortunate marriage.

In her reply to his note, Lady Mary named an afternoon when she would be alone. She was as good as her word, and when MacMaster arrived he found the drawing-room empty. Lady Mary entered shortly after he was announced. She was a tall woman, thin and stiffly jointed; and her body stood out under the folds of her gown with the rigour of cast-iron. This rather metallic suggestion was further carried out in her heavily knuckled hands, her stiff grey hair and long, bold-featured face, which was saved from freakishness only by her alert eyes.

"Really," said Lady Mary, taking a seat beside him and giving him a sort of military inspection through her nose-glasses, "Really, I had begun to fear that I had lost you altogether. It's four years since I saw you at Nice, isn't it? I was in Paris last winter, but I heard nothing from you."

"I was in New York then."

"It occurred to me that you might be. And why are you in London?"

"Can you ask?" replied MacMaster gallantly.

Lady Mary smiled ironically. "But for what else, incidentally?"

"Well, incidentally, I came to see Treffinger's studio and his unfinished picture. Since I've been here, I've decided to stay the summer. I'm even thinking of attempting to do a biography of him."

"So that is what brought you to London?"

"Not exactly. I had really no intention of anything so serious when I came. It's his last picture, I fancy, that has rather thrust it upon me. The notion has settled down on me like a thing destined."

"You'll not be offended if I question the clemency of such a destiny," remarked Lady Mary dryly. "Isn't there rather a surplus of books on that subject already?"

"Such as they are. Oh, I've read them all," here MacMaster faced Lady Mary triumphantly. "He has quite escaped your amiable critics," he added, smiling.

"I know well enough what you think, and I dare say we are not much on art," said Lady Mary with tolerant good humour. "We leave that to people who have no physique. Treffinger made a stir for a time, but it seems that we are not capable of sustained appreciation of such extraordinary methods. In the end we go back to the pictures we find agreeable and unperplexing. He was regarded as an experiment, I fancy; and now it seems that he was rather an unsuccessful one. If you've come to us in a missionary spirit, we'll tolerate you politely, but we'll laugh in our sleeve, I warn you."

"That really doesn't daunt me, Lady Mary," declared MacMaster blandly. "As I told you, I'm a man with a mission."

Lady Mary laughed her hoarse baritone laugh. "Bravo! and you've come to me for inspiration for your panegyric?"

MacMaster smiled with some embarrassment. "Not altogether for that purpose. But I want to consult you, Lady Mary, about the advisability of troubling Lady Ellen Treffinger in the matter. It seems scarcely legitimate to go on without asking her to give some sort of grace to my proceedings, yet I feared the whole subject might be painful to her. I shall rely wholly upon your discretion."

"I think she would prefer to be consulted," replied Lady Mary judicially. "I can't understand how she endures to have the wretched affair continually raked up, but she does. She seems to feel a sort of moral responsibility. Ellen has always been singularly conscientious about this matter, in so far as her light goes,—which rather puzzles me, as hers is not exactly a magnanimous nature. She is certainly trying to do what she believes to be the right thing. I shall write to her, and you can see her when she returns from Italy."

"I want very much to meet her. She is, I hope, quite recovered in every way," queried MacMaster, hesitatingly.

"No, I can't say that she is. She has remained in much the same condition she sank to before his death. He trampled over pretty much whatever there was in her, I fancy. Women don't recover from wounds of that sort; at least, not women in Ellen's grain. They go on bleeding inwardly."

"You, at any rate have not grown more reconciled," MacMaster ventured.

"Oh, I give him his dues. He was a colourist, I grant you; but that is a vague and unsatisfactory quality to marry to; Lady Ellen Treffinger found it so."

"But, my dear Lady Mary," expostulated MacMaster, "and just repress me if I'm becoming too personal—but it must, in the first place, have been a marriage of choice on her part as well as on his."

Lady Mary poised her glasses on her large forefinger and assumed an attitude suggestive of the clinical lecture room as she replied. "Ellen, my dear boy, is an essentially romantic person. She is quiet about it, but she runs deep. I never knew how deep until I came against her on the issue of that marriage. She was always discontented as a girl; she found things dull and prosaic, and the ardour of his courtship was agreeable to her. He met her during her first season in town. She is handsome, and there were plenty of other men, but I grant you your scowling brigand was the most picturesque of the lot. In his courtship, as in everything else, he was theatrical to the point of being ridiculous, but Ellen's sense of humour is not her strongest quality. He had the charm of celebrity, the air of a man who could storm his way through anything to get what he wanted. That sort of vehemence is particularly effective with women like Ellen, who can be warmed only by reflected heat, and she couldn't at all stand out against it. He convinced her of his necessity; and that done, all's done."

"I can't help thinking that, even on such a basis, the marriage should have turned out better," MacMaster remarked reflectively.

"The marriage," Lady Mary continued with a shrug, "was made on the basis of a mutual misunderstanding. Ellen, in the nature of the case, believed that she was doing something quite out of the ordinary in accepting him, and expected concessions which, apparently, it never occurred to him to make. After his marriage he relapsed into his old habits of incessant work, broken by violent and often brutal relaxations. He insulted her friends and foisted his own upon her—many of them well calculated to arouse aversion in any well-bred girl. He had Ghillini constantly at the house—a homeless vagabond, whose conversation was impossible. I don't say, mind you, that he had not grievances on his side. He had probably over-rated the girl's possibilities, and he let her see that he was disappointed in her. Only a large and generous nature could have borne with him, and Ellen's is not that.

She could not at all understand that odious strain of plebeian pride which plumes itself upon not having risen above its sources."

As MacMaster drove back to his hotel, he reflected that Lady Mary Percy had probably had good cause for dissatisfaction with her brother-in-law. Treffinger was, indeed, the last man who should have married into the Percy family. The son of a small tobacconist, he had grown up a sign painter's apprentice; idle, lawless, and practically letterless until he had drifted into the night classes of the Albert League, where Ghillini sometimes lectured. From the moment he came under the eye and influence of that erratic Italian, then a political exile, his life had swerved sharply from its old channel. This man had been at once incentive and guide, friend and master, to his pupil. He had taken the raw clay out of the London streets and moulded it anew. Seemingly he had divined at once where the boy's possibilities lay, and had thrown aside every canon of orthodox instruction in the training of him. Under him Treffinger acquired his superficial, yet facile, knowledge of the classics; had steeped himself in the monkish Latin and mediæval romances which later gave his work so naive and remote a quality. That was the beginning of the wattle fences, the cobble pave, the brown roof beams, the cunningly wrought fabrics that gave to his pictures such a richness of decorative effect.

As he had told Lady Mary Percy, MacMaster had found the imperative inspiration of his purpose in Treffinger's unfinished picture, the *Marriage of Phædra*. He had always believed that the key to Treffinger's individuality lay in his singular education; in the *Roman de la Rose*, in Boccaccio, and Amadis, those works which had literally transcribed themselves upon the blank soul of the London street boy, and through which he had been born into the world of spiritual things. Treffinger had been a man who lived after his imagination; and his mind, his ideals and, as MacMaster believed, even his personal ethics, had to the last been coloured by the trend of his early training. There was in him alike the freshness and spontaneity, the frank brutality and the religious mysticism which lay well back of the fifteenth century. In the *Marriage of Phædra* MacMaster found the ultimate expression of this spirit, the final word as to Treffinger's point of view.

As in all Treffinger's classical subjects, the conception was wholly mediæval. This Phædra, just turning from her husband and maidens to greet her husband's son, giving him her first fearsome glance from under her half lifted veil, was no daughter of Minos. The daughter of *heathenesse* and the early church she was; doomed to torturing visions and scourgings, and the wrangling of soul with flesh. The venerable Theseus might have been victorious Charlemagne, and Phædra's maidens belonged rather in the train of Blanche of Castile than at the Cretan court. In the earlier studies Hippolytus had been done with a more pagan suggestion, but in each successive drawing the glorious figure had been deflowered of something of its serene unconsciousness; until, in the canvas under the skylight, he appeared a very Christian knight. This male figure, and the face of Phædra, painted with such magical preservation of tone under the heavy shadow of the veil, were plainly Treffinger's highest achievements of craftsmanship. By what labour he had reached the seemingly inevitable composition of the picture—with its twenty figures, its plenitude of light and air, its restful distances seen through white porticoes—countless studies bore witness.

From James's attitude toward the picture, MacMaster could well conjecture what the painter's had been. This picture was always uppermost in James's mind; its custodianship formed, in his eyes, his occupation. He was manifestly apprehensive when visitors—not many came now-a-days—lingered near it. "It was the *Marriage* as killed 'im," he would often say, "and for the matter 'o that, it did like to 'av been the death of all of us."

By the end of his second week in London, MacMaster had begun the notes for his study of Hugh Treffinger and his work. When his researches led him occasionally to visit the studios of Treffinger's friends and erstwhile disciples, he found their Treffinger manner fading as the ring of Treffinger's personality died out in them. One by one they were stealing back into the fold of national British art; the hand that had wound them up was still. MacMaster despaired of them and confined himself more and more exclusively to the studio, to such of Treffinger's letters as were available—they were for the most part singularly negative and colourless—and to his interrogation of Treffinger's man.

He could not himself have traced the successive steps by which he was gradually admitted into James's confidence. Certainly most of his adroit strategies to that end failed humiliatingly, and whatever it was that built up an understanding between them, must have been instinctive and intuitive on both sides. When at last James became anecdotal, personal, there was that in every word he let fall which put breath and blood into MacMaster's book. James had so long been steeped in that penetrating personality that he fairly exuded it. Many of his very phrases, mannerisms and opinions were impressions that he had taken on like wet plaster in his daily contact with Treffinger. Inwardly he was lined with cast off epithelia, as outwardly he was clad in the painter's discarded coats. If the painter's letters were formal and perfunctory, if his expressions to his friends had been extravagant, contradictory and often apparently insincere—still, MacMaster felt himself not entirely without authentic sources. It was James who possessed Treffinger's legend; it was with James that he had laid aside his pose. Only in his studio, alone, and face to face with his work, as it seemed, had the man invariably been himself. James had known him in the one attitude in which he was entirely honest; their relation had fallen well within the painter's only indubitable integrity. James's report of Treffinger was distorted by no hallucination of artistic insight, coloured by no interpretation of his own. He merely held what he had heard and seen; his mind was a sort of *camera oscura*. His very limitations made him the more literal and minutely accurate.

One morning when MacMaster was seated before the *Marriage of Phædra*, James entered on his usual round of dusting.

"I've 'eard from Lydy Elling by the post, sir," he remarked, "an' she's give h'orders to 'ave the 'ouse put in readiness. I doubt she'll be 'ere by Thursday or Friday next."

"She spends most of her time abroad?" queried MacMaster; on the subject of Lady Treffinger James consistently maintained a very delicate reserve.

"Well, you could 'ardly say she does that, sir. She finds the 'house a bit dull, I daresay, so durin' the season she stops mostly with Lydy Mary Percy, at Grosvenor Square. Lydy Mary's a h'only sister." After a few moments he continued, speaking in jerks governed by the rigour of his dusting: "Honly this morning I come upon this scarf-pin," exhibiting a very striking instance of that article, "an' I recalled as 'ow Sir 'Ugh give it me when 'e was a-courting of Lydy Elling. Blowed if I ever see a man go in for a 'oman like 'im! 'E was that gone, sir. 'E never went in on anythink so 'ard before nor since, till 'e went in on the *Marriage* there—though 'e mostly went in on things pretty keen; 'ad the measles when 'e was thirty, strong as cholera, an' come close to dyin' of 'em. 'E wasn't strong for Lydy Elling's set; they was a bit too stiff for 'im. A free an' easy gentleman, 'e was; 'e liked 'is dinner with a few friends an' them jolly, but 'e wasn't much on what you might call big affairs. But once 'e went in for Lydy Elling, 'e broke 'imself to new paces. He give away 'is rings an' pins, an' the tylor's man an' the 'aberdasher's man was at 'is rooms continual. 'E got 'imself put up for a club in Piccadilly; 'e starved 'imself thin, an' worrited 'imself white, an' ironed 'imself out, an' drawed 'imself tight as a bow string. It was a good job 'e come a winner, or I don't know w'at'd 'a been to pay."

The next week, in consequence of an invitation from Lady Ellen Treffinger, MacMaster went one afternoon to take tea with her. He was shown into the garden that lay between the residence and the studio, where the tea-table was set under a gnarled pear tree. Lady Ellen rose as he approached—he was astonished to note how tall she was—and greeted him graciously, saying that she already knew him through her sister. MacMaster felt a certain satisfaction in her; in her reassuring poise and repose, in the charming modulations of her voice and the indolent reserve of her full, almond eyes. He was even delighted to find her face so inscrutable, though it chilled his own warmth and made the open frankness he had wished to permit himself impossible. It was a long face, narrow at the chin, very delicately featured, yet steeled by an impassive mask of self-control. It was behind just such finely cut, close-sealed faces, MacMaster reflected, that nature sometimes hid astonishing secrets. But in spite of this suggestion of hardness, he felt that the unerring taste that Treffinger had always shown in larger matters had not deserted him when he came to the choosing of a wife, and he admitted that he could not himself have selected a woman who looked more as Treffinger's wife should look.

While he was explaining the purpose of his frequent visits to the studio, she heard him with courteous interest. "I have read, I think, everything that has been published on Sir Hugh Treffinger's work, and it seems to me that there is much left to be said," he concluded.

"I believe they are rather inadequate," she remarked vaguely. She hesitated for a moment, absently fingering the ribbons of her gown, then continued, without raising her eyes; "I hope you will not think me too exacting if I ask to see the proofs of such chapters of your work as have to do with Sir Hugh's personal life. I have always asked that privilege."

MacMaster hastily assured her as to this, adding, "I mean to touch on only such facts in his personal life as have to do directly with his work—such as his monkish education under Ghillini."

"I see your meaning, I think," said Lady Ellen, looking at him with wide, uncomprehending eyes.

When MacMaster stopped at the studio on leaving the house, he stood for some time before Treffinger's one portrait of himself; that brigand of a picture, with its full throat and square head; the short upper lip blackened by the close-clipped moustache, the wiry hair tossed down over the forehead, the strong white teeth set hard on a short pipe stem. He could well understand what manifold tortures the mere grain of the man's strong red and brown flesh might have inflicted upon a woman like Lady Ellen. He could conjecture, too, Treffinger's impotent revolt against that very repose which had so dazzled him when it first defied his daring; and how once possessed of it, his first instinct had been to crush it, since he could not melt it.

Toward the close of the season, Lady Ellen Treffinger left town. MacMaster's work was progressing rapidly, and he and James wore away the days in their peculiar relation, which by this time had much of friendliness. Excepting for the regular visits of a Jewish picture dealer, there were few intrusions upon their solitude. Occasionally a party of Americans rang at the little door in the garden wall, but usually they departed speedily for the Moorish hall and tinkling fountain of the great show studio of London, not far away.

This Jew, an Austrian by birth, who had a large business in Melbourne, Australia, was a man of considerable discrimination, and at once selected the *Marriage of Phædra* as the object of his especial interest. When, upon his first visit, Lichtenstein had declared the picture one of the things done for time, MacMaster had rather warmed toward him and had talked to him very freely. Later, however, the man's repulsive personality and innate vulgarity so wore upon him that, the more genuine the Jew's appreciation, the more he resented it and the more base he somehow felt it to be. It annoyed him to see Lichtenstein walking up and down before the picture, shaking his head and blinking his watery eyes over his nose-glasses, ejaculating: "Dot is a chem, a chem! It is wordt to gome den dousant miles for such a bainting, eh? To make Eurobe abbreciate such a work of ardt it is necessary to take it away while she is napping. She has never abbreciated until she has lost, but," knowingly, "she will buy back."

James had, from the first, felt such a distrust of the man that he would never leave him alone in the studio for a moment. When Lichtenstein insisted upon having Lady Ellen Treffinger's address, James rose to the point of insolence. "It ay'nt no use to give it, noway. Lydy Treffinger never has nothink to do with dealers." MacMaster quietly repented his rash confidences, fearing that he might indirectly cause Lady Ellen annoyance from this merciless speculator, and he recalled with chagrin that Lichtenstein had extorted from him, little by little, pretty much the entire plan of his book, and especially the place in it which the *Marriage of Phædra* was to occupy.

By this time the first chapters of MacMaster's book were in the hands of his publisher, and his visits to the studio were necessarily less frequent. The greater part of his time was now employed with the engravers who were to reproduce such of Treffinger's pictures as he intended to use as illustrations.

He returned to his hotel late one evening after a long and vexing day at the engravers, to find James in his room, seated on his steamer trunk by the window, with the outline of a great square draped in sheets resting against his knee.

"Why, James, what's up?" he cried in astonishment, glancing enquiringly at the sheeted object.

"Ay'nt you seen the pypers, sir?" jerked out the man.

"No, now I think of it, I haven't even looked at a paper. I've been at the engravers' plant all day. I haven't seen anything."

James drew a copy of the *Times* from his pocket and handed it to him, pointing with a tragic finger to a paragraph in the social column. It was merely the announcement of Lady Ellen Treffinger's engagement to Captain Alexander Gresham.

"Well, what of it, my man? That surely is her privilege."

James took the paper, turned to another page, and silently pointed to a paragraph in the art notes which stated that Lady Treffinger had presented to the X—— gallery the entire collection of paintings and sketches now in her late husband's studio, with the exception of his unfinished picture, the *Marriage of Phædra*, which she had sold for a large sum to an Australian dealer who had come to London purposely to secure some of Treffinger's paintings.

MacMaster pursed up his lips and sat down, his overcoat still on. "Well, James, this is something of a—something of a jolt, eh? It never occurred to me she'd really do it."

"Lord, you don't know 'er, sir," said James bitterly, still staring at the floor in an attitude of abandoned dejection.

MacMaster started up in a flash of enlightenment, "What on earth have you got there, James? It's not—surely it's not—"

"Yes, it is, sir," broke in the man excitedly. "It's the *Marriage* itself. It ayn't a-going to H'australia, no'ow!"

"But man, what are you going to do with it? It's Lichtenstein's property now, as it seems."

"It aynt, sir, that it aynt. No, by Gawd it aynt!" shouted James, breaking into a choking fury. He controlled himself with an effort and added supplicatingly: "Oh, sir, you aynt a-going to see it go to H'australia, w'ere they send convic's?" He unpinned and flung aside the sheets as though to let *Phædra* plead for herself.

MacMaster sat down again and looked sadly at the doomed masterpiece. The notion of James having carried it across London that night rather appealed to his fancy. There was certainly a flavour about such a high-handed proceeding. "However did you get it here?" he queried.

"I got a four-wheeler and come over direct, sir. Good job I 'appened to 'ave the chaynge about me."

"You came up High Street, up Piccadilly, through the Haymarket and Trafalgar Square, and into the Strand?" queried MacMaster with a relish.

"Yes, sir. Of course, sir," assented James with surprise.

MacMaster laughed delightedly. "It was a beautiful idea, James, but I'm afraid we can't carry it any further."

"I was thinkin' as 'ow it would be a rare chance to get you to take the *Marriage* over to Paris for a year or two, sir, until the thing blows over?" suggested James blandly.

"I'm afraid that's out of the question, James. I haven't the right stuff in me for a pirate, or even a vulgar smuggler, I'm afraid." MacMaster found it surprisingly difficult to say this, and he busied himself with the lamp as he said it. He heard James's hand fall heavily on the trunk top, and he discovered that he very much disliked sinking in the man's estimation.

"Well, sir," remarked James in a more formal tone, after a protracted silence; "then there's nothink for it but as 'ow I'll 'ave to make way with it myself."

"And how about your character, James? The evidence would be

heavy against you, and even if Lady Treffinger didn't prosecute, you'd be done for."

"Blow my character!—your pardon, sir," cried James, starting to his feet. "W'at do I want of a character? I'll chuck the 'ole thing, and damned lively, too. The shop's to be sold out, an' my place is gone any'ow. I'm a-going to enlist, or try the gold-fields. I've lived too long with h'artists; I'd never give satisfaction in livery now. You know 'ow it is yourself, sir; there aynt no life like it, no'ow."

For a moment MacMaster was almost equal to abetting James in his theft. He reflected that pictures had been white-washed, or hidden in the crypts of churches, or under the floors of palaces from meaner motives, and to save them from a fate less ignominious. But presently, with a sigh, he shook his head.

"No, James, it won't do at all. It has been tried over and over again, ever since the world has been a-going and pictures a-making. It was tried in Florence and in Venice, but the pictures were always carried away in the end. You see the difficulty is that, although Treffinger told you what was not to be done with the picture, he did not say definitely what was to be done with it. Do you think Lady Treffinger really understands that he did not want it to be sold?"

"Well, sir, it was like this, sir," said James resuming his seat on the trunk and again resting the picture against his knee. "My memory is as clear as glass about it. After Sir 'Ugh got up from 'is first stroke, 'e took a fresh start at the *Marriage*. Before that 'e 'ad been working at it only at night for awhile back; the *Legend* was the big picture then, an' was under the north light w'ere 'e worked of a morning. But one day 'e bid me take the *Legend* down an' put the *Marriage* in its place, an' 'e says, dashin' on 'is jacket, 'Jymes, this is a start for the finish, this time.'

"From that day on 'e worked at the night picture in the mornin'— a thing contrary to 'is custom. The *Marriage* went wrong, and wrong— an' Sir 'Ugh a-gettin' seedier an' seedier every day. 'E tried models an' models, an' smudged an' pynted out on account of 'er face goin' wrong in the shadow. Sometimes 'e layed it on the colours, an' swore at me an' things in general. He got that discouraged about 'imself that on 'is low days 'e used to say to me: 'Jymes, remember one thing; if anythink 'appens to me, the *Marriage* is not to go out of 'ere unfinished. It's worth the lot of 'em, my boy, an' it's not a-going to go shabby for lack of pains.' 'E said things to that effect repeated.

"He was workin' at the picture the last day, before 'e went to 'is club. 'E kept the carriage waitin' near an hour while 'e put on a stroke an' then drawed back for to look at it, an' then put on another, careful like. After 'e 'ad 'is gloves on, 'e come back an' took away the brushes I was startin' to clean, an' put in another touch or two. 'It's a-comin' Jymes,' 'e says, 'by gad if it aynt.' An' with that 'e goes out. It was cruel sudden, w'at come after.

"That night I was lookin' to 'is clothes at the 'ouse when they brought 'im 'ome. He was conscious, but w'en I ran down stairs for to 'elp lift 'im up, I knowed 'e was a finished man. After we got 'im into bed, 'e kept lookin' restless at me and then at Lydy Elling and a-jerkin' of 'is 'and. Finally 'e quite raised it an' shot 'is thumb out towards the wall. 'He wants water; ring Jymes,' says Lydy Elling, placid. But I knowed 'e was pointin' to the shop.

"'Lydy Treffinger,' says I, bold, 'he's pointin' to the studio. He means about the *Marriage;* 'e told me to-day as 'ow 'e never wanted it sold unfinished. Is that it, Sir 'Ugh?'

"He smiled an' nodded slight an' closed 'is eyes. 'Thank you, Jymes,' says Lydy Elling, placid. Then 'e opened 'is eyes an' looked long and 'ard at Lydy Elling.

"'Of course I'll try to do as you'd wish about the pictures, 'Ugh, if that's w'at's troublin' you,' she says quiet. With that 'e closed 'is eyes and 'e never opened 'em. He died unconscious at four that mornin'.

"You see, sir, Lydy Elling was always cruel 'ard on the *Marriage.* From the first it went wrong, an' Sir 'Ugh was out of temper pretty constant. She came into the studio one day and looked at the picture an' asked 'im why 'e didn't throw it up an' quit a-worriting 'imself. He answered sharp, an' with that she said as 'ow she didn't see w'at there was to make such a row about, no'ow. She spoke 'er mind about that picture, free; an' Sir 'Ugh swore 'ot an' let a 'andful of brushes fly at 'is study, an' Lydy Elling picked up 'er skirts careful an' chill, an' drifted out of the studio with 'er eyes calm and 'er chin 'igh. If there was one thing Lydy Elling 'ad no comprehension of, it was the usefulness of swearin'. So the *Marriage* was a sore thing between 'em. She is uncommon calm, but uncommon bitter, is Lydy Elling. She's never come a-near the studio since that day she went out 'oldin' up of 'er skirts. W'en 'er friends goes over she excuses 'erself along o' the strain. Strain—Gawd!" James ground his wrath short in his teeth.

"I'll tell you what I'll do, James, and it's our only hope. I'll see

Lady Ellen to-morrow. The *Times* says she returned to-day. You take the picture back to its place, and I'll do what I can for it. If anything is done to save it, it must be done through Lady Ellen Treffinger herself; that much is clear. I can't think that she fully understands the situation. If she did, you know, she really couldn't have any motive—" He stopped suddenly. Somehow, in the dusky lamplight her small, close-sealed face came ominously back to him. He rubbed his forehead and knitted his brows thoughtfully. After a moment he shook his head and went on: "I am positive that nothing can be gained by high-handed methods, James. Captain Gresham is one of the most popular men in London, and his friends would tear up Treffinger's bones if he were annoyed by any scandal of our making—and this scheme you propose would inevitably result in scandal. Lady Ellen has, of course, every legal right to sell the picture. Treffinger made considerable inroads upon her estate, and, as she is about to marry a man without income, she doubtless feels that she has a right to replenish her patrimony."

He found James amenable, though doggedly sceptical. He went down into the street, called a carriage, and saw James and his burden into it. Standing in the doorway, he watched the carriage roll away through the drizzling mist, weave in and out among the wet, black vehicles and darting cab lights, until it was swallowed up in the glare and confusion of the Strand. "It is rather a fine touch of irony," he reflected, "that he, who is so out of it, should be the one to really care. Poor Treffinger," he murmured as, with a rather spiritless smile, he turned back into his hotel, "Poor Treffinger; *sic transit gloria*."

The next afternoon MacMaster kept his promise. When he arrived at Lady Mary Percy's house he saw preparations for a function of some sort, but he went resolutely up the steps, telling the footman that his business was urgent. Lady Ellen came down alone, excusing her sister. She was dressed for receiving, and MacMaster had never seen her so beautiful. The colour in her cheeks sent a softening glow over her small, delicately cut features.

MacMaster apologized for his intrusion and came unflinchingly to the object of his call. He had come, he said, not only to offer her his warmest congratulations, but to express his regret that a great work of art was to leave England.

Lady Treffinger looked at him in wide-eyed astonishment. Surely, she said, she had been careful to select the best of the pictures for the X—— gallery, in accordance with Sir Hugh Treffinger's wishes.

"And did he—pardon me, Lady Treffinger, but in mercy set my mind at rest—did he or did he not express any definite wish concerning this one picture, which to me seems worth all the others, unfinished as it is?"

Lady Treffinger paled perceptibly, but it was not the pallor of confusion. When she spoke there was a sharp tremor in her smooth voice, the edge of a resentment that tore her like pain. "I think his man has some such impression, but I believe it to be utterly unfounded. I cannot find that he ever expressed any wish concerning the disposition of the picture to any of his friends. Unfortunately, Sir Hugh was not always discreet in his remarks to his servants."

"Captain Gresham, Lady Ellingham and Miss Ellingham," announced a servant, appearing at the door.

There was a murmur in the hall, and MacMaster greeted the smiling Captain and his aunt as he bowed himself out.

To all intents and purposes the *Marriage of Phædra* was already entombed in a vague continent in the Pacific, somewhere on the other side of the world.

A Wagner Matinee

I received one morning a letter, written in pale ink on glassy, blue-lined note-paper, and bearing the postmark of a little Nebraska village. This communication, worn and rubbed, looking as though it had been carried for some days in a coat pocket that was none too clean, was from my uncle Howard and informed me that his wife had been left a small legacy by a bachelor relative who had recently died, and that it would be necessary for her to go to Boston to attend to the settling of the estate. He requested me to meet her at the station and render her whatever services might be necessary. On examining the date indicated as that of her arrival, I found it no later than to-morrow. He had characteristically delayed writing until, had I been away from home for a day, I must have missed the good woman altogether.

The name of my Aunt Georgiana called up not alone her own figure, at once pathetic and grotesque, but opened before my feet a gulf of recollection so wide and deep that, as the letter dropped from my hand, I felt suddenly a stranger to all the present conditions of my existence, wholly ill at ease and out of place amid the familiar surroundings of my study. I became, in short, the gangling farmer-boy my aunt had known, scourged with chilblains and bashfulness, my hands cracked and sore from the corn husking. I felt the knuckles of my thumb tentatively, as though they were raw again. I sat again before her parlour organ, fumbling the scales with my stiff, red hands, while she, beside me, made canvas mittens for the huskers.

The next morning, after preparing my landlady somewhat, I set out for the station. When the train arrived I had some difficulty in finding my aunt. She was the last of the passengers to alight, and it was not until I got her into the carriage that she seemed really to

recognize me. She had come all the way in a day coach; her linen duster had become black with soot and her black bonnet grey with dust
during the journey. When we arrived at my boarding-house the landlady put her to bed at once and I did not see her again until the next
morning.

Whatever shock Mrs. Springer experienced at my aunt's appearance, she considerately concealed. As for myself, I saw my aunt's misshapen figure with that feeling of awe and respect with which we be-
hold explorers who have left their ears and fingers north of Franz
Josef Land, or their health somewhere along the Upper Congo. My
Aunt Georgiana had been a music teacher at the Boston Conservatory, somewhere back in the latter sixties. One summer, while visiting in the little village among the Green Mountains where her ancestors had dwelt for generations, she had kindled the callow fancy of
the most idle and shiftless of all the village lads, and had conceived
for this Howard Carpenter one of those extravagant passions which a
handsome country boy of twenty-one sometimes inspires in an angular, spectacled woman of thirty. When she returned to her duties in
Boston, Howard followed her, and the upshot of this inexplicable infatuation was that she eloped with him, eluding the reproaches of her
family and the criticisms of her friends by going with him to the Nebraska frontier. Carpenter, who, of course, had no money, had taken
a homestead in Red Willow County, fifty miles from the railroad. There
they had measured off their quarter section themselves by driving
across the prairie in a wagon, to the wheel of which they had tied a
red cotton handkerchief, and counting off its revolutions. They built a
dugout in the red hillside, one of those cave dwellings whose inmates
so often reverted to primitive conditions. Their water they got from
the lagoons where the buffalo drank, and their slender stock of provi-
sions was always at the mercy of bands of roving Indians. For thirty
years my aunt had not been farther than fifty miles from the homestead.

But Mrs. Springer knew nothing of all this, and must have been
considerably shocked at what was left of my kinswoman. Beneath the
soiled linen duster which, on her arrival, was the most conspicuous
feature of her costume, she wore a black stuff dress, whose ornamen-
tation showed that she had surrendered herself unquestioningly into
the hands of a country dressmaker. My poor aunt's figure, however,
would have presented astonishing difficulties to any dressmaker.

Originally stooped, her shoulders were now almost bent together over her sunken chest. She wore no stays, and her gown, which trailed unevenly behind, rose in a sort of peak over her abdomen. She wore ill-fitting false teeth, and her skin was as yellow as a Mongolian's from constant exposure to a pitiless wind and to the alkaline water which hardens the most transparent cuticle into a sort of flexible leather.

I owed to this woman most of the good that ever came my way in my boyhood, and had a reverential affection for her. During the years when I was riding herd for my uncle, my aunt, after cooking the three meals—the first of which was ready at six o'clock in the morning—and putting the six children to bed, would often stand until midnight at her ironing-board, with me at the kitchen table beside her, hearing me recite Latin declensions and conjugations, gently shaking me when my drowsy head sank down over a page of irregular verbs. It was to her, at her ironing or mending, that I read my first Shakspere, and her old text-book on mythology was the first that ever came into my empty hands. She taught me my scales and exercises, too—on the little parlour organ which her husband had bought her after fifteen years, during which she had not so much as seen any instrument, but an accordion that belonged to one of the Norwegian farm-hands. She would sit beside me by the hour, darning and counting, while I struggled with the "Joyous Farmer," but she seldom talked to me about music, and I understood why. She was a pious woman; she had the consolations of religion and, to her at least, her martyrdom was not wholly sordid. Once when I had been doggedly beating out some easy passages from an old score of *Euryanthe* I had found among her music books, she came up to me and, putting her hands over my eyes, gently drew my head back upon her shoulder, saying tremulously, "Don't love it so well, Clark, or it may be taken from you. Oh! dear boy, pray that whatever your sacrifice may be, it be not that."

When my aunt appeared on the morning after her arrival, she was still in a semi-somnambulant state. She seemed not to realize that she was in the city where she had spent her youth, the place longed for hungrily half a lifetime. She had been so wretchedly train-sick throughout the journey that she had no recollection of anything but her discomfort, and, to all intents and purposes, there were but a few hours of nightmare between the farm in Red Willow County and my study on Newbury Street. I had planned a little pleasure for her that afternoon, to repay her for some of the glorious moments she had given me when we used to milk together in the strawthatched cowshed and she, because I was more than usually tired, or because her husband had spoken sharply to me, would tell me of the splendid performance of the *Huguenots* she had seen in Paris, in her youth. At two o'clock the Symphony Orchestra was to give a Wagner programme, and I intended to take my aunt; though, as I conversed with her, I grew doubtful about her enjoyment of it. Indeed, for her own sake, I could only wish her taste for such things quite dead, and the long struggle mercifully ended at last. I suggested our visiting the Conservatory and the Common before lunch, but she seemed altogether too timid to wish to venture out. She questioned me absently about various changes in the city, but she was chiefly concerned that she had forgotten to leave instructions about feeding half-skimmed milk to a certain weakling calf, "old Maggie's calf, you know, Clark," she explained, evidently having forgotten how long I had been away. She was further troubled because she had neglected to tell her daughter about the freshly-opened kit of mackerel in the cellar, which would spoil if it were not used directly.

I asked her whether she had ever heard any of the Wagnerian operas, and found that she had not, though she was perfectly familiar with their respective situations, and had once possessed the piano score of *The Flying Dutchman*. I began to think it would have been best to get her back to Red Willow County without waking her, and regretted having suggested the concert.

From the time we entered the concert hall, however, she was a trifle less passive and inert, and for the first time seemed to perceive her surroundings. I had felt some trepidation lest she might become aware of the absurdities of her attire, or might experience some painful embarrassment at stepping suddenly into the world to which she had been dead for more than a quarter of a century. But, again, I found how superficially I had judged her. She sat looking about her with eyes as impersonal, almost as stony, as those with which the granite Rameses in a museum watches the froth and fret that ebbs and flows about his pedestal—separated from it by the lonely stretch of centuries. I have seen this same aloofness in old miners who drift into the Brown Hotel at Denver, their pockets full of bullion, their linen soiled, their haggard faces unshaven; standing in the thronged corridors as solitary as though they were still in a frozen camp on the Yukon, conscious that certain experiences have isolated them from their fellows by a gulf no haberdasher could bridge.

We sat at the extreme left of the first balcony, facing the arc of our own and the balcony above us, veritable hanging gardens, brilliant as tulip beds. The matinée audience was made up chiefly of women. One lost the contour of faces and figures, indeed any effect of line what-ever, and there was only the colour of bodices past counting, the shim-mer of fabrics soft and firm, silky and sheer; red, mauve, pink, blue, lilac, purple, ecru, rose, yellow, cream, and white, all the colours that an impressionist finds in a sunlit landscape, with here and there the dead shadow of a frock coat. My Aunt Georgiana regarded them as though they had been so many daubs of tube-paint on a palette.

When the musicians came out and took their places, she gave a little stir of anticipation, and looked with quickening interest down over the rail at that invariable grouping, perhaps the first wholly fa-miliar thing that had greeted her eye since she had left old Maggie and her weakling calf. I could feel how all those details sank into her soul, for I had not forgotten how they had sunk into mine when I came fresh from ploughing forever and forever between green aisles of corn, where, as in a treadmill, one might walk from daybreak to dusk with-out perceiving a shadow of change. The clean profiles of the musi-cians, the gloss of their linen, the dull black of their coats, the beloved shapes of the instruments, the patches of yellow light thrown by the green shaded lamps on the smooth, varnished bellies of the 'cellos and the bass viols in the rear, the restless, wind-tossed forest of fiddle necks and bows—I recalled how, in the first orchestra I had ever heard, those long bow strokes seemed to draw the heart out of me, as a con-jurer's stick reels out yards of paper ribbon from a hat.

The first number was the *Tannhäuser* overture. When the horns drew out the first strain of the Pilgrim's chorus, my Aunt Georgiana clutched my coat sleeve. Then it was I first realized that for her this broke a silence of thirty years; the inconceivable silence of the plains. With the battle between the two motives, with the frenzy of the Ve-nusberg theme and its ripping of strings, there came to me an over-whelming sense of the waste and wear we are so powerless to combat; and I saw again the tall, naked house on the prairie, black and grim as a wooden fortress; the black pond where I had learned to swim, its margin pitted with sun-dried cattle tracks; the rain gullied clay banks about the naked house, the four dwarf ash seedlings where the dish-cloths were always hung to dry before the kitchen door. The world there was the flat world of the ancients; to the east, a cornfield that stretched to daybreak; to the west, a corral that reached to sunset; between, the conquests of peace, dearer bought than those of war.

The overture closed, my aunt released my coat sleeve, but she said nothing. She sat staring at the orchestra through a dullness of thirty years, through the films made little by little by each of the three hundred and sixty-five days in every one of them. What, I wondered, did she get from it? She had been a good pianist in her day I knew, and her musical education had been broader than that of most music teachers of a quarter of a century ago. She had often told me of Mo-zart's operas and Meyerbeer's, and I could remember hearing her sing, years ago, certain melodies of Verdi's. When I had fallen ill with a fever in her house she used to sit by my cot in the evening—when the cool, night wind blew in through the faded mosquito netting tacked over the window and I lay watching a certain bright star that burned red above the cornfield—and sing "Home to our mountains, O, let us return!" in a way fit to break the heart of a Vermont boy near dead of homesickness already.

I watched her closely through the prelude to *Tristan and Isolde*, trying vainly to conjecture what that seething turmoil of strings and winds might mean to her, but she sat mutely staring at the violin bows that drove obliquely downward, like the pelting streaks of rain in a summer shower. Had this music any message for her? Had she enough left to at all comprehend this power which had kindled the world since she had left it? I was in a fever of curiosity, but Aunt Georgiana sat silent upon her peak in Darien. She preserved this utter immobility throughout the number from *The Flying Dutchman*, though her fin-gers worked mechanically upon her black dress, as though, of them-selves, they were recalling the piano score they had once played. Poor old hands! They had been stretched and twisted into mere tentacles to hold and lift and knead with; the palm, unduly swollen, the fingers bent and knotted—on one of them a thin, worn band that had once been a wedding ring. As I pressed and gently quieted one of those groping hands, I remembered with quivering eyelids their services for me in other days.

Soon after the tenor began the "Prize Song," I heard a quick drawn breath and turned to my aunt. Her eyes were closed, but the tears were glistening on her cheeks, and I think, in a moment more, they were in my eyes as well. It never really died, then—the soul that can suffer so excruciatingly and so interminably; it withers to the outward eye only; like that strange moss which can lie on a dusty shelf half a century and yet, if placed in water, grows green again. She wept so throughout the development and elaboration of the melody.

During the intermission before the second half of the concert, I questioned my aunt and found that the "Prize Song" was not new to her. Some years before there had drifted to the farm in Red Willow County a young German, a tramp cow-puncher, who had sung in the chorus at Bayreuth, when he was a boy, along with the other peasant boys and girls. Of a Sunday morning he used to sit on his gingham-sheeted bed in the hands' bedroom which opened off the kitchen, cleaning the leather of his boots and saddle, singing the "Prize Song," while my aunt went about her work in the kitchen. She had hovered about him until she had prevailed upon him to join the country church, though his sole fitness for this step, in so far as I could gather, lay in his boyish face and his possession of this divine melody. Shortly afterward he had gone to town on the Fourth of July, been drunk for several days, lost his money at a faro table, ridden a saddled Texas steer on a bet, and disappeared with a fractured collar-bone. All this my aunt told me huskily, wanderingly, as though she were talking in the weak lapses of illness.

"Well, we have come to better things than the old *Trovatore* at any rate, Aunt Georgie?" I queried, with a well meant effort at jocularity.

Her lip quivered and she hastily put her handkerchief up to her mouth. From behind it she murmured, "And you have been hearing this ever since you left me, Clark?" Her question was the gentlest and saddest of reproaches.

The second half of the programme consisted of four numbers from the *Ring*, and closed with Siegfried's funeral march. My aunt wept quietly, but almost continuously, as a shallow vessel overflows in a rain-storm. From time to time her dim eyes looked up at the lights which studded the ceiling, burning softly under their dull glass globes; doubtless they were stars in truth to her. I was still perplexed as to what measure of musical comprehension was left to her, she who had heard nothing but the singing of Gospel Hymns at Methodist services in the square frame school-house on Section Thirteen for so many years.

I was wholly unable to gauge how much of it had been dissolved in soapsuds, or worked into bread, or milked into the bottom of a pail.

The deluge of sound poured on and on; I never knew what she found in the shining current of it; I never knew how far it bore her, or past what happy islands. From the trembling of her face I could well believe that before the last numbers she had been carried out where the myriad graves are, into the grey, nameless burying grounds of the sea; or into some world of death vaster yet, where, from the beginning of the world, hope has lain down with hope and dream with dream and, renouncing, slept.

The concert was over; the people filed out of the hall chattering and laughing, glad to relax and find the living level again, but my kinswoman made no effort to rise. The harpist slipped its green felt cover over his instrument; the flute-players shook the water from their mouthpieces; the men of the orchestra went out one by one, leaving the stage to the chairs and music stands, empty as a winter cornfield.

I spoke to my aunt. She burst into tears and sobbed pleadingly. "I don't want to go, Clark, I don't want to go!"

I understood. For her, just outside the door of the concert hall, lay the black pond with the cattle-tracked bluffs; the tall, unpainted house, with weather-curled boards; naked as a tower, the crook-backed ash seedlings where the dish-cloths hung to dry; the gaunt, moulting turkeys picking up refuse about the kitchen door.

Paul's Case

A Study in Temperament

It was Paul's afternoon to appear before the
faculty of the Pittsburgh High School to account for his various mis-
demeanours. He had been suspended a week ago, and his father had
called at the Principal's office and confessed his perplexity about his
son. Paul entered the faculty room suave and smiling. His clothes were
a trifle out-grown and the tan velvet on the collar of his open overcoat
was frayed and worn; but for all that there was something of the dandy
about him, and he wore an opal pin in his neatly knotted black four-
in-hand, and a red carnation in his button-hole. This latter adornment
the faculty somehow felt was not properly significant of the contrite
spirit befitting a boy under the ban of suspension.

Paul was tall for his age and very thin, with high, cramped shoulders and a narrow chest. His eyes were remarkable for a certain hysterical brilliancy, and he continually used them in a conscious, theatrical sort of way, peculiarly offensive in a boy. The pupils were
abnormally large, as though he were addicted to belladonna, but there
was a glassy glitter about them which that drug does not produce.

When questioned by the Principal as to why he was there, Paul
stated, politely enough, that he wanted to come back to school. This
was a lie, but Paul was quite accustomed to lying; found it, indeed,
indispensable for overcoming friction. His teachers were asked to state
their respective charges against him, which they did with such a rancour and aggrievedness as evinced that this was not a usual case. Disorder and impertinence were among the offences named, yet each of
his instructors felt that it was scarcely possible to put into words the
real cause of the trouble, which lay in a sort of hysterically defiant
manner of the boy's; in the contempt which they all knew he felt for
them, and which he seemingly made not the least effort to conceal.

Once, when he had been making a synopsis of a paragraph at the blackboard, his English teacher had stepped to his side and attempted to guide his hand. Paul had started back with a shudder and thrust his hands violently behind him. The astonished woman could scarcely have been more hurt and embarrassed had he struck at her. The insult was so involuntary and definitely personal as to be unforgettable. In one way and another, he had made all his teachers, men and women alike, conscious of the same feeling of physical aversion. In one class he habitually sat with his hand shading his eyes; in another he always looked out of the window during the recitation; in another he made a running commentary on the lecture, with humorous intention.

His teachers felt this afternoon that his whole attitude was symbolized by his shrug and his flippantly red carnation flower, and they fell upon him without mercy, his English teacher leading the pack. He stood through it smiling, his pale lips parted over his white teeth. (His lips were continually twitching, and he had a habit of raising his eyebrows that was contemptuous and irritating to the last degree.) Older boys than Paul had broken down and shed tears under that baptism of fire, but his set smile did not once desert him, and his only sign of discomfort was the nervous trembling of the fingers that toyed with the buttons of his overcoat, and an occasional jerking of the other hand that held his hat. Paul was always smiling, always glancing about him, seeming to feel that people might be watching him and trying to detect something. This conscious expression, since it was as far as possible from boyish mirthfulness, was usually attributed to insolence or "smartness."

As the inquisition proceeded, one of his instructors repeated an impertinent remark of the boy's, and the Principal asked him whether he thought that a courteous speech to have made a woman. Paul shrugged his shoulders slightly and his eyebrows twitched.

"I don't know," he replied. "I didn't mean to be polite or impolite, either. I guess it's a sort of way I have of saying things regardless."

The Principal, who was a sympathetic man, asked him whether he didn't think that a way it would be well to get rid of. Paul grinned and said he guessed so. When he was told that he could go, he bowed gracefully and went out. His bow was but a repetition of the scandalous red carnation.

His teachers were in despair, and his drawing master voiced the feeling of them all when he declared there was something about the boy which none of them understood. He added: "I don't really believe that smile of his comes altogether from insolence; there's something sort of haunted about it. The boy is not strong, for one thing. I happen to know that he was born in Colorado, only a few months before his mother died out there of a long illness. There is something wrong about the fellow."

The drawing master had come to realize that, in looking at Paul, one saw only his white teeth and the forced animation of his eyes. One warm afternoon the boy had gone to sleep at his drawing-board, and his master had noted with amazement what a white, blue-veined face it was; drawn and wrinkled like an old man's about the eyes, the lips twitching even in his sleep, and stiff with a nervous tension that drew them back from his teeth.

His teachers left the building dissatisfied and unhappy; humiliated to have felt so vindictive toward a mere boy, to have uttered this feeling in cutting terms, and to have set each other on, as it were, in the grewsome game of intemperate reproach. Some of them remembered having seen a miserable street cat set at bay by a ring of tormentors.

As for Paul, he ran down the hill whistling the Soldiers' Chorus from *Faust* looking wildly behind him now and then to see whether some of his teachers were not there to writhe under his lightheartedness. As it was now late in the afternoon and Paul was on duty that evening as usher at Carnegie Hall, he decided that he would not go home to supper. When he reached the concert hall the doors were not yet open and, as it was chilly outside, he decided to go up into the picture gallery—always deserted at this hour—where there were some of Raffaelli's gay studies of Paris streets and an airy blue Venetian scene or two that always exhilarated him. He was delighted to find no one in the gallery but the old guard, who sat in one corner, a newspaper on his knee, a black patch over one eye and the other closed. Paul possessed himself of the place and walked confidently up and down, whistling under his breath. After a while he sat down before a blue Rico and lost himself. When he bethought him to look at his watch, it was after seven o'clock, and he rose with a start and ran downstairs, making a face at Augustus, peering out from the cast-room, and an evil gesture at the Venus of Milo as he passed her on the stairway.

When Paul reached the ushers' dressing-room half-a-dozen boys were there already, and he began excitedly to tumble into his uniform. It was one of the few that at all approached fitting, and Paul thought it very becoming—though he knew that the tight, straight coat accentuated his narrow chest, about which he was exceedingly sensitive. He was always considerably excited while he dressed, twanging all over to the tuning of the strings and the preliminary flourishes of the horns in the music-room; but to-night he seemed quite beside himself, and he teased and plagued the boys until, telling him that he was crazy, they put him down on the floor and sat on him.

Somewhat calmed by his suppression, Paul dashed out to the front of the house to seat the early comers. He was a model usher; gracious and smiling he ran up and down the aisles; nothing was too much trouble for him; he carried messages and brought programmes as though it were his greatest pleasure in life, and all the people in his section thought him a charming boy, feeling that he remembered and admired them. As the house filled, he grew more and more vivacious and animated, and the colour came to his cheeks and lips. It was very much as though this were a great reception and Paul were the host. Just as the musicians came out to take their places, his English teacher arrived with checks for the seats which a prominent manufacturer had taken for the season. She betrayed some embarrassment when she handed Paul the tickets, and a *hauteur* which subsequently made her feel very foolish. Paul was startled for a moment, and had the feeling of wanting to put her out; what business had she here among all these fine people and gay colours? He looked her over and decided that she was not appropriately dressed and must be a fool to sit downstairs in such togs. The tickets had probably been sent her out of kindness, he reflected as he put down a seat for her, and she had about as much right to sit there as he had.

When the symphony began Paul sank into one of the rear seats with a long sigh of relief, and lost himself as he had done before the Rico. It was not that symphonies, as such, meant anything in particular to Paul, but the first sigh of the instruments seemed to free some hilarious and potent spirit within him; something that struggled there like the Genius in the bottle found by the Arab fisherman. He felt a sudden zest of life; the lights danced before his eyes and the concert hall blazed into unimaginable splendour. When the soprano soloist came on, Paul forgot even the nastiness of his teacher's being there and gave himself up to the peculiar stimulus such personages always had for him. The soloist chanced to be a German woman, by no means in her first youth, and the mother of many children; but she wore an elaborate gown and a tiara, and above all she had that indefinable air of achievement, that world-shine upon her, which, in Paul's eyes, made her a veritable queen of Romance.

After a concert was over Paul was always irritable and wretched until he got to sleep, and to-night he was even more than usually restless. He had the feeling of not being able to let down, of its being impossible to give up this delicious excitement which was the only thing that could be called living at all. During the last number he withdrew and, after hastily changing his clothes in the dressing-room, slipped out to the side door where the soprano's carriage stood. Here he began pacing rapidly up and down the walk, waiting to see her come out.

Over yonder the Schenley, in its vacant stretch, loomed big and square through the fine rain, the windows of its twelve stories glowing like those of a lighted card-board house under a Christmas tree. All the actors and singers of the better class stayed there when they were in the city, and a number of the big manufacturers of the place lived there in the winter. Paul had often hung about the hotel, watching the people go in and out, longing to enter and leave school-masters and dull care behind him forever.

At last the singer came out, accompanied by the conductor, who helped her into her carriage and closed the door with a cordial *auf wiedersehen*, which set Paul to wondering whether she were not an old sweetheart of his. Paul followed the carriage over to the hotel, walking so rapidly as not to be far from the entrance when the singer alighted and disappeared behind the swinging glass doors that were opened by a negro in a tall hat and a long coat. In the moment that the door was ajar, it seemed to Paul that he, too, entered. He seemed to feel himself go after her up the steps, into the warm, lighted building, into an exotic, a tropical world of shiny, glistening surfaces and basking ease. He reflected upon the mysterious dishes that were brought into the dining-room, the green bottles in buckets of ice, as he had seen them in the supper party pictures of the *Sunday World* supplement. A quick gust of wind brought the rain down with sudden vehemence, and Paul was startled to find that he was still outside in the slush of the gravel driveway; that his boots were letting in the water and his scanty overcoat was clinging wet about him; that the lights in front of the concert hall were out, and that the rain was driving in sheets between him and the orange glow of the windows above him. There it was, what he wanted—tangibly before him, like the fairy world of a Christmas pantomime, but mocking spirits stood guard at the doors, and, as the rain beat in his face, Paul wondered whether he were destined always to shiver in the black night outside, looking up at it.

He turned and walked reluctantly toward the car tracks. The end had to come sometime; his father in his night-clothes at the top of the stairs, explanations that did not explain, hastily improvised fictions that were forever tripping him up, his upstairs room and its horrible yellow wall-paper, the creaking bureau with the greasy plush collar-box, and over his painted wooden bed the pictures of George Washington and John Calvin, and the framed motto, "Feed my Lambs," which had been worked in red worsted by his mother.

Half an hour later, Paul alighted from his car and went slowly down one of the side streets off the main thoroughfare. It was a highly respectable street, where all the houses were exactly alike, and where business men of moderate means begot and reared large families of children, all of whom went to Sabbath-school and learned the shorter catechism, and were interested in arithmetic; all of whom were as exactly alike as their homes, and of a piece with the monotony in which they lived. Paul never went up Cordelia Street without a shudder of loathing. His home was next the house of the Cumberland minister. He approached it to-night with the nerveless sense of defeat, the hopeless feeling of sinking back forever into ugliness and commonness that he had always had when he came home. The moment he turned into Cordelia Street he felt the waters close above his head. After each of these orgies of living, he experienced all the physical depression which follows a debauch; the loathing of respectable beds, of common food, of a house permeated by kitchen odours; a shuddering repulsion for the flavourless, colourless mass of every-day existence; a morbid desire for cool things and soft lights and fresh flowers.

The nearer he approached the house, the more absolutely unequal Paul felt to the sight of it all; his ugly sleeping chamber; the cold bathroom with the grimy zinc tub, the cracked mirror, the dripping spiggots; his father, at the top of the stairs, his hairy legs sticking out from his night-shirt, his feet thrust into carpet slippers. He was so much later than usual that there would certainly be inquiries and re-

proaches. Paul stopped short before the door. He felt that he could
not be accosted by his father to-night; that he could not toss again on
that miserable bed. He would not go in. He would tell his father that
he had no car fare, and it was raining so hard he had gone home with
one of the boys and stayed all night.

Meanwhile, he was wet and cold. He went around to the back of
the house and tried one of the basement windows, found it open, raised
it cautiously, and scrambled down the cellar wall to the floor. There
he stood, holding his breath, terrified by the noise he had made, but
the floor above him was silent, and there was no creak on the stairs.
He found a soap-box, and carried it over to the soft ring of light that
streamed from the furnace door, and sat down. He was horribly afraid
of rats, so he did not try to sleep, but sat looking distrustfully at the
dark, still terrified lest he might have awakened his father. In such
reactions, after one of the experiences which made days and nights
out of the dreary blanks of the calendar, when his senses were dead-
ened, Paul's head was always singularly clear. Suppose his father had
heard him getting in at the window and had come down and shot him
for a burglar? Then, again, suppose his father had come down, pistol
in hand, and he had cried out in time to save himself, and his father
had been horrified to think how nearly he had killed him? Then, again,
suppose a day should come when his father would remember that night,
and wish there had been no warning cry to stay his hand? With this
last supposition Paul entertained himself until daybreak.

The following Sunday was fine; the sodden November chill was
broken by the last flash of autumnal summer. In the morning Paul had
to go to church and Sabbath-school, as always. On seasonable Sunday
afternoons the burghers of Cordelia Street always sat out on their
front "stoops," and talked to their neighbours on the next stoop, or
called to those across the street in neighbourly fashion. The men usually sat on gay cushions placed upon the steps that led down to the
sidewalk, while the women, in their Sunday "waists," sat in rockers
on the cramped porches, pretending to be greatly at their ease. The
children played in the streets; there were so many of them that the
place resembled the recreation grounds of a kindergarten. The men
on the steps—all in their shirt sleeves, their vests unbuttoned—sat
with their legs well apart, their stomachs comfortably protruding,
and talked of the prices of things, or told anecdotes of the sagacity of
their various chiefs and overlords. They occasionally looked over the

multitude of squabbling children, listened affectionately to their high-pitched, nasal voices, smiling to see their own proclivities reproduced in their offspring, and interspersed their legends of the iron kings with remarks about their sons' progress at school, their grades in arithmetic, and the amounts they had saved in their toy banks.

On this last Sunday of November, Paul sat all the afternoon on the lowest step of his "stoop," staring into the street, while his sisters, in their rockers, were talking to the minister's daughters next door about how many shirt-waists they had made in the last week, and how many waffles some one had eaten at the last church supper. When the weather was warm, and his father was in a particularly jovial frame of mind, the girls made lemonade, which was always brought out in a red-glass pitcher, ornamented with forget-me-nots in blue enamel. This the girls thought very fine, and the neighbours always joked about the suspicious colour of the pitcher.

To-day Paul's father sat on the top step, talking to a young man who shifted a restless baby from knee to knee. He happened to be the young man who was daily held up to Paul as a model, and after whom it was his father's dearest hope that he would pattern. This young man was of a ruddy complexion, with a compressed, red mouth, and faded, near-sighted eyes, over which he wore thick spectacles, with gold bows that curved about his ears. He was clerk to one of the magnates of a great steel corporation, and was looked upon in Cordelia Street as a young man with a future. There was a story that, some five years ago—he was now barely twenty-six—he had been a trifle dissipated, but in order to curb his appetites and save the loss of time and strength that a sowing of wild oats might have entailed, he had taken his chief's advice, oft reiterated to his employees, and at twenty-one had married the first woman whom he could persuade to share his fortunes. She happened to be an angular school-mistress, much older than he, who also wore thick glasses, and who had now borne him four children, all near-sighted, like herself.

The young man was relating how his chief, now cruising in the Mediterranean, kept in touch with all the details of the business, arranging his office hours on his yacht just as though he were at home, and "knocking off work enough to keep two stenographers busy." His father told, in turn, the plan his corporation was considering, of putting in an electric railway plant at Cairo. Paul snapped his teeth; he had an awful apprehension that they might spoil it all before he got there. Yet he rather liked to hear these legends of the iron kings, that were told and retold on Sundays and holidays; these stories of palaces in Venice, yachts on the Mediterranean, and high play at Monte Carlo appealed to his fancy, and he was interested in the triumphs of these cash boys who had become famous, though he had no mind for the cash-boy stage.

After supper was over, and he had helped to dry the dishes, Paul nervously asked his father whether he could go to George's to get some help in his geometry, and still more nervously asked for car fare. This latter request he had to repeat, as his father, on principle, did not like to hear requests for money, whether much or little. He asked Paul whether he could not go to some boy who lived nearer, and told him that he ought not to leave his school work until Sunday; but he gave him the dime. He was not a poor man, but he had a worthy ambition to come up in the world. His only reason for allowing Paul to usher was, that he thought a boy ought to be earning a little.

Paul bounded upstairs, scrubbed the greasy odour of the dish-water from his hands with the ill-smelling soap he hated, and then shook over his fingers a few drops of violet water from the bottle he kept hidden in his drawer. He left the house with his geometry conspicuously under his arm, and the moment he got out of Cordelia Street and boarded a downtown car, he shook off the lethargy of two deadening days, and began to live again.

The leading juvenile of the permanent stock company which played at one of the downtown theatres was an acquaintance of Paul's, and the boy had been invited to drop in at the Sunday-night rehearsals whenever he could. For more than a year Paul had spent every available moment loitering about Charley Edwards's dressing-room. He had won a place among Edwards's following not only because the young actor, who could not afford to employ a dresser, often found him useful, but because he recognized in Paul something akin to what churchmen term "vocation."

It was at the theatre and at Carnegie Hall that Paul really lived; the rest was but a sleep and a forgetting. This was Paul's fairy tale, and it had for him all the allurement of a secret love. The moment he inhaled the gassy, painty, dusty odour behind the scenes, he breathed like a prisoner set free, and felt within him the possibility of doing or saying splendid, brilliant, poetic things. The moment the cracked orchestra beat out the overture from *Martha*, or jerked at the serenade from *Rigoletto*, all stupid and ugly things slid from him, and his senses were deliciously, yet delicately fired.

Perhaps it was because, in Paul's world, the natural nearly always wore the guise of ugliness, that a certain element of artificiality seemed to him necessary in beauty. Perhaps it was because his experience of life elsewhere was so full of Sabbath-school picnics, petty economies, wholesome advice as to how to succeed in life, and the unescapable odours of cooking, that he found this existence so alluring, these smartly-clad men and women so attractive, that he was so moved by these starry apple orchards that bloomed perennially under the lime-light.

It would be difficult to put it strongly enough how convincingly the stage entrance of that theatre was for Paul the actual portal of Romance. Certainly none of the company ever suspected it, least of all Charley Edwards. It was very like the old stories that used to float about London of fabulously rich Jews, who had subterranean halls there, with palms, and fountains, and soft lamps and richly apparelled women who never saw the disenchanting light of London day. So, in the midst of that smoke-palled city, enamoured of figures and grimy toil, Paul had his secret temple, his wishing carpet, his bit of blue-and-white Mediterranean shore bathed in perpetual sunshine.

Several of Paul's teachers had a theory that his imagination had been perverted by garish fiction, but the truth was that he scarcely ever read at all. The books at home were not such as would either tempt or corrupt a youthful mind, and as for reading the novels that some of his friends urged upon him—well, he got what he wanted much more quickly from music; any sort of music, from an orchestra to a barrel organ. He needed only the spark, the indescribable thrill that made his imagination master of his senses, and he could make plots and pictures enough of his own. It was equally true that he was not stage-struck—not, at any rate, in the usual acceptation of that expression. He had no desire to become an actor, any more than he had to become a musician. He felt no necessity to do any of these things; what he wanted was to see, to be in the atmosphere, float on the wave of it, to be carried out, blue league after blue league, away from everything.

After a night behind the scenes, Paul found the school-room more than ever repulsive; the bare floors and naked walls; the prosy men who never wore frock coats, or violets in their button-holes; the women with their dull gowns, shrill voices, and pitiful seriousness about prepositions that govern the dative. He could not bear to have the other pupils think, for a moment, that he took these people seriously; he must convey to them that he considered it all trivial, and was there only by way of a jest, anyway. He had autograph pictures of all the members of the stock company which he showed his classmates, telling them the most incredible stories of his familiarity with these people, of his acquaintance with the soloists who came to Carnegie Hall, his suppers with them and the flowers he sent them. When these stories lost their effect, and his audience grew listless, he became desperate and would bid all the boys good-bye, announcing that he was going to travel for awhile; going to Naples, to Venice, to Egypt. Then, next Monday, he would slip back, conscious and nervously smiling; his sister was ill, and he should have to defer his voyage until spring.

Matters went steadily worse with Paul at school. In the itch to let his instructors know how heartily he despised them and their homilies, and how thoroughly he was appreciated elsewhere, he mentioned once or twice that he had no time to fool with theorems; adding—with a twitch of the eyebrows and a touch of that nervous bravado which so perplexed them—that he was helping the people down at the stock company; they were old friends of his.

The upshot of the matter was, that the Principal went to Paul's father, and Paul was taken out of school and put to work. The manager at Carnegie Hall was told to get another usher in his stead; the doorkeeper at the theatre was warned not to admit him to the house; and Charley Edwards remorsefully promised the boy's father not to see him again.

The members of the stock company were vastly amused when some of Paul's stories reached them—especially the women. They were hard-working women, most of them supporting indigent husbands or brothers, and they laughed rather bitterly at having stirred the boy to such fervid and florid inventions. They agreed with the faculty and with his father that Paul's was a bad case.

The east-bound train was ploughing through a January snow-storm; the dull dawn was beginning to show grey when the engine whistled a mile out of Newark. Paul started up from the seat where he had lain curled in uneasy slumber, rubbed the breath-misted window glass with his hand, and peered out. The snow was whirling in curling eddies above the white bottom lands, and the drifts lay already deep in the fields and along the fences, while here and there the long dead grass and dried weed stalks protruded black above it. Lights shone from the scattered houses, and a gang of labourers who stood beside the track waved their lanterns.

Paul had slept very little, and he felt grimy and uncomfortable. He had made the all-night journey in a day coach, partly because he was ashamed, dressed as he was, to go into a Pullman, and partly because he was afraid of being seen there by some Pittsburgh business man, who might have noticed him in Denny & Carson's office. When the whistle awoke him, he clutched quickly at his breast pocket, glancing about him with an uncertain smile. But the little, clay-bespattered Italians were still sleeping, the slatternly women across the aisle were in open-mouthed oblivion, and even the crumby, crying babies were for the nonce stilled. Paul settled back to struggle with his impatience as best he could.

When he arrived at the Jersey City station, he hurried through his breakfast, manifestly ill at ease and keeping a sharp eye about him. After he reached the Twenty-third Street station, he consulted a cabman, and had himself driven to a men's furnishing establishment that was just opening for the day. He spent upward of two hours there, buying with endless reconsidering and great care. His new street suit he put on in the fitting-room; the frock coat and dress clothes he had bundled into the cab with his linen. Then he drove to a hatter's and a shoe house. His next errand was at Tiffany's, where he selected his silver and a new scarf-pin. He would not wait to have his silver marked, he said. Lastly, he stopped at a trunk shop on Broadway, and had his purchases packed into various traveling bags.

It was a little after one o'clock when he drove up to the Waldorf, and after settling with the cabman, went into the office. He registered from Washington; said his mother and father had been abroad, and that he had come down to await the arrival of their steamer. He told his story plausibly and had no trouble, since he volunteered to pay for them in advance, in engaging his rooms; a sleeping-room, sitting-room and bath.

Not once, but a hundred times Paul had planned this entry into New York. He had gone over every detail of it with Charley Edwards, and in his scrap book at home there were pages of description about New York hotels, cut from the Sunday papers. When he was shown to his sitting-room on the eighth floor, he saw at a glance that everything was as it should be; there was but one detail in his mental picture that the place did not realize, so he rang for the bell boy and sent him down for flowers. He moved about nervously until the boy returned, putting away his new linen and fingering it delightedly as he did so. When the flowers came, he put them hastily into water, and then tumbled into a hot bath. Presently he came out of his white bathroom, resplendent in his new silk underwear, and playing with the tassels of his red robe. The snow was whirling so fiercely outside his windows that he could scarcely see across the street, but within the air was deliciously soft and fragrant. He put the violets and jonquils on the taboret beside the couch, and threw himself down, with a long sigh, covering himself with a Roman blanket. He was thoroughly tired; he had been in such haste, he had stood up to such a strain, covered so much ground in the last twenty-four hours, that he wanted to think how it had all come about. Lulled by the sound of the wind, the warm air, and the cool fragrance of the flowers, he sank into deep, drowsy retrospection.

It had been wonderfully simple; when they had shut him out of the theatre and concert hall, when they had taken away his bone, the whole thing was virtually determined. The rest was a mere matter of opportunity. The only thing that at all surprised him was his own courage—for he realized well enough that he had always been tormented by fear, a sort of apprehensive dread that, of late years, as the meshes of the lies he had told closed about him, had been pulling the muscles of his body tighter and tighter. Until now, he could not remember the time when he had not been dreading something. Even when he was a little boy, it was always there—behind him, or before, or on either side. There had always been the shadowed corner, the dark place into which he dared not look, but from which something seemed always to be watching him—and Paul had done things that were not pretty to watch, he knew.

But now he had a curious sense of relief, as though he had at last thrown down the gauntlet to the thing in the corner.

Yet it was but a day since he had been sulking in the traces; but yesterday afternoon that he had been sent to the bank with Denny & Carson's deposit, as usual—but this time he was instructed to leave the book to be balanced. There was above two thousand dollars in checks, and nearly a thousand in the bank notes which he had taken from the book and quietly transferred to his pocket. At the bank he had made out a new deposit slip. His nerves had been steady enough to permit of his returning to the office, where he had finished his work and asked for a full day's holiday to-morrow, Saturday, giving a perfectly reasonable pretext. The bank book, he knew, would not be returned before Monday or Tuesday, and his father would be out of town for the next week. From the time he slipped the bank notes into his pocket until he boarded the night train for New York, he had not known a moment's hesitation. It was not the first time Paul had steered through treacherous waters.

How astonishingly easy it had all been; here he was, the thing done; and this time there would be no awakening, no figure at the top of the stairs. He watched the snow flakes whirling by his window until he fell asleep.

When he awoke, it was three o'clock in the afternoon. He bounded up with a start; half of one of his precious days gone already! He spent more than an hour in dressing, watching every stage of his toilet carefully in the mirror. Everything was quite perfect; he was exactly the kind of boy he had always wanted to be.

When he went downstairs, Paul took a carriage and drove up Fifth Avenue toward the Park. The snow had somewhat abated; carriages and tradesmen's wagons were hurrying soundlessly to and fro in the winter twilight; boys in woolen mufflers were shovelling off the doorsteps; the avenue stages made fine spots of colour against the white street. Here and there on the corners were stands, with whole flower gardens blooming under glass cases, against the sides of which the snow flakes stuck and melted; violets, roses, carnations, lilies of the valley—somehow vastly more lovely and alluring that they blossomed thus unnaturally in the snow. The Park itself was a wonderful stage winter-piece.

When he returned, the pause of the twilight had ceased, and the tune of the streets had changed. The snow was falling faster, lights streamed from the hotels that reared their dozen stories fearlessly up into the storm, defying the raging Atlantic winds. A long, black stream of carriages poured down the avenue, intersected here and there by other streams, tending horizontally. There were a score of cabs about the entrance of his hotel, and his driver had to wait. Boys in livery were running in and out of the awning stretched across the sidewalk, up and down the red velvet carpet laid from the door to the street.

Above, about, within it all was the rumble and roar, the hurry and toss of thousands of human beings as hot for pleasure as himself, and on every side of him towered the glaring affirmation of the omnipotence of wealth.

The boy set his teeth and drew his shoulders together in a spasm of realization; the plot of all dramas, the text of all romances, the nerve-stuff of all sensations was whirling about him like the snow flakes. He burnt like a faggot in a tempest.

When Paul went down to dinner, the music of the orchestra came floating up the elevator shaft to greet him. His head whirled as he stepped into the thronged corridor, and he sank back into one of the chairs against the wall to get his breath. The lights, the chatter, the perfumes, the bewildering medley of colour—he had, for a moment, the feeling of not being able to stand it. But only for a moment; these were his own people, he told himself. He went slowly about the corridors, through the writing-rooms, smoking-rooms, reception-rooms, as though he were exploring the chambers of an enchanted palace, built and peopled for him alone.

When he reached the dining-room he sat down at a table near a window. The flowers, the white linen, the many-coloured wine glasses, the gay toilettes of the women, the low popping of corks, the undulating repetitions of the *Blue Danube* from the orchestra, all flooded Paul's dream with bewildering radiance. When the roseate tinge of his champagne was added—that cold, precious bubbling stuff that creamed and foamed in his glass—Paul wondered that there were honest men in the world at all. This was what all the world was fighting for, he reflected; this was what all the struggle was about. He doubted the reality of his past. Had he ever known a place called Cordelia Street, a place where fagged-looking business men got on the early car; mere rivets in a machine they seemed to Paul,—sickening men, with combings of children's hair always hanging to their coats, and the smell of cooking in their clothes. Cordelia Street—Ah! that belonged to another time and country; had he not always been thus, had he not sat here night after night, from as far back as he could remember, looking pensively over just such shimmering textures, and slowly twirling the stem of a glass like this one between his thumb and middle finger? He rather thought he had.

He was not in the least abashed or lonely. He had no especial desire to meet or to know any of these people; all he demanded was the right to look on and conjecture, to watch the pageant. The mere stage properties were all he contended for. Nor was he lonely later in the evening, in his loge at the Metropolitan. He was now entirely rid of his nervous misgivings, of his forced aggressiveness, of the imperative desire to show himself different from his surroundings. He felt now that his surroundings explained him. Nobody questioned the purple; he had only to wear it passively. He had only to glance down at his attire to reassure himself that here it would be impossible for any one to humiliate him.

He found it hard to leave his beautiful sitting-room to go to bed that night, and sat long watching the raging storm from his turret window. When he went to sleep, it was with the lights turned on in his bedroom; partly because of his old timidity, and partly so that, if he should wake in the night, there would be no wretched moment of doubt, no horrible suspicion of yellow wall-paper, or of Washington and Calvin above his bed.

Sunday morning the city was practically snow-bound. Paul breakfasted late, and in the afternoon he fell in with a wild San Francisco boy, a freshman at Yale, who said he had run down for a "little flyer" over Sunday. The young man offered to show Paul the night side of the town, and the two boys went out together after dinner, not returning to the hotel until seven o'clock the next morning. They had started out in the confiding warmth of a champagne friendship, but their parting in the elevator was singularly cool. The freshman pulled himself together to make his train, and Paul went to bed. He awoke at two o'clock in the afternoon, very thirsty and dizzy, and rang for ice-water, coffee, and the Pittsburgh papers.

On the part of the hotel management, Paul excited no suspicion. There was this to be said for him, that he wore his spoils with dignity and in no way made himself conspicuous. Even under the glow of his wine he was never boisterous, though he found the stuff like a magician's wand for wonder-building. His chief greediness lay in his ears and eyes, and his excesses were not offensive ones. His dearest pleasures were the grey winter twilights in his sitting-room; his quiet enjoyment of his flowers, his clothes, his wide divan, his cigarette and his sense of power. He could not remember a time when he had felt so at peace with himself. The mere release from the necessity of petty lying, lying every day and every day, restored his self-respect. He had never lied for pleasure, even at school; but to be noticed and admired, to assert his difference from other Cordelia Street boys; and he felt a good deal more manly, more honest, even, now that he had no need for boastful pretensions, now that he could, as his actor friends used to say, "dress the part." It was characteristic that remorse did not occur to him. His golden days went by without a shadow, and he made each as perfect as he could.

On the eighth day after his arrival in New York, he found the whole affair exploited in the Pittsburgh papers, exploited with a wealth of detail which indicated that local news of a sensational nature was at a low ebb. The firm of Denny & Carson announced that the boy's father had refunded the full amount of the theft, and that they had no intention of prosecuting. The Cumberland minister had been interviewed, and expressed his hope of yet reclaiming the motherless lad, and his Sabbath-school teacher declared that she would spare no effort to that end. The rumour had reached Pittsburgh that the boy had been seen in a New York hotel, and his father had gone East to find him and bring him home.

Paul had just come in to dress for dinner; he sank into a chair, weak to the knees, and clasped his head in his hands. It was to be worse than jail, even; the tepid waters of Cordelia Street were to close over him finally and forever. The grey monotony stretched before him in hopeless, unrelieved years; Sabbath-school, Young People's Meeting, the yellow-papered room, the damp dish-towels; it all rushed back upon him with a sickening vividness. He had the old feeling that the orchestra had suddenly stopped, the sinking sensation that the play was over. The sweat broke out on his face, and he sprang to his feet, looked about him with his white, conscious smile, and winked at himself in the mirror. With something of the old childish belief in miracles with which he had so often gone to class, all his lessons unlearned, Paul dressed and dashed whistling down the corridor to the elevator.

He had no sooner entered the dining-room and caught the measure of the music than his remembrance was lightened by his old elastic power of claiming the moment, mounting with it, and finding it all sufficient. The glare and glitter about him, the mere scenic accessories had again, and for the last time, their old potency. He would show himself that he was game, he would finish the thing splendidly. He doubted, more than ever, the existence of Cordelia Street, and for the first time he drank his wine recklessly. Was he not, after all, one of those fortunate beings born to the purple, was he not still himself and in his own place? He drummed a nervous accompaniment to the Pagliacci music and looked about him, telling himself over and over that it had paid.

He reflected drowsily, to the swell of the music and the chill sweetness of his wine, that he might have done it more wisely. He might have caught an outbound steamer and been well out of their clutches before now. But the other side of the world had seemed too far away and too uncertain then; he could not have waited for it; his need had been too sharp. If he had to choose over again, he would do the same thing to-morrow. He looked affectionately about the dining-room, now gilded with a soft mist. Ah, it had paid indeed!

Paul was awakened next morning by a painful throbbing in his head and feet. He had thrown himself across the bed without undressing, and had slept with his shoes on. His limbs and hands were lead heavy, and his tongue and throat were parched and burnt. There came upon him one of those fateful attacks of clear-headedness that never occurred except when he was physically exhausted and his nerves hung loose. He lay still and closed his eyes and let the tide of things wash over him.

His father was in New York; "stopping at some joint or other," he told himself. The memory of successive summers on the front stoop fell upon him like a weight of black water. He had not a hundred dollars left; and he knew now, more than ever, that money was everything, the wall that stood between all he loathed and all he wanted. The thing was winding itself up; he had thought of that on his first glorious day in New York, and had even provided a way to snap the thread. It lay on his dressing-table now; he had got it out last night when he came blindly up from dinner, but the shiny metal hurt his eyes, and he disliked the looks of it.

He rose and moved about with a painful effort, succumbing now and again to attacks of nausea. It was the old depression exaggerated; all the world had become Cordelia Street. Yet somehow he was not afraid of anything, was absolutely calm; perhaps because he had looked into the dark corner at last and knew. It was bad enough, what he saw there, but somehow not so bad as his long fear of it had been. He saw everything clearly now. He had a feeling that he had made the best of it, that he had lived the sort of life he was meant to live, and for half an hour he sat staring at the revolver. But he told himself that was not the way, so he went downstairs and took a cab to the ferry.

When Paul arrived at Newark, he got off the train and took another cab, directing the driver to follow the Pennsylvania tracks out of the town. The snow lay heavy on the roadways and had drifted deep in the open fields. Only here and there the dead grass or dried weed stalks projected, singularly black, above it. Once well into the country, Paul dismissed the carriage and walked, floundering along the tracks, his mind a medley of irrelevant things. He seemed to hold in his brain an actual picture of everything he had seen that morning. He remembered every feature of both his drivers, of the toothless old woman from whom he had bought the red flowers in his coat, the agent from whom he had got his ticket, and all of his fellow-passengers on the ferry. His mind, unable to cope with vital matters near at hand, worked feverishly and deftly at sorting and grouping these images. They made for him a part of the ugliness of the world, of the ache in his head, and the bitter burning on his tongue. He stooped and put a handful of snow into his mouth as he walked, but that, too, seemed hot. When he reached a little hillside, where the tracks ran through a cut some twenty feet below him, he stopped and sat down.

The carnations in his coat were drooping with the cold, he noticed; their red glory all over. It occurred to him that all the flowers he had seen in the glass cases that first night must have gone the same way, long before this. It was only one splendid breath they had, in spite of their brave mockery at the winter outside the glass; and it was a losing game in the end, it seemed, this revolt against the homilies by which the world is run. Paul took one of the blossoms carefully from his coat and scooped a little hole in the snow, where he covered it up. Then he dozed a while, from his weak condition, seeming insensible to the cold.

The sound of an approaching train awoke him, and he started to his feet, remembering only his resolution, and afraid lest he should be too late. He stood watching the approaching locomotive, his teeth chattering, his lips drawn away from them in a frightened smile; once or twice he glanced nervously sidewise, as though he were being watched. When the right moment came, he jumped. As he fell, the folly of his haste occurred to him with merciless clearness, the vastness of what he had left undone. There flashed through his brain, clearer than ever before, the blue of Adriatic water, the yellow of Algerian sands.

He felt something strike his chest, and that his body was being thrown swiftly through the air, on and on, immeasurably far and fast, while his limbs were gently relaxed. Then, because the picture making mechanism was crushed, the disturbing visions flashed into black, and Paul dropped back into the immense design of things.

THE END

Abbreviations

MV   Magazine version:
"'A Death in the Desert,'"
Scribner's 33 (January 1903):
109–21.
"Paul's Case," *McClure's* 25 (May
1905): 74–83.
"The Sculptor's Funeral,"
McClure's 24 (January 1905):
329–36.
"A Wagner Matinee," *Everybody's
Magazine* 10 (February 1904):
324–26.

NS   *The Novels and Stories of Willa
Cather* (Boston: Houghton
Mifflin Co., 1937–41).

TG   *The Troll Garden* (New York:
McClure, Phillips and Co.,
1905).

YBM   *Youth and the Bright Medusa*
(New York: Alfred A. Knopf,
1920).

Notes to the Text

"Flavia and Her Artists"

7.24   Ecole des Chartes/ *École nationale des Chartes* is one of the French *grandes écoles* founded in 1821 to carry on the historical research of eighteenth-century savants. At the time Cather made use of it, the school trained librarians and archivists.

10.18   *aves rares*/ rare birds. Cather takes liberties with the Latin here, which should be *aves raras*, if Flavia intends it as the object (in accusative case) of the preposition "of."

10.33   like the suitors in the halls of Penelope/ An allusion to the faithful wife of Odysseus, who fended off a pack of suitors pending her husband's return from the Trojan War in Homer's *Odyssey*.

10.35   ambition hath a knapsack at his back/ This is an altered version of Ulysses' speech in Shakespeare's *Troilus and Cressida* 3.3.145–46: "Time hath, my lord, a wallet at his back, / Wherein he puts alms for oblivion."

17.8   Rolla/ The title character of a poem by Alfred de Musset (1810–57). Rolla lives a life of debauchery, then murders his illegitimate sister and commits suicide.

17.35   *Une Méduse*/ A Medusa, a reference to the Gorgon Medusa of Greek mythology, who was slain by Perseus.

17.38   Rudel of Tripoli/ Gauffre Rudel was not from Tripoli but was a twelfth-century French troubadour poet who is supposed to have searched the Middle East for the beautiful Princess of Tripoli. When he found her, he was so overcome by her beauty that he dropped dead, whereupon she had him buried and then entered a convent.

18.5   Mrs. Browning . . . Mme. Dudevant/ Although Elizabeth Barrett Browning hardly needs identification here, Amandine-Aurore-Lucie Dupin, Baronne Dudevant, the nineteenth-century French novelist, is better known under her pen name George Sand.

19.31   the Little Mermaid/ by Hans Christian Andersen

21.36   Maeterlinck/ Maurice Maeterlinck (1862–1949), Belgian poet and dramatist.

22.7   mother of the Gracchi/ A reference to the second-century B.C. Roman matron Cornelia, wife of Tiberius Sempronius Gracchus, by whom she had twelve children. After her husband's death she refused to remarry and devoted her time to the education of her sons, whom she presented as her jewels.

26.24   Lay of the Jabberwock/ The Jabberwock is a fictitious monster and the title of a poem in Lewis Carroll's *Through the Looking-Glass.*

26.26   Erl-King music/ *Erlkoenig,* songs by Schubert (1821) based on poems by Goethe.

30.17   seed of Banquo kings/ Allusion to the witches' prophecy in *Macbeth* 1.3.67: "Thou shalt get kings, though thou be none."

31.31   Gaius Marius among the ruins of Carthage/ Gaius Marius, although elected consul of Rome seven times and a great general, was banished by the Roman Senate late in his career, and when he tried to visit Carthage, the Roman governor refused to allow him to enter. In Plutarch's *Lives* he is reported to have told the governor's messenger: "Go tell him that you have seen Gaius Marius sitting in exile among the ruins of Carthage."

"The Sculptor's Funeral"

32.18 and   Grand Army and G.A.R./ The Grand Army of the Re-
33.8   public was the veterans organization for ex–Union Army

soldiers of the Civil War, founded in Decatur, Illinois, in 1866.

34.8–9   palm leaf/ The palm leaf here may signify that Harvey Merrick is an *officier d'académie*, a holder of the *palmes académiques* for distinguished instruction in sculpture. (Note the later reference to the palm leaf and his stay in France.)

35.20   Rogers Group/ John Rogers (1829–1904) was a popular American sculptor who specialized in creating small groups illustrating literary, historical, and humorous subjects. Thousands of small plaster copies of his groups were sold in the nineteenth-century.

42.22   wine when it was red/ Prov. 21:31–32: "Look not thou upon the wine when it is red, when it giveth his colour in the cup, *when* it moveth itself aright. At the last it biteth like a serpent, and stingeth like an adder" (King James Version).

"The Garden Lodge"

46.16   Freya/ The Norse goddess of love in Richard Wagner's *Das Rheingold*, without whose presence flowers wither and trees refuse to bear fruit.

50.6   Klingsor's garden/ Klingsor is the magician in whose enchanted garden the climactic battle of act 2 of Wagner's *Parsifal* takes place. Parsifal strikes Klingsor dead and ends the magician's evil power.

54.30   *Walküre/ Die Walküre* (1870) is the second opera in Wagner's *Ring of the Niebelungs*.

55.1   *Sieglinde/* The complications in *Die Walküre* result from the irresistible attraction between Sieglinde, the wife of Hunding, and her long-lost brother Siegmund.

"'A Death in the Desert'"

57   [title]/ The title of this story comes from a poem by Robert Browning.

57.9   Holdrege/ A person traveling directly west from Chi-
                cago would have taken the Union Pacific via Omaha,
                Grand Island, and Kearney, Nebraska, to Cheyenne.
                Cather's travelers are following the route that she and
                her brother took from Red Cloud to Cheyenne in 1898,
                which involved changing trains at Holdrege from the
                Burlington main line that went to Denver to a branch
                line that went into Cheyenne via Sterling, Colorado.

63.19   Camille entrance/ The allusion is to Alexander Dumas
                (fils), *La dame aux camelias* (1852), given in its English
                translation the title *Camille* for its doomed heroine whose
                pathetic story Cather thought one of the great
                nineteenth-century plays. Verdi's *La traviata* is based
                on the same play.

64.22   Gibbon's 'Decline and Fall'/ Edward Gibbon, *The His-
                tory of the Decline and Fall of the Roman Empire* (1776–
                88), one of the great historical works of the eighteenth-
                century. It actually appeared in six volumes.

65.3   *Rheingold/ Das Rheingold* (1869), the first opera in Rich-
                ard Wagner's *Ring of the Niebelungs*.

65.27   'an earthen vessel in love with a star'/This quotation
                may be a somewhat garbled version of "The desire of
                the moth for the star," a line that occurs in Shelley's "To
                ———," which is a love poem beginning: "One word is
                too often profaned."

67.12–13   'The Baggage Coach Ahead' and 'She is My Baby's
                Mother'/ These are fictitious titles.

70.3–4   Heine's 'Florentine Nights'/ Heinrich Heine (1797–1856),
                important German Romantic poet to whose work Cather
                was introduced by her Pittsburgh friend George Seibel
                in the 1890s.

72.3–4   "swift feet of the runners"/ This sounds like a para-
                phrase of the reference in Lucretius's *De rerum natura*
                to "the swift runners who hand over the lamp of life."
                Cather was fairly well read in Latin literature and at
                the beginning of her high school teaching career in
                Pittsburgh taught Latin.

72.18   Brunhilda/ Brunhilda is one of the Valkyries (warrior-

maidens) who protect Walhalla in Wagner's *Die Walküre*. She is the leading lady in the third *Ring* opera,
Siegfried, and becomes the wife of the protagonist.

73.20   *'and in the book we read . . . '*/ This is a free translation
of Francesca da Rimini's account of her tragic love affair
with Paolo in *The Divine Comedy*, *Inferno* 5.138: "quel
giorno più non vi leggemmo avante" ("that day we read
no farther"). Paolo and Francesca were reading a book
about Lancelot's love life when Paolo, overcome with
emotion, kissed Francesca passionately. Thereupon
Francesca recalls that they stopped reading.

75.12–14   *"For ever and for ever . . . "*/ Brutus speaks these lines in
Shakespeare's *Julius Caesar*, 5.1.117–19, just before
Cassius is killed and he commits suicide.

76.27   *lieber Freund*/ dear friend.

"The Marriage of Phædra"

83.25–26   *Roman de la Rose*/ Long French metrical romance of the
thirteenth-century embodying the ideals of courtly love,
part of which was translated by Chaucer.

83.26   Boccaccio and Amadis/ Giovanni Boccaccio (1313?–75),
Italian prose romancer and poet. Amadis is a romance
of chivalry, *Amadis de Gaula*, which probably originated in Portugal in the fourteenth-century.

83.37   Phædra/ In Greek mythology Phædra, the daughter of
King Minos of Crete, marries Theseus but falls in love
with Theseus's son Hippolytus. She hangs herself when
Hippolytus repulses her advances but before dying leaves
a scroll making false charges against him, an act that
causes Theseus to bring about the destruction of his son.

84.1   *heathenesse*/ A middle English word found in Chaucer,
for example, meaning the state of being a heathen.
Chaucer's spelling is *hethenesse*.

84.3   Charlemagne/ Charles the Great or Charles I (742–814),
king of the Franks.

84.4   Blanche of Castille/ (1187?–1252), daughter of Alfonso

IX, king of Castille, queen of France during the reign of Louis VIII, and later queen regent during the minority of her son Louis IX.

92.25   *sic transit gloria/ sic transit gloria mundi* ("so passes the glory of the earth").

"A Wagner Matinee"

96.26   *Euryanthe/* A now-forgotten opera by Carl Maria von Weber (1786–1826).

97.5   *Huguenots/* A popular nineteenth-century opera by Giacomo Meyerbeer (1791–1864).

97.23   *The Flying Dutchman/ Der Fliegende Holländer* (1841), one of Wagner's early operas.

98.30   *Tannhäuser/* Opera by Richard Wagner (1845).

99.21   *Tristan and Isolde/* One of Wagner's greatest operas (1865).

99.38   "Prize Song"/ The song by which Walter von Stolzing (tenor) wins the hand of Eva Pogner (soprano) in the song festival that concludes Wagner's one comic opera, *Die Meistersinger*.

100.11   Bayreuth/ After marrying Franz Liszt's daughter Cosima, Wagner settled in Bayreuth in 1870 and founded his own theater, which opened with the *Ring* in 1876. Cather never managed to spell Bayreuth correctly. It is "Baireuth" in MV, "Beyruth" in TG, and "Beyreuth" in YBM and NS.

100.24   *Trovatore/ Il trovatore*, an early opera (1853) by Giuseppe Verdi.

100.31   *Ring/ Der Ring des Nibelungen (The Ring of the Niebelungs)*, Wagner's cycle of four operas based on Northern European mythology found in the *Nibelungenlied*.

"Paul's Case"

104.21   *Faust/* Charles Gounod's popular opera first produced in Paris in 1859.

104.28	Raffaelli's gay studies/ Jean Francois Raffaelli (1850–1924), a very minor French impressionist.
104.34	Rico/ Martin Rico (1835–1908), Spanish landscape painter influenced by the French Barbizon school.
104.36	Augustus/ Cather clarifies this reference by adding "Caesar" to the text of YBM. Augustus (27 B.C.–A.D. 14) was the first Roman emperor. Paul was looking at a plaster cast of a bust or statue of Augustus.
104.37	Venus of Milo/ Venus de Milo, famous Greek statue of the Hellenistic Period, the original of which is in the Louvre.
106.24–25	*auf wiedersehen/* good-by.
110.39	*Martha/* Romantic opera by Friedrich von Flotow (1847).
111.1	*Rigoletto/* One of Verdi's most popular operas (1851).
116.22	*Blue Danube/* Famous waltz by Johann Strauss (1825–1899).
119.3	Pagliacci music/ This reference to Leoncavallo's well-known opera *I Pagliacci* (1892) is appropriately used, for Paul is playing a role that ends in tragedy, just as the strolling actors' performance does in the opera.

Textual Commentary

The aim of this edition is twofold: to produce an authoritative text of *The Troll Garden* (TG) as Willa Cather intended it to appear when it was published in 1905 and to record all of the revisions that took place in four of the seven stories in successive versions over a span of thirty-four years. Three of the stories ("Flavia and Her Artists," "The Garden Lodge," and "The Marriage of Phædra") were neither published in magazines before book publication nor ever reprinted in Cather's lifetime. Thus they exist in a unique printing in TG. On the other hand, "The Sculptor's Funeral," "'A Death in the Desert,'" "A Wagner Matinee," and "Paul's Case" all were first published in magazines (MV), revised for TG, further revised for inclusion in *Youth and the Bright Medusa* (YBM) in 1920, and all but one reworked for Cather's collected writings, *The Novels and Stories of Willa Cather* (NS) brought out between 1937 and 1941. The fourth story, "'A Death in the Desert,'" was omitted from NS. Thus there are four versions of three stories and three versions of one.

The problem of establishing the text for the three stories never reprinted is not difficult. Apparently no manuscripts exist, and there was only one printing of TG. There is no evidence that any corrections were ever made in the plates or corrected copies printed after the original issue. When the firm of McClure, Phillips and Company, the original publisher, was dissolved in 1906, the remainder of the edition was sold to Doubleday, Page and Company. Doubleday then issued the original McClure, Phillips sheets without even redoing the title page. Doubleday did, however, print its own name on the spine of the cover. This then is the second issue of the book.

All copies examined of the McClure, Phillips edition have a cancel as the title leaf for "The Marriage of Phædra" (11_6, pp. 155–56), whereas the second issue of the edition has this leaf integral. This condition means that a new gathering 11 was bound into the unbound sheets sold to Doubleday, Page and Company. There are no textual variants in the new gathering 11, however, and apparently only the defective title leaf that had required the insertion of a cancel in the copies issued by McClure, Phillips and Company was redone.

I have collated copies of *The Troll Garden* owned by the University of California, Davis, and the universities of Oregon, Idaho, and Colorado and found no textual variants. Joan Crane, Cather's bibliographer, has examined the four copies owned by the University of Virginia Library and also found no variants. All copies examined show the same type batter in lines 2, 4 of page 127 and such obvious misprints, as, for example, "his" for "this" (83.18), the omission of a question mark (76.12), the printing of "lodge" for "loge" (244.16), "least" for "lest" (226.4), and "offencive" for "offensive" (246.7). In fact, the text of TG was not very well proofread. There are in all some sixty-seven misspellings, typographical errors, inconsistencies, or omissions scattered throughout the book. All of them are errors that careful proofreading should have caught, and in editing the stories I have corrected these obvious lapses.

Cather began to find infelicities of style in her book as soon as it came out. The University of Virginia Library owns a presentation copy inscribed to an old friend, Mrs. A. K. Goudy, in which Cather made seven marginal emendations, all of which occur between pages 109 and 153. In editing this text I have incorporated all of these suggested changes.

The editing of the four stories that underwent revisions ("The Sculptor's Funeral," "'A Death in the Desert,'" "A Wagner Matinee," and "Paul's Case") presents more of a problem. W. W. Greg's theory of copy-text holds that the manuscript or first printing of a work supplies the most authoritative copy text for the accidentals (capitalization, spelling, punctuation), because in each subsequent reprinting of a text corruption takes place because of editorial meddling or typesetting carelessness. Greg's theory also calls for the incorporation into the copy text of all later substantive revisions that can be shown authorially sanctioned. The edited result then is an eclectic text unlike any that ever actually existed. Following Greg's theory for TG, then, an editor would select as copy-text the serial versions of "The Sculptor's Funeral," "A Wagner Matinee," "'A Death in the Desert,'" and

"Paul's Case," and the TG version of "Flavia and Her Artists," "The Garden Lodge," and "The Marriage of Phædra."

Nevertheless, I have rejected the magazine versions of the four stories previously printed in favor of TG as the copy-text for this entire edition. While no one would doubt that Cather was responsible for the hundreds of substantive revisions made between MV and TG, a case needs to be argued for adopting TG as the copy-text for the accidentals. I believe it can be demonstrated beyond reasonable doubt that Cather made the changes that resulted in the many variants existing between the accidentals of MV and TG. The demonstration has to rest on internal evidence, however, as there are no extant MSS either of the stories published serially or the stories published in TG. Nor are there any letters that throw light on the editing or printing of this material. The first point to note is that the accidentals in all seven stories in TG are consistent. It is clear that someone made an effort to achieve this uniformity, and the most likely person was Cather herself. The only possible copy-text for the three stories not previously published, as I have noted, is TG, and it seems inescapable that the text of the four MV stories showing the most consistency with the text of the three TG stories should be the copy-text. The scores of changes made in the accidentals of MV before book publication were made for the purpose of achieving uniformity in TG. Moreover, the stories published in magazines are not consistent with each other, a fact suggesting strongly that house style was imposed on Cather's texts when the stories appeared in magazines.

For example, in all seven stories in TG Cather regularly spells the *or* words (*honor, humor, favor, splendor, odor, arbor, labor,* and others) with a *u* (*honour, humour, favour,* and so forth). (This practice in TG is also consistent with Cather's practice in her later books.) The word *gray* in MV has been changed to *grey* in TG, and this spelling is consistent with the spelling *grey* in the stories that appear only in TG. Titles of such things as books, operas, and magazines appear consistently in italics in all the stories in TG, whereas these titles appear sometimes with and sometimes without quotation marks in the serial versions. Punctuation practices that differ between MV and TG also follow consistent patterns. For example, commas used in MV are replaced frequently by semicolons in TG. These occur in compound sentences that contain commas within the two independent clauses. They also occur in appositives attached to the ends of sentences. This latter practice is something of an idiosyncrasy in Cather, and the fact that it occurs consistently throughout TG argues strongly for authorial sanction for the accidentals in TG. There are in addition other punctuation changes that strongly suggest authorial revision. The dash, for example, that occurs in TG (127.18) replaces a comma in MV. The dash here has almost the effect of a substantive change, and it seems very unlikely that anyone but the author would have been responsible for it. Again, in TG (197.8) one finds "Franz-Joseph-Land" spelled with hyphens and with the "ph" on "Josef." If Cather had checked this region in an atlas, she would have found it listed as "Franz-Joseph Land" or "Franz Josef Land," which is indeed the way it appears in the *Everybody's Magazine* version of the story. One conjectures that "Franz-Joseph-Land" is the way the place originally appeared in Cather's MS submitted to the magazine and that an editor made the correction. Then when Cather prepared this story for book publication, she apparently let stand her original misspelling, which was repeated in YBM. A correct spelling did not appear until NS. It is unlikely that anyone but Cather was responsible for "Franz-Joseph-Land" in TG.

The internal evidence, I think, is overwhelming that the accidentals in all the stories of TG have authorial sanction and that the accidentals in MV are at best a collaboration between Cather and the editors of the magazines that published her stories. Thus the copytext for the accidentals should be TG. It is possible that some of the accidentals of TG may have been imposed by a McClure, Phillips editor, but there is no way of knowing which, if any, and one can assume that Cather had a chance, as is normal publishing practice, to read proof on her book and to accept changes or to restore original accidentals. It would be bizarre indeed to follow the accidentals of MV for four stories and TG for three, as this would result in the spelling of *humor* and *favor* and *gray*, for example, in the four stories originally published in magazines and *humour, favour,* and *grey* in the other three. And there would be similar inconsistencies in the punctuation, italics, and capitalization. Furthermore, it would have been impossible for Cather to make the extensive substantive changes she made in preparing her stories for book publication without recopying or retyping the entire MS. Thus she undoubtedly had a chance to rethink and redo her accidentals.

There are two possible texts for the stories printed in YBM: the 1920 edition and a 1945 reprinting when the book was reset and new plates were made. Cather could have made revisions for this new edition, but there is no evidence that she did. My collation of these two texts reveals no differences other than an occasional printer's error in the resetting. The 1920 text was apparently used as the printer's copy for the 1945 resetting.

Emendations

The following list records all changes in substantives and accidentals introduced here into the copy-text. The reading of the present edition appears to the left of the bracket; the source or sources of that reading come next in chronological order, followed by a semicolon. The copy-text reading then follows with its symbol and those symbols of another reading or other readings that may concur. After that, if necessary, come other variant readings in chronological order. Within an entry the curved dash (∼) represents the same word that appears before the bracket and is used in recording punctuation variants. The symbol N (New) indicates an emendation made for the first time in the present edition, and the symbol WC indicates a correction Cather made in her presentation copy to Mrs. Goudy (see Textual Commentary). *Om.* means that the reading to the left of the bracket is omitted in the text or texts cited to the right of the semicolon. An asterisk (*) indicates that the reading is discussed in the Notes on the Emendations. A slash through a hyphen (as in "cattle⁄farms") means that the word was divided at the end of a line.

"Flavia and Her Artists"

11.21	perseverance] N; perseverence TG
14.24	Willard";] N; ∼;" TG
15.27	exclusive] N; exculsive TG
15.37	purplish] N; purpleish TG
17.26	'Mes] N; "∼ TG
17.27	Femmes,'] N; ∼ ," TG

*17.30	madame] N; madam TG
*17.35	madame] N; madam TG
*18.10	madame] N; madam TG
23.25	Emile] N; Emil TG
24.6	futilely] N; futily TG
27.4	hate] N; heat TG
28.34	altogether] N; altogther TG
29.35	She] N; she TG
31.31	Gaius] N; Caius TG

"The Sculptor's Funeral"

*35.25	panels] MV, YBM, NS;~, TG
35.29	curls,] MV, YBM, NS;~TG
35.36	even;] MV, YBM, NS;~, TG
36.30	lawyer,] MV, YBM, NS;~TG
*39.24	word] TG, YBM, NS; wand MV
41.2	cattle-farms] YBM;~-/~MV, TG;~ranch NS
41.2	farms,] MV, YBM, NS;~TG
41.12	then?"] MV, YBM, NS;~." TG
41.20	'Cal] YBM; "~TG; '~. MV; "~NS
41.21	trunk.'"] MV, YBM;~." TG;~.'" NS
41.23	yet,] MV, YBM, NS;~TG
42.8	say,] MV, YBM, NS;~TG
43.20	civilization] MV, YBM, NS;~, TG
*44.28	this] MV, YBM, NS; his TG

"The Garden Lodge"

48.19	as] N; at TG
48.26	ebullitions] N; ebulitions TG
49.35	Street] N; street TG
54.35	duet] N; duett TG
55.2	repellent] N; repellant TG
56.19	self-respect so much. She could scarcely] WC; self-respect so much. As it was, she was without even the extenuation of an outer impulse, and she could scarcely TG

"'A Death in the Desert'"

*57.9	Holdrege] N; Holdridge TG; Holdredge MV, YBM
57.18	by] WC; *om.* TG, MV, YBM
*57.26	Holdrege] N; Holdridge TG; Holdredge MV, YBM
60.20	more] WC; *om.* MV, TG, YBM
*61.2	flicking] N; flecking MV, TG, YBM
62.22	which] WC; that MV, TG, YBM
63.32	eyes,] MV, YBM;~TG
64.21	bad. He has read] WC; bad. His English never offends me, and he MV, TG; *om.* YBM
74.7	shall] WC; will MV, TG, YBM
76.4	upon] WC; on MV, TG, YBM

"The Marriage of Phædra"

*77–20	*Phædra*] N; *Phœdra* TG
80–1	bus] N; buss TG
81.8	people] N; peoples TG
81.15	doesn't] N; dosen't TG
81.16	blandly.] N;~, TG
83.24	*Phædra*] N; *Phœdra* TG
83.34	*Phædra*] N; *Phœdra* TG
84.27	ring of] N; ring TG
85.17	*camera oscura*] N; camera obscura TG
85.20	*Phædra*] N; *Phœdra* TG
86.4	'aberdasher's] N; 'abberdasher's TG
87.26	*Phædra*] N; *Phœdra* TG
87.38	"she] N; "She TG
88.10	*Phædra*] N; *Phœdra* TG
88.34	*Phædra*] N; *Phœdra* TG
89.13	*Phædra*] N; *Phœdra* TG
90.29	time.'] N;~.'" TG
*90.30	day] N; *om.* TG
*90.35	in] N; *om.* TG
90.39	repeated.] N;~." TG
91.23	morning.'] N;~'."
93.16	*Phædra*] N; *Phœdra* TG

"A Wagner Matinee"

94.16	deep] MV, YBM, NS;~, TG
*95.9–10	Franz Josef Land] MV; Franz-Joseph-Land TG, YBM; Franz-Josef Land NS
95.31	farther] MV, YBM, NS; further TG
96.18	organ] MV, YBM, NS;~, TG
96.21	counting,] MV, YBM, NS;~TG
96.32	to] MV, YBM, NS; *om.* TG
97.3	tired] MV, YBM, NS; tried TG
97.7	her,] YBM, NS;~MV, TG
97.23	*Dutchman.*] YBM;~TG; Dutchman." MV; Dutchman.' NS
97.28	lest] MV, YBM, NS; least TG
*97.31	for more than] NS; for MV, TG, YBM
97.37	Brown Hotel] MV; Brown hotel TG, YBM; Brown Palace Hotel NS
98.8	counting,] MV, YBM, NS;~TG
98.30	*Tannhäuser*] N; *Tannhauser* TG, YBM; Tannhäuser MV; 'Tannhäuser' NS
99.29	*The*] YBM; the MV, TG, 'The NS (see 97.23)
100.10	cow-puncher] MV, YBM, NS;~⁄~TG
100.10	in] MV, YBM, NS; *om.* TG
100.11	Bayreuth] N; Beyruth TG; Baireuth MV; Beyreuth YBM, NS
100.20	Texas] MV, YBM, NS; Texan TG

"Paul's Case"

102.14	brilliancy,] MV, YBM, NS;~TG
104.28	Raffaelli] Raffelli TG, YBM, NS; *om.* MV
106.25	*wiedersehen,*] MV;~TG;~,—YBM;~—NS
*107.31	permeated] YBM, NS; penetrated MV, TG
107.38	night-shirt] MV; ~⁄~ TG, YBM; ~~ NS
108.14	lest] YBM, NS; least TG, MV
109.26	dissipated,] MV; '~,' YBM, NS;~TG
111.31	stage-struck] MV, YBM, NS; ~⁄~TG
111.39	button-holes] MV; ~⁄~TG, YBM; ~~NS
117.3	loge] YBM, NS; lodge TG; *loge* MV

117.12	sleep,] MV, YBM, NS;~TG
117.33	offensive] MV, YBM, NS; offencive TG
120.33	lest] MV, YBM, NS; least TG

Notes on the Emendations

"Flavia and Her Artists"

17.30, 35; 18.10	Three times Cather allowed "madam" to stand in her text; once she wrote "madame" (18.23). Because M. Roux is French, I believe Cather, if aware of this discrepancy, would have changed all uses of the word to the French spelling; thus I have adopted the final *e* in all instances. This decision is reinforced by Cather's use of "madame" in all three versions of the final paragraph of "'A Death in the Desert.'"

"The Sculptor's Funeral"

35.25	The comma at this point in TG is clearly an error, and because MV, YBM, and NS all omit it, I have emended the copy-text. In seventeen other instances like this one, I also have emended accidentals in the copy-text.
39.24	word] Cather wrote in MV ". . . if ever a man had the magic wand in his finger-tips, it was Merrick." I suspect that "wand" became "word" by typographical error in TG. Then later when Cather revised the TG text for inclusion in YBM, she discovered the error and decided to let it stand on grounds that the change converted a trite metaphor into a much more complex and interesting one. This is something like the printer's error that produced "soiled fish of the sea" in Melville's *White-Jacket*.
44.28	The "his" in TG is clearly an error, and because MV, YBM, and NS all correct this error, I have emended the copy-text. In nine other similar instances I have made substantive emendations.

"'A Death in the Desert'"

57.9, 26   Holdrege, Nebraska, has been given its correct spelling (see also Notes to the Text). "Holdridge" in TG is probably a typographical error. Cather must have thought there was a second "d" in the name, as she spelled it "Holdredge" in MV, YBM, and NS, and never bothered to look it up. She spelled it correctly in a letter she wrote Mrs. George Seibel from there while waiting to change trains on 20 August 1898.

61.2   Although "flecking" went through all three versions of this story, it clearly is the wrong word in this context.

"The Marriage of Phædra"

77.20   Scrutiny of the copy-text and consultation with the book designer indicates that the italic digraph æ in "Phædra" was most probably set as the italic digraph œ. In many fonts the two are barely distinguishable with a magnifying glass, and the copy-text has no other italic digraphs of æ or œ that would permit comparison that would certify exact identification.

90.30   Whether the insertion of "day" is correct or not is conjectural; the "that" might have been mistaken by the typesetter for "then," in which case there would have been no omission. If the "that" is correct, something must have been omitted. Possibly the sentence should have begun "From that time on . . . "

90.35   Here I have supplied "in" to make sense out of "things general."

"A Wagner Matinee"

95.9–10   See discussion of this reading in the Textual Commentary. I have adopted the spelling of geographical places that one finds in standard atlases, even though Cather consistently misspelled some of them, such as "Josef" here, "Bayreuth," Germany, and "Holdrege," Nebraska, elsewhere.

97.31   Here I have adopted a substantive revision made when Cather prepared her stories for her collected works. The addition of "more than" corrects an error in the story's chronology, as 95.30 says that the narrator's aunt had not been more than fifty miles from the homestead for thirty years.

"Paul's Case"

107.31   I have adopted the substantive from YBM and NS because I conclude that Cather simply used the wrong word in MV and TG and did not catch the error until she revised TG for YBM. Because both the story and the book were in press at about the same time, it is not surprising to find "penetrated" unchanged in both MV and TG.

Table of Revisions

The following pages record the evolution of the four stories that went through successive revisions over a period of many years. Substantive changes only are listed. The readings are arranged in chronological order: magazine version (MV), *The Troll Garden* (TG), *Youth and the Bright Medusa* (YBM), and *The Novels and Stories* (NS). When substantive readings from two or three versions are identical but the accidentals differ, I have recorded the accidentals from TG, using the 1905 edition. However, the revisions are keyed to the presently established text in the following table.

"The Sculptor's Funeral"

32.8	open MV, TG, YBM; open (they never buttoned them) NS
32.24	which MV; that TG, YBM, NS
33.9	shuffled back to MV, TG; rejoined YBM, NS
33.21–22	often stirred in his boyhood the man who was coming home to-night MV; often stirred the man who was coming home to-night, in his boyhood TG, YBM; often, in his boyhood, stirred the man who was coming home to-night NS
33.23	out of MV; from out TG, YMB, NS
33.26	still, pale MV; pale TG, YBM, NS
33.34	spare MV, TG; *om.* YBM, NS

33.38   and shuffled MV, TG; *om.* YBM, NS
34.2   body MV, TG, YBM; remains NS
34.13   Bostonian MV, TG, YBM; stranger NS
35.22   some horrible MV, TG; a YBM, NS
35.24   painfully about over MV, TG; at YBM, NS
35.27   have conceivably MV; conceivably have TG, YBM, NS
35.29   over MV; above TG, YBM, NS
36.20   orgy of grief MV, TG, YBM; behaviour NS
36.21   *om.* MV; so TG, YBM, NS
36.23   with a cry MV, TG; *om.* YBM, NS
36.31   trembling and MV, TG; *om.* YBM, NS
36.35   beautiful and chaste repose which MV, TG; repose YBM, NS
37.2   and holy MV, TG; *om.* YBM, NS
37.8   ever MV, TG, YBM; just NS
38.9–10   for demonstrative piety and ingenious cruelty MV, TG; *om.* YBM, NS
38.12   so MV, TG; *om.* YBM, NS
38.15   true and MV, TG; *om.* YBM, NS
38.27–28   Oh, he comprehended well enough now the gentle bitterness MV; Oh, he comprehended well enough now the quiet bitterness TG, YBM; *om.* NS
38.28–29   of the smile that he had seen so often on his master's lips MV, TG, YBM; *om.* NS
38.30   He remembered that once MV, TG; Once YBM, NS
38.31   feeling and MV, TG, YBM; *om.* NS
38.34   sustained MV; held up TG, YBM, NS
39.3   red beard MV; beard TG, YBM, NS
39.4   he MV, TG; Jim Laird YBM, NS
39.12   sure-footed MV, TG; sure YBM, NS
39.20   tastes were refined beyond the limits of the reasonable—whose mind was MV, TG; mind was to become YBM, NS
39.21   impressions MV, YBM, NS; impressions, and TG
39.24   wand MV; word TG, YBM, NS
39.25–27   liberated it from enchantment and restored it to its pristine loveliness, like the Arabian prince who fought the enchantress spell for spell MV, TG; liberated it from

enchantment and restored it to its pristine loveliness YBM; *om.* NS

| 39.27–29 | Upon whatever he had come in contact with, he had left a beautiful record of the experience—a sort of ethereal signature; a scent, a sound, a colour that was his own MV, TG, YBM; *om.* NS |

39.32   these MV, TG; anything else YBM, NS

40.1   doubtless; as for me MV, TG; *om.* YBM, NS

40.7   room MV; dining-room TG, YBM, NS

40.10   table MV; side table TG, YBM, NS

41.2   dozen cattle-farms MV, TG, YBM; cattle ranch NS

41.13   Every one chuckled MV, TG; The company laughed discreetly YBM, NS

41.22   gleefully MV, TG; *om.* YBM, NS

41.29   he argued that sunset was oncommon fine MV, TG; *om.* YBM, NS

41.32   trapseing to Paris and all such folly MV, TG; nonsense YBM, NS

42.9   The wings of the Victory, in there"—with a weak gesture toward his studio—"will not shelter me MV, TG; *om.* YBM, NS

42.22   red, also variegated MV, TG, YBM; red NS

42.26   His red face was convulsed with anger, and MV, TG; *om.* YBM, NS

42.31   gently MV, TG; *om.* YBM, NS

43.15   boys, worse luck MV, TG; boys YBM, NS

43.27   Nimrod, here MV, TG; Nimrod YBM, NS

43.38   in dead MV; dead in TG, YBM, NS

44.8   old MV, TG; *om.* YBM, NS

44.11–12   and that's why I'm not afraid to plug the truth home to you this once MV, TG; *om.* YBM, NS

44.20–21   doing his great work and MV, TG; *om.* YBM, NS

44.21   big MV, TG, YBM; *om.* NS

44.24–25   Harvey Merrick wouldn't have given one sunset over your marshes for all you've got put together, and you know it MV, TG, YBM; *om.* NS

44.27   genius MV, TG, YBM; man like Harvey NS

44.35   had found MV; had had TG, YBM, NS

"'A Death in the Desert'"

Note—Cather's character Everett Hilgarde in TG and
YBM is named Windermere Hilgarde in MV. There are
fifty-nine instances in which this name has been changed
throughout the story. The following table of revisions
does not record this particular emendation unless it is
part of other substantive revisions.

57.10	only other MV; only TG, YBM
57.20	were kept alive only by continual hypodermic injections of water from the tank where the engines were watered MV; made TG, YBM
58.26	on MV; upon TG, YBM
58.38	Windermere MV; Everett TG; him YBM
59.13–14	Suddenly the MV, TG; the YBM
59.23–24	by women, but this cry out of the night had shaken him MV, TG; from women YBM
59.29	of nervous MV; of TG, YBM
60.1	Mr. Hilgarde MV, TG; *om.* YBM
60.2	apologize. MV, TG; explain. YBM
60.4	the MV, TG; an YBM
60.5	apology, and I make it to you most sincerely MV; apology." TG, YBM
60.6	on MV; of TG, YBM
60.12	Now it's you who have given me a turn MV, TG; *om.* YBM
60.14	said Gaylord, grimly filling MV, TG; Gaylord grimly filled YBM
60.15	knew MV, TG; know YBM
60.17	No, I had never heard a word of that MV, TG; No YBM
60.20–21	There are many [more] reasons why I should be concerned than I can tell you MV; There are many [more] reasons why I am concerned than I can tell you TG; *om.* YBM
60.24	I hate to ask you, but she's so set on it. MV, TG; She's set on it. YBM
60.26	"I can go now, and it will give me real pleasure to do so," MV, TG; "At once then. YBM

60.27   Windermere, quickly MV; Everett, quickly TG; *om.* YBM

60.31   You see MV, TG; *om.* YBM

60.36   pupils, and that when MV, TG; pupils. When YBM

60.37   turned my head sadly MV, TG; quite turned my head YBM

60.38–61.2   quite engrossed by his grief. He was wrought up to the point where his reserve and sense of proportion had quite left him, and his trouble was the one vital thing in the world. MV, TG; entirely taken up by his grief. YBM

61.6–7   where she went up like lightning MV, TG; *om.* YBM

61.11   very MV, TG; *om.* YBM

61.11   that you are MV, TG; you're YBM

61.19   you know MV, TG; *om.* YBM

61.21   days until the end MV; days TG, YBM

61.23   all MV, TG; *om.* YBM

61.25   and that to go East would be dying twice MV, TG; *om.* YBM

61.30   sleep!" He stopped with a gulp and half closed his eyes. MV; sleep!" TG, YBM

61.33–39   and the brakeman's frank avowal of sentiment. Presently Gaylord went on:

             "You can understand how she has outgrown her family. We're all a pretty common sort, railroaders from away back. My father was a conductor. He died when we were kids. Maggie, my other sister, who lives with me, was a telegraph operator here while I was getting my grip on things. We had no education. MV, TG; *om.* YBM.

61.39   *om.* MV; to speak of TG; *om.* YBM

61.39–62.7   I have to hire a stenographer because I can't spell straight—the Almighty couldn't teach me to spell. The things that make up life to Kate are all Greek to me, and there's scarcely a point where we touch any more, except in our recollections of the old times when we were all young and happy together, and Kate sang in a church choir in Bird City. But I believe, Mr. Hilgarde, that if she can see just one person like you, who knows about the things and people MV, TG; *om.* YBM

actly as Adriance would have had them. MV; personality. TG, YBM

63.1 thoroughly sophisticated and MV, TG; *om.* YBM

63.5–7 and the bravado of her smile could not conceal the shadow of an unrest that was almost discontent. MV, TG; *om.* YBM

63.7 discontent. Perhaps that, too, was only the scar of the struggle of which her brother had spoken; perhaps the long warfare against adverse conditions had brought about an almost antagonistic and distrustful attitude of mind. MV; discontent. TG; *om.* YBM

63.9 sunlight; generous, fearless MV; sunlight TG, YBM

63.10 glowed with sympathy and good cheer for all living things MV; glowed with TG; glowed with a perpetual YBM

63.10 Her head, Windermere MV; Her head, Everett TG; *om.* YBM

63.11–14 remembered as peculiarly well shaped and proudly poised. There had been always a little of the imperatrix about her, and her pose in the photograph revived all his old impressions of her unattachedness, of how absolutely and valiantly she stood alone. MV, TG; *om.* YBM

63.20 with the cough MV, TG; *om.* YBM

63.25 disguise MV; conceal TG, YBM

63.26 emaciated MV, TG; *om.* YBM

63.28 nor MV; or TG, YBM

63.30 touch as water-flowers. Her chest, that full, proud singer's chest, that had swelled like the bellows of an organ when she took her high notes, was fallen and flat. MV; touch. TG, YBM

63.35 arranging MV; to arrange TG, YBM

63.36 "I know I'm not an inspiring object to look upon MV, TG; "Of course I'm ill, and I look it YBM

64.6 not content with reading the prayers for the sick MV, TG; *om.* YBM

64.8–9 Of course, he disapproves of my profession, and I think he takes it for granted that I have a dark past. MV, TG; *om.* YBM

64.10 vocation MV, TG; profession YBM

64.11–13 condoning it, you know—and trying to patch up my peace with my conscience by suggesting possible noble uses for what he kindly calls my talent." MV, TG; *om.* YBM

64.14   Windermere MV; Everett TG; *om.* YBM

64.14–18   laughed. "Oh! I'm afraid I'm not the person to call after such a serious gentleman—I can't sustain the situation. At my best I don't reach higher than low comedy. Have you decided to which one of the noble uses you will devote yourself?"

Katharine lifted her hands in a gesture of renunciation and MV, TG; *om.* YBM

64.19   went on MV; exclaimed TG; *om.* YBM

64.19–20   "I'm not equal to any of them, not even the least noble. I didn't study that method. MV, TG; *om.* YBM

64.20   method. Neither Marchesi nor your brother taught me the moral purpose of singing the scales." MV; method. TG; *om.* YBM

64.21   Katharine laughed indulgently MV; She laughed and went on nervously TG; *om.* YBM

64.21–23   "The parson's not so bad. His English never offends me, and he has read Gibbon's 'Decline and Fall,' all five volumes, and that's something. Then, he has been to New York, and that's a great deal. MV, TG; *om.* YBM

64.27–28   Who conspicuously walks the Rialto now, and what does he or she wear? MV, TG; *om.* YBM

64.29–30   on the Garden Theatre MV, TG; *om.* YBM

64.30   vestal MV, TG; *om.* YBM

64.32   above MV; about TG, YBM

64.34–35   I love MV; I'm homesick for TG; *om.* YBM

64.35   it all, from the Battery to Riverside MV, TG; *om.* YBM

65.1   on the back of an old envelope he found in his pocket MV, TG; *om.* YBM

65.9–10   and he felt as though a crisis of some sort had been met and tided over MV, TG; *om.* YBM

65.13   Napoleon—there's no possibility of living up to the part. I really believe it kept me out of a scrape or two when I was in college, and MV; Napoleon—But TG, YBM

65.16   smiled and MV, TG; *om.* YBM

65.19   if they paid you back in your own coin MV, TG; *om.* YBM

66.35	as nearly an Arab as possible MV, TG; an Arab YBM
66.36–38	Probably he was playing Arab to himself all the time. I remember he was a sixteenth-century duke in Florence once for weeks together MV, TG; *om.* YBM
67.2	that."

"Well, he had a piano carted out into the desert somehow, and was living in a tent beside a dried water-course grown up with dwarf oleanders. MV; that." TG, YBM

67.6	a letter MV, TG; an envelope YBM
67.6	about MV, TG; *om.* YBM
67.7–8	It's chiefly about his new opera which is to be brought out in London next winter. MV, TG; *om.* YBM
67.9–10	"I think I shall keep it as a hostage, so that I may be sure you will come again. MV, TG; "Thanks. I shall keep it as a hostage. YBM
67.11–13	For nine months I have heard nothing but 'The Baggage Coach Ahead' and 'She is My Baby's Mother.'" MV, TG; *om.* YBM
67.16	consisted. Windermere was not even a handsome man, and everyone admitted that his brother was. Katharine MV; consisted. She TG; *om.* YBM
67.16–17	She told herself that it was very much as though a sculptor's finished work had been rudely copied in wood. MV, TG; *om.* YBM
67.18–19	his shoulders were broad and heavy, while those of his brother were slender and rather girlish. MV, TG; much heavier. YBM
67.20	But it MV, TG; It YBM
67.26	face that was MV, TG; face YBM
67.29	words or music, and responded to the nerve-centres of his sensitive brain as the keyboard to the touch. MV; words. TG, YBM
67.30–31	had once said of him MV, TG; once said YBM
67.31	sang under the oaks MV; sang TG, YBM
67.32–33	and the comparison had been appropriated by a hundred shyer women who preferred to quote. MV, TG; *om.* YBM
67.34	As Windermere MV; As Everett TG; Everett YBM
67.35	night, he was MV, TG; night YBM
67.35	to random MV, TG; of mournful YBM

67.38–68.1	and had long disturbed his bachelor dreams. He was painfully timid in everything relating to the emotions, and his hurt had withdrawn him from the society of women. MV, TG; *om.* YBM
68.4	He bethought himself of something MV, TG; *om.* YBM
68.4	something that Stevenson had said MV; something he had read about TG; *om.* YBM
68.4–6	"sitting by the hearth and remembering the faces of women without desire," and felt himself an octogenarian. MV, TG; *om.* YBM
68.11–12	after the last number, watching the roses go MV, TG; and the flowers went YBM
68.15	song, as he had read in some Greek lyric. MV; song. TG, YBM
68.16–17	a circle of flame set about those splendid children of genius. MV, TG; *om.* YBM
68.19	resolving MV, TG; resolved YBM
68.20–21	and realizing more keenly than ever before how far this glorious world of MV, TG; *om.* YBM
68.21	of production and MV; of TG; *om.* YBM
68.21	beautiful creations lay MV, TG; *om.* YBM
68.21–22	beyond the prow of the merchant marines. MV; from the paths of men like himself. TG; *om.* YBM
68.21–22	He told himself that he had in common with this woman only the baser uses of life. MV, TG; *om.* YBM
68.22	life. That sixth sense, the passion for perfect expression, and the lustre of her achievement were like a rosy mist veiling her, such as the goddesses of the elder days wrapped about themselves when they vanished from the arms of men. MV; life. TG. *om.* YBM
68.25	passed as swiftly as the sands through an hour-glass. MV; passed swiftly. TG, YBM
68.28–29	and in the evening he sat in his room writing letters or reading. MV, TG; *om.* YBM
68.30	*om.* MV; he reflected TG, YBM
68.34	Windermere Hilgarde MV; Everett TG, YBM
68.34	life, and whatever career he embarked upon he drifted back always to the same harbor, refused by the high seas, and found himself doing the work of all his several

friends and serving every purpose save his own. MV; life. TG, YBM

69.7   he felt Katharine Gaylord's need for him and MV, TG; *om.* YBM

69.9   demands on him grow more imperious, her MV, TG; *om.* YBM

69.12   *om.* MV, YBM; and smaller TG

69.12   he saw MV, TG; *om.* YBM

69.13–14   He understood all that his physical resemblance meant to her. MV, TG; *om.* YBM

69.16   trick MV; illusion TG, YBM

69.17–18   her disease fed upon it; that it sent MV, TG; *om.* YBM

69.18   a shudder MV; shudders TG; *om.* YBM

69.18   of remembrance through her MV, TG; *om.* YBM

69.18–19   her and quickened nerves that the grave had already chilled; that all the womanhood in her cried out for this MV; her and TG; *om.* YBM

69.22–23   The question which most perplexed him was, "How much shall I know? How much does she wish me to know?" MV, TG; *om.* YBM

69.25   had MV, TG; *om.* YBM

69.28–30   His phrases took the colour of the moment and the then present condition, so that they never savoured of perfunctory compliment or frequent usage. MV, TG; *om.* YBM

69.30   always MV, TG; *om.* YBM

69.31   effluvium MV; suggestion TG, YBM

70.2   school-girl MV, TG; girl YBM

70.5   as Heine did MV, TG; *om.* YBM

70.6   and looked searchingly up into his face MV, TG; *om.* YBM

70.10–12   "Why, what have I done now?" he asked, lamely, "I can't remember having sent you any stale candy or champagne since yesterday." MV, TG; *om.* YBM

70.14   copy of *"Fort comme la Mort"* MV; book TG, YBM

70.18   a pastoral MV; the new TG, YBM

70.19   the most ambitious thing he has ever done MV, TG; *om.* YBM

70.20   though it looks horribly intricate MV, TG; *om.* YBM

70.23   sat MV; reclined TG, YBM

70.23   her, and, playing with the lace on her sleeve, he MV;
             her. He TG, YBM
70.25   and beautiful and MV; and TG, YBM
70.29   Lindaraxa. In the orange and box and citron trees about
             him the nightingales were singing all the unwritten and
             unwritable music in the world, and "*Je pense à mon amie*,"
             he wrote. MV; Lindaraxa. TG, YBM
70.35   The subtleties of Arabic decoration had cast an unholy
             spell over him MV, TG; *om.* YBM.
70.36   and Christian art and the brutal exaggerations of Gothic
             architecture here no more for him. The soul of Théo-
             phile Gautier had entered into him, and Western civili-
             zation was a bad dream, easily forgotten. MV; and the
             brutal exaggerations of Gothic art were a bad dream,
             easily forgotten. TG; *om.* YBM
70.37–39   The Alhambra itself had, from the first, seemed per-
             fectly familiar to him, and he knew that he must have
             trod that court, sleek and brown and obsequious, cen-
             turies before Ferdinand rode into Andalusia. MV, TG;
             om. YBM
71.2–4   and of her own work, still so warmly remembered and
             appreciatively discussed everywhere he went. MV, TG;
             om. YBM
71.5   the letter MV, TG; it YBM
71.8   wanted. He wondered whether all the gift-bearers, all
             the sons of genius, broke what they touched and blighted
             what they caressed thus. MV; wanted. TG, YBM
71.13   quietly, and Windermere felt in her voice the softness
             of the south wind in the spring. MV; quietly. TG, YBM
71.17   the dear boyishness that MV, TG; what YBM
71.20   I have often felt so about him myself. MV, TG; *om.* YBM
71.21   those creative MV; those TG, YBM
71.23   the feverish earnestness of her speech MV; feverish
             earnestness TG, YBM
71.25–26   He can kindle marble, strike fire from putty, but is it
             worth what it costs him?" MV, TG; *om.* YBM
71.26   Certainly there is a sacred and dignified selfishness which
             properly belongs to art and religion. You know how he
             wastes his time and strength in those idiotic social ob-

ligations which he takes so seriously—in chivalrous attentions to vapid old women who knew his mother, and in writing wedding-marches for every pink-and-white thing who asks him." MV; him?" TG; *om.* YBM

71.27   alarmed MV, TG; now alarmed YBM

71.29   movement of the sonata MV; movement TG, YBM

71.30   his lofty and MV; his TG, YBM

71.31   was dedicated to Brahms, and was the most classic work MV; was the most ambitious work TG, YBM

71.31   time. It marked, indeed MV; time, and marked TG, YBM

71.32   purely MV, TG; early YBM

71.33   style by which he will live MV; style TG, YBM

71.33   intelligently, without the least affectation of virtuosity, but MV; intelligently and TG, YBM

71.33   that MV; a TG, YBM

71.37   grown! Heavens, how he has grown!" MV; grown!" TG, YBM

71.37   cried. "This thing is entirely great. There is not a trace of that persistent saccharine quality that was always creeping into his earlier work. The theme, the whole conception, is big, and serene. How firm the texture is! and surely he never wrote such harmonies before. MV; cried. TG, YBM

71.39–72.1   the soul, the shadow co-existent with the soul. This is the tragedy of MV, TG; *om.* YBM

72.2   spent by the white race course MV; spent by the race-course TG; *om.* YBM

72.5   straining MV, TG; *om.* YBM

72.6   quickly MV, TG; *om.* YBM

72.7–8   before given voice to the bitterness of her own defeat beyond an occasional ironic jest. MV; before, beyond an occasional ironic jest, given voice to the bitterness of her own defeat. TG, YBM

72.9–10   and to see it going sickened him. MV, TG; *om.* YBM

72.12   We mustn't speak of that; it's too tragic and too vast." MV, TG; *om.* YBM

72.13   the MV; a TG, YBM

72.15   be so ungenerous MV, TG; *om.* YBM

72.15–16   the watches of MV, TG; *om.* YBM

72.16–21   Now you may mix me another drink of some sort. For-
            merly, when it was not *if* I should ever sing Brunhilda,
            but quite simply when I *should* sing Brunhilda, I was
            always starving myself, and thinking what I might drink
            and what I might not. But broken music-boxes may drink
            whatsoever they list, and no one cares whether they
            lose their figure. MV, TG; *om.* YBM
72.21–22   shepherd-boy theme at the beginning again MV; theme
            at the beginning again TG; theme at the beginning again,
            will you? YBM
72.22   That at least is not new. MV, TG; *om.* YBM
72.25–26   and the paleness of the Adriatic oppressed him MV, TG;
            om. YBM
72.26   winter, and MV, TG; winter. He YBM
72.27   the theme MV, TG; his idea, I suppose YBM
72.30   I was in Nice filling a concert engagement MV, TG; I
            was singing at Monte Carlo YBM
73.1   so MV, TG; *om.* YBM
73.2   not gay, as he usually is, but just contented and tired
            MV, TG; *om.* YBM
73.4–5   for the pain of all the world MV, TG; *om.* YBM
73.5–6   branches of the shivering olives MV, TG; garden YBM
73.6   palace. There was a concert piano in the room, and he
            played that prelude of Chopin's with the ceaseless pelt-
            ing of rain-drops in the bass. He wrote it, you know,
            when George Sand carried him off to Majorca and shut
            him up in a damp grotto in the hill-side, and it rained
            forever and ever, and he had only goat's milk to drink.
            Adriance had been to Majorca, you know, and had slept
            in their grotto. MV; palace. TG, YBM
73.8   fire which MV, TG; fire. It YBM
73.8   upon the hard features of the bronze Dante MV, TG; on
            the black walls and floor YBM
73.9–10   flames, and threw long black shadows about us MV, TG;
            flame YBM
73.10   all. How heavy and impenetrable were those shadows!
            quite like the darkness of the under world, where it will
            be resting time indeed, and the last strokes will have
            been put to the last score, and we shall all be together,

resting in the common darkness, after it is all over. Suddenly Adriance stopped playing and MV; all. Adriance TG, YBM

73.20   returned from Paris MV; returned TG, YBM

73.23   like a mask MV, TG; *om.* YBM

73.24   even MV, TG; *om.* YBM

73.24   completely MV, TG; *om.* YBM

73.26   Sometimes, while looking at the mask she wore, Windermere had thought of Richard's lines, "the shadow of my sorrow hath destroyed the shadow of my face." He MV; Everett TG, YBM

73.27   and sat looking at the rug MV, TG; *om.* YBM

73.29–30   with a long-drawn sigh of relief; and lying perfectly still, she went on MV, TG; *om.* YBM

73.32–35   I used to want to shriek it out to the world in the long nights when I could not sleep. It seemed to me that I could not die with it. It demanded some sort of expression. And now that MV, TG; *om.* YBM

73.35   do know MV; know TG; *om.* YBM

73.35   you would scarcely believe how much less sharp the MV, TG; *om.* YBM

73.36   agony MV; anguish TG; *om.* YBM

74.1–5   I flatter myself that I have been able to conceal it when I chose, though I suppose women always think that. The more observing ones may have seen, but discerning people are usually discreet and often kind, for we usually bleed a little before we begin to discern. But I wanted you to know; MV, TG; *om.* YBM

74.8   for we none of us dare to pity MV; for we none of us dare pity TG; *om.* YBM

74.8–9   Since it was what my life has chiefly meant, I should like him to know. On the whole, I am not ashamed of it. I have fought a good fight." MV, TG; *om.* YBM

74.15   and is miserable about it MV, TG; *om.* YBM

74.15–16   every one MV, TG; every woman YBM

74.16–18   Granted youth and cheerfulness, and a moderate amount of wit and some tact, and Adriance will always be glad to see you coming round the corner. MV, TG; *om.* YBM

74.22–23   I have pretty well used up my life up at standing pun-
            ishment. MV, TG; *om.* YBM
74.27   him. His early music was the first that ever really took
            hold of me. When I was a child out in Iowa, and Charley
            was braking on the road, I used to lie out under the
            apple trees and dream about him. I had seen his picture
            in some magazine or other, and I always fancied him in
            Paris leading the gilded existence of a Ouida hero. I had
            a tough pull to get started; it was a long jump from Bird
            City to Chicago, and a longer one from Chicago to New
            York. MV; him. TG, YBM
74.32   may never be to your glory in this world, perhaps MV,
            TG; *om.* YBM
74.33   but it will stand to your credit in the land to which I
            travel. I wax quotational. MV; but TG; *om.* YBM
74.33–34   it's been the mercy of heaven to me and it MV, TG; *om.*
            YBM
74.35   be. 'Unto one of the least of these,' you remember." MV;
            be. TG, YBM
74.36   Windermere MV; Everett TG; He YBM
74.38   met MV, TG; knew YBM
75.2   the tragedy of life MV; of tragedy TG; tragedy YBM
75.2–3   God knows: don't show me any more just as the curtain
            is going down. No, no, MV, TG; *om.* YBM
75.5–7   If some fancy of that sort had been left over from boy-
            hood, this would rid you of it, and that were well. MV,
            TG; *om.* YBM
75.8   will you not?" MV, TG; *om.* YBM
75.9   that lifted the mask from her soul MV, TG; *om.* YBM
75.10   courage and sadness, hope MV; courage TG, YBM
75.10   *om.* MV; as TG, YBM
75.25   aroused MV, TG; roused YBM
75.27   the roughness MV; the delays and the roughness TG,
            YBM
75.27   road, and to declare that she would never travel by that
            line again. MV; road. TG, YBM
75.31   on the foot of the bed, MV, TG; *om.* YBM
75.33–34   smiling and debonair, with his boyish face and the touch

	of silver grey in his hair. MV, TG; *om.* YBM
75.35	roses MV, TG; flowers YBM
76.1	prima donna MV, TG; singer YBM
76.5–6	laid her hands lightly on his hair and MV, TG; *om.* YBM
76.16	*om.* MV; so TG, YBM
76.21–22	in a broad South German MV; in a broad German TG; *om.* YBM
76.22–23	dialect, and a massive woman whose figure persistently escaped from her stays in the most improbable places MV, TG; and a stout woman YBM
76.23	places and whose florid face was marked by good living and champagne as by fine tide lines, MV; places TG; *om.* YBM
76.24	her blond hair disordered by the wind, and MV, TG; *om.* YBM
76.25	surprise she MV, TG; surprise and YBM
76.26	emotionally. MV, TG; *om.* YBM
76.27	quickly withdrew his arm, and MV, TG; *om.* YBM
76.28	but MV, TG; *om.* YBM
76.29	he said, quietly, and MV, TG; *om.* YBM

"A Wagner Matinee"

94.3	village MV, TG, YBM; town NS
94.5	Howard. It MV; Howard and TG, YBM, NS
94.6–7	who had recently died MV, TG; *om.* YBM, NS
94.7	had become MV; would be TG, YBM, NS
94.7	come MV; go TG, YBM, NS
94.9	prove MV; be TG, YBM, NS
94.12	the good woman MV, TG; my aunt YBM, NS
94.14–15	called up not alone her own figure, at once pathetic and grotesque, but opened before my feet MV, TG; opened before me YBM, NS
94.16	recollections MV; recollection TG, YBM, NS
94.18	*om.* MV; familiar TG, YBM, NS
94.21	raw MV; sore TG, YBM, NS
94.21–22	I felt the knuckles of my thumb tentatively, as though they were raw again. MV, TG; *om.* YBM, NS

tioningly into the hands of a country dressmaker. My poor aunt's figure, however, would have presented astonishing difficulties to any dressmaker. MV, TG; *om.* YBM, NS

96.1–3   dressmaker. MV; dressmaker. Originally stooped, her shoulders were now almost bent together over her sunken chest. She wore no stays, and her gown, which trailed unevenly behind, rose in a sort of peak over her abdomen. TG; *om.* YBM, NS

96.3–6   Her skin was yellow as a Mongolian's from constant exposure to a pitiless wind, and to the alkaline water, which transforms the most transparent cuticle into a sort of flexible leather. She wore ill-fitting false teeth. The most striking thing about her physiognomy, however, was an incessant twitching of the mouth and eyebrows, a form of nervous disorder resulting from isolation and monotony, and from frequent physical suffering. MV; She wore ill-fitting false teeth, and her skin was as yellow as a Mongolian's from constant exposure to a pitiless wind and to the alkaline water which hardens the most transparent cuticle into a sort of flexible leather. TG; *om.* YBM, NS

96.7–8   In my boyhood this affliction had possessed a sort of horrible fascination for me, of which I was secretly very much ashamed, for in those days I owed to this woman most of the good that ever came my way MV; I owed to this woman most of the good that ever came my way in my boyhood TG, YBM, NS

96.8   three winters MV; years TG, YBM, NS

96.9–10   three meals for half a dozen farm-hands MV; the three meals—the first of which was ready at six o'clock in the morning TG, YBM, NS

96.12   hearing MV; with TG, YBM, NS

96.12–13   *om.* MV; hearing me TG, YBM, NS

96.13   conjugations, and MV; conjugations, TG, YBM, NS

96.16   of MV; on TG, YBM, NS

96.17   too MV, TG; *om.* YBM, NS

96.19   any instrument, MV, TG; a musical instrument. YBM, NS

96.19	except MV; but TG; *om.* YBM, NS
96.20	an accordion that belonged to one of the Norwegian farmhands. MV, TG; *om.* YBM, NS
96.22	"Harmonious Blacksmith" MV; "Joyous Farmer" TG, YBM, NS
96.23–25	She was a pious woman; she had the consolations of religion and, to her at least, her martyrdom was not wholly sordid. MV, TG; *om.* YBM, NS
96.29–30	Oh! dear boy, pray that whatever your sacrifice MV, TG; *om.* YBM, NS
96.30	be it is not that MV; may be, it be not that TG; *om.* YBM, NS
96.31	arrival MV, TG; arrival in Boston YBM, NS
96.34	hungrily for MV; hungrily TG, YBM, NS
97.5	Meyerbeer's "Huguenots" MV; the *Huguenots* TG, YBM, NS
97.6	Boston Symphony MV; Symphony TG, YBM, NS
97.8–10	Indeed, for her own sake, I could only wish her taste for such things quite dead, and the long struggle mercifully ended at last. MV, TG; *om.* YBM, NS
97.18	that MV; which TG, YBM, NS
97.27	seemed to begin MV; for the first time seemed TG, YBM, NS
97.29	absurdities of her attire MV, TG; her queer country clothes YBM, NS
97.31	for a MV, TG, YBM; for more than a NS
97.38	unshorn, and who stand MV; unshaven; standing TG, YBM, NS
98.2	Yukon, or in the yellow blaze of the Arizona desert MV; Yukon TG, YBM, NS
98.2–3	conscious that certain experiences have isolated them from their fellows by a gulf no haberdasher could MV, TG; *om.* YBM, NS
98.3	conceal MV; bridge TG; *om.* YBM, NS
98.4–6	*om.* MV; We sat at the extreme left of the first balcony, facing the arc of our own and the balcony above us, veritable hanging gardens, brilliant as tulip beds. TG; *om.* YBM, NS
98.6	*om.* MV; matinée TG, YBM, NS

98.8	color contrast MV; colour TG, YBM, NS
98.8	shimmer and shading MV; shimmer TG, YBM, NS
98.9	sheer, resisting and yielding MV; sheer TG, YBM, NS
98.12	dead black MV; dead TG, YBM, NS
98.22	change in one's environment. I reminded myself of the impression made on me by MV; change. TG, YBM, NS
98.24–25	thrown by the green-shaded stand-lamps MV; thrown by the green shaded lamps TG; *om.* YBM, NS
98.28	soul MV; heart TG, YBM, NS
98.29	*om.* MV; yards of TG, YBM, NS
98.30	violins MV; horns TG, YBM, NS
98.32	was that MV; was TG, YBM, NS
98.32	this singing of basses and stinging frenzy of lighter strings MV; this TG, YBM, NS
98.33	years; the inconceivable silence of the plains MV, TG; *om.* YBM, NS
98.34	With the battle between the two motifs MV; With the battle between the two motives TG, YBM; *om.* NS
98.34	with the bitter frenzy MV; with the frenzy TG, YBM; *om.* NS
98.34–35	of the Venusberg theme and its ripping of strings MV, TG, YBM; *om.* NS
98.35	came MV; there came TG, YBM; *om.* NS
98.35–36	to me an overwhelming sense of the waste and wear we are so powerless to combat MV, TG, YBM; *om.* NS
98.37	*om.* MV; and TG, YBM; *om.* NS
98.38–39	*om.* MV; its margin pitted with sun-dried cattle tracks TG, YBM, NS
98.39	*om.* MV; banks TG, YBM, NS
99.1	on which MV; where TG, YBM, NS
99.3	is MV; was TG, YBM, NS
99.4	stretched MV; reached TG, YBM, NS
99.5	sordid conquests MV; conquests TG, YBM, NS
99.5	more merciless MV; dearer bought TG, YBM, NS
99.7–9	staring at the orchestra through a dullness of thirty years, through the films made little by little by each of the three hundred and sixty-five days in every one of them. MV, TG; staring dully at the orchestra. YBM; quietly looking at the orchestra. NS

99.15   *om.* MV; in her house TG, YBM, NS
99.15   while MV; when TG, YBM, NS
99.17   *om.* MV; certain TG, YBM, NS
99.22   what that warfare of motifs, MV; what TG, YBM, NS
99.23–24   *om.* MV; but she sat mutely staring down at the violin
           bows that drove obliquely downward like the TG, YBM,
           NS
99.24   *om.* MV; pelting TG, YBM; *om.* NS
99.24–25   *om.* MV; streaks of rain in a summer shower. TG, YBM,
           NS
99.25–27   Did or did not a new planet swim into her ken? Wagner
           had been a sealed book to Americans before the sixties.
           Had she anything left with which to comprehend this
           glory that had flashed around the world since she had
           gone from it? MV; Had she enough left to at all compre-
           hend this power which had kindled the world since she
           had left it? TG, YBM, NS
99.30   though MV, TG; if YBM, NS
99.32   were MV; had been TG, YBM, NS
99.32   and pulled and twisted MV; and twisted TG, YBM, NS
99.33   the palms MV; the palm TG; *om.* YBM, NS
99.33–34   unduly swollen, the fingers bent and knotted MV, TG;
           om. YBM, NS
100.2   dies, then, the soul? MV; died, then—the soul TG, YBM,
           NS
100.2   *om.* MV; that TG; which YBM, NS
100.2–3   *om.* MV; can suffer so excruciatingly and so intermina-
           bly; TG, YBM, NS
100.5–6   My aunt wept gently MV; She wept so TG, YBM; *om.*
           NS
100.6   throughout the development and elaboration of the mel-
           ody. MV, TG, YBM; *om.* NS
100.12   his blue MV; his TG, YBM, NS
100.14   saddle, and MV; saddle, TG, YBM, NS
100.17   so far MV; in so far TG, YBM, NS
100.21–22 *om.* MV; All this my aunt told me huskily, wanderingly
           TG, YBM, NS
100.22–23 *om.* MV; as though she were talking in the weak lapses
           of illness. TG, YBM; during the intermission. NS

100.25   queried with well-meant MV; queried, with a well-meant
            effort at TG, YBM; asked, with a well-meant effort at
            NS

100.27   you've MV; you have TG, YBM, NS

100.29   reproaches.
            "But do you get it, Aunt Georgiana, the astonishing
            structure of it all?" I persisted.
            "Who could?" she said, absently; "why should one?"
            MV; *om.* TG, YBM, NS

100.31   Ring. This was followed by the forest music from Sieg-
            fried, and the programme MV; *Ring*, and TG, YBM, NS

100.31–32   My aunt wept quietly but almost continuously MV, TG,
            YBM; Throughout these I felt that my aunt had drifted
            quite away from me NS

100.32–33   *om.* MV; as a shallow vessel overflows in a rain-storm
            TG, YBM; *om.* NS

100.33   *om.* MV; From time to time her dim eyes TG, YBM;
            From time to time her eyes NS

100.33–34   *om.* MV; looked up at the lights which studded the ceil-
            ing TG; looked up at the lights YBM, NS

100.34   *om.* MV; burning softly under their dull glass globes
            TG, YBM, NS

100.35   *om.* MV; doubtless they were stars in truth to her TG;
            om. YBM, NS

100.35   I was MV; I was still TG; *om.* YBM, NS

100.35–36   perplexed as to what measure of musical comprehen-
            sion was left to her MV, TG; *om.* YBM, NS

100.36–38   to her who had heard nothing for so many years but the
            singing of gospel hymns in the Methodist services at the
            square frame school-house on Section Thirteen MV; she
            who had heard nothing but the singing of gospel hymns
            at Methodist services in the square frame school-house
            on Section Thirteen for so many years TG; *om.* YBM,
            NS

101.1   I was MV; I was wholly TG; *om.* YBM, NS

101.1–2   unable to guage how much of it had been dissolved in
            soapsuds, or worked into bread, or milked into the bot-
            tom of a pail. MV, TG; *om.* YBM, NS

101.3   know MV; knew TG, YBM, NS

101.5   islands, or under what skies. MV; islands. TG, YBM, NS

101.6   the Siegfried march, at least, carried her out MV; before the last numbers she had been carried out TG, YBM, NS

101.7   out into MV; into TG, YBM, NS

101.7   *om.* MV; nameless TG, YBM, NS

101.13   rise. MV; rise. The harpist slipped TG, YBM, NS

101.13   *om.* MV; its TG; the YBM, NS

101.13–16   *om.* MV; green felt cover over his instrument; the flute-players shook the water from their mouthpieces; the men of the orchestra went out one by one, leaving the stage to the chairs and music stands, empty as a winter cornfield. TG, YBM, NS

101.17   gently to her, MV; to my aunt. TG, YBM, NS

101.17–18   She burst into tears and sobbed pleadingly, "I don't want to go, Clark, I don't want to go MV, TG, YBM; She turned to me with a sad little smile. 'I don't want to go, Clark. I suppose we must NS

101.19   the door of the MV, TG; *om.* YBM, NS

101.21   naked as a tower, with weather-curled boards MV; with weather-curled boards; naked as a tower TG, YBM, NS

"Paul's Case"

102.22   *om.* MV; against him TG, YBM, NS

102.23   an MV; a TG, YBM, NS

103.9–12   *om.* MV; In one class he habitually sat with his hand shading his eyes; in another he always looked out of the window during the recitation; in another he made a running commentary on the lecture, with humorous TG, YBM, NS

103.12   *om.* MV; intention TG; intent YBM, NS

103.15   *om.* MV; his English teacher leading the pack. TG, YBM, NS

103.34   Principal, who was a sympathetic man MV, TG; Principal YBM, NS

104.4–6   I happen to know that he was born in Colorado, only a few months before his mother died out there of a long illness. MV, TG; *om.* YBM, NS

104.13–14   and stiff with a nervous tension that drew them back from his teeth MV, TG; *om.* YBM, NS

104.15–18   *om.* MV; His teachers left the building dissatisfied and unhappy; humiliated to have felt so vindictive toward a mere boy, to have uttered this feeling in cutting terms, and to have set each other on, as it were, in the grewsome game of intemperate reproach. TG, YBM, NS

104.18   *om.* MV; some TG; one YBM, NS

104.18–19   *om.* MV; of them remembered having seen a miserable street cat set at bay by a ring of tormentors.

104.21   wildly MV, TG, YBM; *om.* NS

104.22   writhe under MV, TG; witness YBM, NS

104.25–26   supper, but would hang about an Oakland tabacconist's shop until it was time to go to the concert hall. MV; supper. When he reached the concert hall the doors were not yet open TG, YBM, NS

104.26   *om.* MV, YBM, NS; and as TG

104.26   *om.* MV; it was chilly outside TG; It was chilly outside, and YBM, NS

104.26–30   *om.* MV; decided to go up into the picture gallery—always deserted at this hour—where there were some of Raffelli's gay studies of Paris streets and an airy blue Venetian scene or two that always exhilarated him. He was delighted to find no one in the gallery but the old guard, who sat in TG, YBM, NS

104.30   *om.* MV; one TG; the YBM, NS

104.30–36   *om.* MV; corner, a newspaper on his knee, a black patch over one eye and the other closed. Paul possessed himself of the place and walked confidently up and down, whistling under his breath. After a while he sat down before a blue Rico and lost himself. When he bethought him to look at his watch, it was after seven o'clock, and he rose with a start and ran downstairs, making a face at Augustus TG, YBM, NS

104.36   *om.* MV, TG; Caesar YBM, NS

104.36–38   *om.* MV; peering out from the cast-room, and an evil gesture at the Venus of Milo as he passed her on the stairway. TG, YBM, NS

104.39   When Paul reached the ushers' dressing-room at about half-past seven that evening MV; When Paul reached the ushers' dressing-room TG, YBM, NS

105.1   Paul MV; he TG, YBM, NS

105.2   he MV; Paul TG, YBM, NS

105.5   considerably MV, TG; *om.* YBM, NS

105.19–29   *om.* MV; Just as the musicians came out to take their places, his English teacher arrived with checks for the seats which a prominent manufacturer had taken for the season. She betrayed some embarrassment when she handed Paul the tickets, and a *hauteur* which subsequently made her feel very foolish. Paul was startled for a moment, and had the feeling of wanting to put her out; what business had she here among all these fine people and gay colours? He looked her over and decided that she was not appropriately dressed and must be a fool to sit downstairs in such togs. The tickets had probably been sent her out of kindness, he relected as he put down a seat for her, and she had about as much right to sit there as he had. TG, YBM, NS

105.31–32   *om.* MV; and lost himself as he had done before the Rico. TG, YBM, NS

105.38   half closed his eyes MV; forgot even the nastiness of his teacher's being there TG, YBM, NS

105.39   stimulus MV, TG; intoxication YBM, NS

106.3   elaborate MV, TG; satin YBM, NS

106.4–5   in Paul's eyes, made her a veritable queen of Romance. MV, TG; which always blinded Paul to any possible defects. YBM, NS

106.12   soprano's MV, TG; singer's YBM, NS

106.18   the better class MV, TG; any importance YBM, NS

106.35   *World* MV, TG; *om.* YBM, NS

107.4–5   but mocking spirits stood guard at the doors, and MV, TG; *om.* YBM, NS

107.15   mother. MV, TG; mother, whom Paul could not remember. YBM, NS

107.16	his MV, TG; the Negley Avenue YBM, NS
107.31	penetrated MV, TG; permeated YBM, NS
108.4	he had had MV; he had TG, YBM, NS
108.18	*om.* MV; had TG, YBM, NS
108.30–31	usually sat MV, TG; sat placidly YBM, NS
109.16	sat on the top step, MV, TG; on the top step, was YBM, NS
110.4	these MV, TG; *om.* YBM, NS
110.30	the services of a MV; a TG, YBM, NS
110.30	the boy very MV; him TG, YBM, NS
110.38	poetic MV, TG; *om.* YBM, NS
111.12	put MV; put it TG, YBM, NS
111.17	there MV, TG; *om.* YBM, NS
111.23	that MV, TG; *om.* YBM, NS
112.12	Venice MV, TG; California YBM, NS
113.7–8	partly because he was ashamed, dressed as he was, to go into a Pullman, and partly MV, TG; *om.* YBM, NS
113.9	of being seen there MV, TG; if he took a Pullman he might be seen YBM, NS
113.10	might have MV, TG; had YBM, NS
113.15	nonce MV, TG, YBM; time NS
113.17	Paul MV; he TG, YBM, NS
113.20	that MV, TG; which YBM, NS
113.24	linen MV, TG; new shirts YBM, NS
113.25–26	his silver and a new MV, TG; silver-mounted brushes and a YBM, NS
114.37	deposits MV; deposit TG, YBM, NS
114.38	were MV; was TG, YBM, NS
115.9–10	It was not the first time Paul had steered through treacherous waters. MV, TG; *om.* YBM, NS
115.15	three MV, TG; four YBM, NS
115.16	half of MV, TG; *om.* YBM, NS
115.17	more than MV, TG; nearly YBM, NS
115.22	*om.* MV; soundlessly TG, YBM, NS
115.25	were stands, with MV, TG; *om.* YBM, NS
115.26	under glass cases MV, TG; behind glass windows YBM, NS
115.26	the sides of MV, TG; *om.* YBM, NS
115.33	dozen MV, TG; many YBM, NS

115.38	that was stretched MV; stretched TG, YBM, NS
116.9–10	came floating MV, TG; floated YBM, NS
116.10	His head whirled MV, TG; *om.* YBM, NS
116.11	and MV, TG; *om.* YBM, NS
116.17	was MV; were TG, YBM, NS
116.23	rosy MV; roseate TG, YBM, NS
116.29	got on MV, TG; boarded YBM, NS
117.3	Metropolitan MV, TG; Opera YBM, NS
117.3	now MV, TG; *om.* YBM, NS
117.17	Sunday MV, TG; On Sunday YBM, NS
117.30–32	Even under the glow of his wine he was never boisterous, though he found the stuff like a magician's wand for wonder-building. MV, TG; *om.* YBM, NS
118.13	boy MV; lad TG, YBM, NS
119.2	born to the purple MV, TG; *om.* YBM, NS
119.17	and burnt MV, TG; *om.* YBM, NS
119.31	looks of the thing MV; looks of it TG; look of it, anyway YBM, NS
120.12	of MV, TG; *om.* YBM, NS
120.18	of MV; on TG, YBM, NS
120.26	and MV, TG; *om.* YBM, NS
120.30	a little MV; a while TG, YBM, NS
121.3	and that MV, TG; *om.* YBM, NS

Word Divisions

The compounds or possible compounds in List A are hyphenated at the end of the line in the copy-text (TG) and were resolved as hyphenated or one word as listed below. The resolution was made on the basis of Cather's preferences and usages at other points in the copy-text. List B records compounds or possible compounds that are hyphenated at the end of the line in the present text; if the compound or possible compound does not appear there, it should be transcribed as one word.

List A

15.12	gypsy-dago	75.23	cattle-farms
19.22	five-and-thirty	76.23	ladylike
22.8	forehead	80.22	grandfathers
28.6	childhood	81.12	cattle-farms
30.21	smoking-jacket	82.17	real-estate
33.11	carriage-house	87.7	blue-and-white
41.20	eyebrows	88.24	cold-bloodedly
43.19	music-room	90.1	self-commiseration
46.9	tip-toe	90.10	life-long
52.7	middle-class	90.25	twenty-five
58.11	to-night	92.14	dining-room
59.25	world-wide	97.17	Heat-lightning
61.21	stoop-shouldered	98.2	candlesticks
62.26	sidewalk	104.13	self-deprivations
73.26	dining-room	114.15	shirt-sleeves
75.2	pocket-knife	117.15	head-light

117.22	handkerchief	233.25	button-holes
122.25	railroaders	235.15	hard-working
129.8	homesick	238.5	sitting-room
142.3	note-paper	241.21	winter-piece
152.14	night-lamp	242.17	nerve-stuff
159.3	mutton-chops	243.23	fagged-looking
170.2	brother-in-law	244.25	sitting-room
173.2	now-a-days	245.9	snow-bound
178.23	close-clipped		
189.16	lamplight		
196.8	farmer-boy		**List B**
196.17	landlady		
198.24	dressmaker	7.23	well-sounding
200.1	farm-hands	12.33	half-consumed
203.20	tube-paint	20.29	breakfast-room
205.9	dish-cloths	27.7	night-clothes
207.25	cow-puncher	51.27	self-defiance
209.12	school-house	55.14	well-ordered
210.7	flute-players	57.16	sage-brush
210.19	dish-cloths	75.7	to-morrow
213.7	out-grown	83.4	brother-in-law
213.12	button-holes	99.1	dish-cloths
218.22	downstairs	100.12	gingham-sheeted
222.7	school-masters	104.22	light-heartedness
225.8	night-shirt	107.12	collar-box
228.7	forget-me-nots	109.28	twenty-one
231.3	Sunday-night	111.10	lime-light
233.13	stage-struck	111.20	blue-and-white